CONQUISTADOR

Quetzal let his eyes wander over his friend's body. Axatan's skin was a deep, dark brown. His hair was the black of burnt wood and his limbs were like those of a wild animal, powerful and ready for the chase. His cock lay lazily, thick and heavy, in the bush of dark hair round his groin. His hands were delicate like a girl's, but Quetzal knew they could break bones.

Together, they splashed into the blue waves. Quetzal dived down under the surface and glided there, feeling the cool currents against his skin.

He jumped as Axatan grabbed his leg and pulled him down. Quetzal kicked out to get him off, but Axatan kept his grip until he had put his hands between his legs and turned him round so that they were facing each other in the water.

They kissed and Quetzal closed his eyes so that all he could hear was the water lapping against the shore and the sound of their breathing. Axatan's tongue pushed inside him and he let himself be taken over by the beautiful strength of his lover.

CONQUISTADOR

Jeff Hunter

To O

First published in Great Britain in 1998 by
Idol
an imprint of Virgin Publishing Ltd
332 Ladbroke Grove
London W10 5AH

Copyright © Jeff Hunter 1998

The right of Jeff Hunter to be identified as the Author of this
Work has been asserted by him in accordance with the Copyright,
Designs and Patents Act 1988.

ISBN 0 352 33244 1

Cover photograph by Colin Clarke Photography

Typeset by SetSystems Ltd, Saffron Walden, Essex
Printed and bound in Great Britain by
Cox & Wyman Ltd, Reading, Berks

This book is sold subject to the condition that it shall not, by way
of trade or otherwise, be lent, resold, hired out or otherwise
circulated without the publisher's prior written consent in any
form of binding or cover other than that in which it is published
and without a similar condition, including this condition, being
imposed on the subsequent purchaser.

SAFER SEX GUIDELINES

These books are sexual fantasies – in real life, everyone needs to think about safe sex.

While there have been major advances in the drug treatments for people with HIV and AIDS, there is still no cure for AIDS or a vaccine against HIV. Safe sex is still the only way of being sure of avoiding HIV sexually.

HIV can only be transmitted through blood, come and vaginal fluids (but no other body fluids) – passing from one person (with HIV) into another person's bloodstream. It cannot get through healthy, undamaged skin. The only real risk of HIV is through anal sex without a condom – this accounts for almost all HIV transmissions between men.

Being Safe:
Even if you don't come inside someone, there is still a risk to both partners from blood (tiny cuts in the arse) and pre-come. Using strong condoms and water-based lubricant greatly reduces the risk of HIV. However, condoms can break or slip off, so:
* Make sure that condoms are stored away from hot or damp places.
* Check the expiry date – condoms have a limited life.
* Gently squeeze the air out of the tip.
* Check the condom is put on the right way up and unroll it down the erect cock.
* Use plenty of water-based lubricant (lube), up the arse and on the condom.
* While fucking, check occasionally to see the condom is still in one piece (you could also add more lube).
* When you withdraw, hold the condom tight to your cock as you pull out.

* Never re-use a condom or use the same condom with more than one person.
* If you're not used to condoms you might practise putting them on.
* Sex toys like dildos and plugs are safe. But if you're sharing them use a new condom each time or wash the toys well.

For the safest sex, make sure you use the strongest condoms, such as Durex Ultra Strong, Mates Super Strong, HT Specials and Rubberstuffers packs. Condoms are free in many STD (Sexually Transmitted Disease) clinics (sometimes called GUM clinics) and from many gay bars. It's also essential to use lots of water-based lube such as KY, Wet Stuff, Slik or Liquid Silk. Never use come as a lubricant.

Oral Sex:
Compared with fucking, sucking someone's cock is far safer. Swallowing come does not necessarily mean that HIV gets absorbed into the bloodstream. While a tiny fraction of cases of HIV infection have been linked to sucking, we know the risk is minimal. But certain factors increase the risk:
* Letting someone come in your mouth
* Throat infections such as gonorrhoea
* If you have cuts, sores or infections in your mouth and throat

So what is safe?
There are so many things you can do which are absolutely safe: wanking each other; rubbing your cocks against one another; kissing, sucking and licking all over the body; rimming – to name but a few.

If you're finding safe sex difficult, call a helpline or speak to someone you feel you can trust for support. The Terrence Higgins Trust Helpline, which is open from noon to 10pm every day, can be reached on 0171 242 1010.

Or, if you're in the United States, you can ring the Center for Disease Control toll free on 1 800 458 5231.

Prologue

He awoke to find his hands and feet tied to a hard wooden cross. Above him, the double-headed dragon face of Quetzalcoatl, god of the storms, stared down at him from the ceiling, fangs gleaming, eyes on fire. On either side of him, charcoal braziers gave off a dark heat and the smell of incense. Along one wall, propped up on long shelves, were row upon row of human skulls. He was naked.

The room was dark. In front of him, a doorway led on to a small balcony and out into the warm night air. He could see a man silhouetted against the stars, a broad black shape darker than the night. He was looking to the east; to the hills where the Priests of the Sun were preparing their victim for slaughter. He could hear their drums heralding the night.

His mouth was dry. He remembered being given the sacred cup as he had presented himself at the Palace, ready to be admitted to the Stable. He remembered the strong arms of his fellow warriors holding him as his knees went from under him and everything turned black. He remembered nothing after that.

The ropes were biting into his hands and feet. They had taken him inside the Palace gates, but where this room lay he couldn't tell. Through the window he could only see the mountains.

Behind him, a deep cough told him that someone else was in the room. He craned his neck around and saw a small group of warriors, older than him, standing there exchanging hushed whispers.

His cock stirred. He realised that a thong had been wound around his balls and fastened to the floor so that he was pinned there like a butterfly on display, and he liked the idea of these men, these warrior champions, sizing him up to see if he could be one of their own. From the window, a warm breeze played around his arse, teasing him with invisible fingers. He imagined the night to come. He had heard stories of the Stable initiation ceremony but knew no details. Whatever happened tonight would change him for ever.

The figure in the window turned and the other warriors formed a circle around him. He saw for the first time that they were naked. They were muscular; men of strength and war.

All eyes were on him. He felt them exploring his body with their minds, their eyes running up and down his lean torso before resting on his long, young cock. He knew they were imagining the dark secrets of his arse.

Their own cocks hung heavily between their legs. He loved the size of them. At the House of Youth, some of the other boys had had long, heavy cocks, but these men were magnificent and he longed to take them in his mouth and show them he was worthy of being their servant.

Some of the warriors had tied leather straps around the bases of their cocks, making their shafts swell and gorge with blood. Others were slowly sliding their foreskins up and down their shafts, making themselves hard. The smell of sex was beginning to fill the room and his own cock grew hard in response. He was to be the plaything of the Stable; the Sun Prince's private elite.

He closed his eyes and felt a cock brush against his arm. Another touched his hand. The warriors were closing in on him, circling around and inspecting their prey. He loved the feeling of their cock heads as they brushed over him, their soft moistness promising him pleasures to come.

A hand found his nipple and he felt a finger scratch over it, making it hard and sending throbbing signals down through his body. Another hand brushed across his chest and started to pull on his other nipple. They took turns — first gently scratching one nipple and making it hard before twisting it until he arched his back with the pain. Then they would let him down and begin on the other one.

His cock was throbbing now and he felt it lift off his belly as one of the warriors reached between his legs and started to pull on the thong attached to his balls. He flicked it, and his balls spasmed with pleasure as the first drop of precome oozed out of his dick and dropped on to his belly.

He stretched out, opening himself up to the hands and minds of the Stable warriors. Hands were all over him now — brushing his body, pinching on his flesh, stroking the end of his cock. He started to grind his hips, feeling the come rising in his shaft, desperate to wank his cock and make his seed fly into the air and cover them all. But just as he thought he would explode, the warriors withdrew and he was left quivering and shaking in the ropes, exposed for punishment.

He opened his eyes.

Montezuma, Lord of the Aztecs, Sun Prince and King of the Mexica, had stepped through the balcony door and was looking down on him.

He was naked except for a mask which hid his face, its deep, black eye sockets revealing only darkness. His powerful legs gleamed in the moonlight, their covering of thick black hair making him look as much an animal as a human god. His cock was massive and swung, half hard, between his legs, surrounded at the base by a thick silver ring. His balls were huge and hung heavily between his thighs.

The captive pulled on his ropes, but two warriors held him still as the prince clapped his hands.

'Let the ceremony begin.'

A young warrior stepped up to him and handed him a steaming bowl of scented oil.

'First we will clean you and make you pure.'

He watched as the Prince took a small brush, dipped it into the bowl and began to brush the hot liquid between his legs. His heart beat faster as the oil seeped into the hairs around his cock and he froze as the Prince held up a shining bone-headed knife.

The blade was cold as he leant forward and began to shave away the hair on his balls, filling him with wild sensations and making his cock rear up with pleasure. The Prince worked methodically, making the young warrior's balls smooth and scraping away at the hairs around the base of his shaft. The others looked on, idly stroking their cocks. No one spoke.

As the blade moved up his cock, he found himself filled with sensations he couldn't control. He writhed in his bonds, pulling on the ropes, but the two guards just held him even more firmly and he knew he had to surrender himself to their strength.

The Prince became rougher and moved between his legs, forcing open his cheeks and scraping the hair away from around his arsehole. He felt the black wiry hair falling away from his crack, leaving him soft and smooth and open for these men's pleasure.

The Prince walked around him and began on his chest. The brush flicked over his nipples and the blade scraped away at the sprinkling of dark hairs that covered his chest and up under his arms. He bit his lip as the blade moved from one nipple to the other, stripping him clean and taking him back to when he was a boy. The wind blew over his body and he looked down at his cock, huge without its bed of hair, hard on his stomach. The warrior had been stripped. Now he was ready to face his comrades.

'Warrior hero. In training you have excelled yourself. In battle you have taken many captives.' The Prince's voice boomed out, filling the room with his presence. 'Now you are my captive. You will serve me and I will be your conqueror.'

He gave the signal, and four guards took hold of him and tied his hands and feet to a rope sling which hung from the ceiling.

The Prince stepped forward and brushed the end of his giant

cock against the young man's lips. It was soft and warm and left a trail of saltiness against his tongue.

He thrust his head forward to take it within him, but the Prince pulled back and the guards grabbed his hair and held him still.

'Young warrior. You think you are still in the training house. You think you still have the other boys worshipping you. But here I am your god. I decide whether you stay in or go out, whether you devote yourself to pleasuring me, or go out and find the company of others like you. I decide whether to use your mouth or your arse, whether you kiss my balls or drink the come that streams from my cock, whether you live or die. I am your ruler. Everyone in the Stable is mine.'

The warrior's heart was pounding with fear but the Prince stepped forward and again brushed his cock against the young man's mouth. This time he knew to hold still and let his Prince push forward and slip the thick head inside him.

The Prince let out a groan and the warrior felt the thick shaft push deeper into his mouth. The end was oozing precome and the initiate swallowed eagerly as the saltiness seeped on to his tongue.

Someone produced a blindfold and he was plunged into darkness. Suddenly, hands were all over him again; stroking his body, feeling his cock, pulling on his balls. The Prince had withdrawn and he felt other cocks brushing across his face and against the crack of his arse. He stuck his tongue out to take what he could into his mouth. Cocks brushed against his face. Fingers explored his hole and tongues and teeth found their way to his nipples.

Someone began to beat on a drum and the warriors gradually took up the rhythm, stamping on the ground and filling the cavern with the crashing of their feet against stone.

A finger pushed against his hole and he relaxed, letting it slide in and explore the soft tissues of his arse. Another joined it and he arched his back as these men took control of him and tested him – the young supplicant who dared to crave admittance to the Stable.

A cock pushed past his lips. He thought at first that it was Montezuma again, but this cock felt different; fatter and more gnarled. He gobbled it greedily as more fingers pushed into his arse and the shaft in his mouth pumped down into his throat, the rough skin running up and down his tongue.

More hands were playing with his nipples and stroking his cock. A tongue found its way up under his balls and he writhed with pleasure as it flicked against his scrotum, sending his cock into spasms of ecstasy.

He pulled on the ropes but the guards held him firm as more fingers pushed inside him and one cock in his mouth was replaced by another as warrior after warrior used him for their games.

Then a low moan of the conch shell filled the room and all was still again. He hung there in the sling, disorientated and unsure who was where.

'Hold him.'

His blindfold was removed and he saw Montezuma standing there, magnificent between his legs. His body was like a wild beast's and the warrior knew he was to be his prey. The Prince's cock was long and thick and hard, and he had greased it with oil so that it glistened in the half-light. He looked down on the warrior with lust and animal desire.

The guards held him as the Prince pushed the end of his cock against his hole. It was hot and powerful, like a spear ready to drive inside him and fill him with molten pleasure. The thick tool began to push into him and he felt like he was being torn apart. The warriors were stamping again and he breathed in the heady air of their sweat and let his head swim with the mesmerising rhythm of their drums and feet. Montezuma groaned with pleasure as his cock drove its way deep inside him.

The others began to wank themselves, mesmerised by the sight of the Prince's thick shaft pushing inside the young warrior's arse and thrilled to see another young soldier initiated into their caste. Montezuma's cock was deep inside the young man's arse now, and for a moment the Prince held it there, allowing the warrior to feel the huge mass inside him and relish his ruler's flesh.

And then, instead of pulling back, Montezuma pushed slowly at the ropes that held him, so that the sling swung back and the warrior felt himself being pulled away from the Prince, his ruler's cock tearing out of his arse as it withdrew, filling him with pleasure and longing. There was a pause as his arse craved the thickness of his flesh once more, and then the sling changed direction and he was brought back down on to his Prince's cock, feeling it slam inside him and fill him with its weight.

Again they held still for a moment until the ropes began their journey back, pulling the Prince's cock out of him and leaving his arsehole open and begging for more. The sling changed direction and he swung down again, fucking the Prince with his open arsehole and begging to be filled again with his massive cock.

He knew he was close to coming. The seed was stirring in his balls and he felt it being pushed up towards his cockhead. Precome was dripping over his stomach and he held his arsehole tight, longing to bring Montezuma to climax; to show his love for his master and be filled with his Prince's come.

All around him his fellow warriors were frantically wanking their cocks. It was an amazing sight. Some knelt in front of others, desperate to taste come in their mouths. Others had opened up their arses to their battlemates and were being pounded by their thick, hard cocks.

The ropes swung down once more and he let out a mighty roar as Montezuma pushed hard inside him, making his balls contract and his cock explode, shooting come high in the air and down in a hot shower over his face, chest and arms.

The Prince caught some of the spunk in his hand and made one final thrust before coming inside him, his come oozing out of the young warrior's arsehole on to the floor. All around them, the Stable warriors were shooting their come and the air was filled with the sound of ecstasy and the smell of men and come and sex.

The Prince looked down upon him.

'You have served us well, warrior hero. You have pleased the gods. Welcome, Axatan, son of Tolec, prince of the Aztecs. Welcome to the Stable.'

One

Axatan woke and went down the narrow stairs into the Great Courtyard, where the women were cooking *tamales*, the little corn patties he loved to eat for breakfast. The sun was still low in the sky, but summer had come and it promised another scorching day.

The Stable's quarters took up one corner of the Royal Palace, and from the whitewashed ramparts he could see the whole city spread out below him. Tenochtitlan, magnificent with its wide squares and gleaming canals, was just waking up. Down at the lakeside he could see the fishermen unloading their night catch, their canoes bumping into each other as they brought their wares ashore. In the marketplace, the traders were already setting up their stalls, and out across the water on the far shore of the lake he could see a herdsman taking his flock up into the mountains.

He looked to the north and towards the Great Temple of Tlaloc and Huitzilopochtli, its twin towers dark and foreboding. A small group of priests, their hair long and matted and their skin scarred with numberless self-mutilations from the blood sacrifices to the gods, climbed slowly up the huge stairway which led to the killing stone. The dark stains of blood which splashed up even as far as the statues of the gods reminded him of the sacrifices that had become daily now. How much longer could they go on? Why were the gods so angry with them?

It had started ten years ago when a terrible star was seen crossing the night sky. It was like a dragon with its tail on fire. Axatan remembered it well, even though he was just a boy, playing with his friends in the marketplace. The whole city had been afraid and he remembered his mother barricading their small house in the *chinampas* to keep out the evil spirits.

Then the Great Temple itself had caught fire. They had all rushed out to see the statue of Huitzilopochtli glaring with fury as the flames ate away at his stone face. A year later, the lake had begun to boil and the lower part of the city was flooded, sweeping people away so that their bodies were never found and their grieving relatives had to wander the countryside paying penance on their behalf.

After that, bad omens were everywhere – ghostly cries heard in empty streets, a bird brought to the palace on whose head a round mirror revealed a vision of armed men riding deer, mysterious deaths in the *chinampas* where men would go out to work the fields and never return. That was when the priests had decreed that the sacrifices would have to be doubled. The warriors made almost daily expeditions into the countryside, bringing back hundreds of captives, some of them just children, to lead up to the killing stone and slaughter with the flint knife, their still-beating hearts torn from their chests and thrown into the fires of the Eagle Brazier.

He remembered that time well. They would all come to line the streets and gawp at the captives being led to their deaths. Some of them were just his age and he wondered what they were thinking as they walked silently up the temple steps to their terrible fate. He knew they were destined for the Humming Bird Paradise, but he could never completely accept that some of his friends claimed they would willingly go to the killing stone themselves. Even now he understood the workings of the world some more, he would never volunteer to make the final sacrifice.

And then they had arrived. The *telpolli* – the natural outcome of all these bad omens.

The first reports were of a mountain moving through the water on the eastern shore of the empire. And then people started talking of men with pale hands and faces marching through the jungle, killing with strange fire sticks wherever they went.

He had been in the Stable three years then, and he could see that the Prince was worried. The Council of War met almost every day and the regular ritual of the temple was changed to a more desperate pleading for help and guidance.

He watched the priests make their ascent. It was the first ritual of the day, the pouring out of blood to the rising sun. Did they know what was happening any more than he did? he wondered.

He glanced to the east. The jungle stretched out before him, the great volcanoes towering over a carpet of green. They were in there somewhere, the *telpolli* foe, the pale men who rode on deer. Were they gods? Had Quetzalcoatl returned from his centuries-old sleep to reclaim his kingdom? Or were they the forces of the night, rallying to destroy the city and tear the flesh from their bones with sharp claws and teeth which would never stop biting?

'Oi, dreamer!' One of the women had come up the stairs on to the ramparts and was offering him a *tamale* wrapped in a maize leaf. 'Eat your breakfast or you won't be strong enough for one of us girls.'

She laughed and he laughed with her. The women knew what went on in the Stable: the nights of passion, the friendships that came and went, the world of men loving men. But they liked to tease, and at the great public festivals, when everyone came together and danced the ritual dances, they would come up to him and put their hands down the front of his loincloth, squeezing him, laughing and running their tongues round their tiny white teeth.

'Oh, Axatan, when will you come to us and find yourself a bride?'

And he'd laugh and push their hands away and carry on with

the dance. They knew he would never find a bride. He liked the women, but his heart was elsewhere.

The *tamale* was good and he went down into the courtyard for a cup of chocolate, silently mouthing the thank you prayer to Xilonen, the tender maize god, a prayer he had learnt at school and never forgotten. He knew that their food was controlled by the gods; that plenty today could become famine tomorrow. He knew when to show his appreciation.

He thanked the women and walked back to the Stable, pausing only to look out again into the jungle. They were there somewhere, but what were their intentions?

Today was a rest day and he had risen early and dressed in the simple blue mantle and breeches of the Stable uniform, his sandals marking him out as a member of the warrior class.

As he strode through the Stable courtyard he thought of the battles that had prepared him for the rank of Stable warrior and he glanced around at the sumptuousness of the Stable barracks, the gifts from the Prince, and the many trophies brought back from conquests of an earlier time.

Each man had his own bedchamber which opened out along two sides of a sheltered courtyard – a beautiful colonnaded area which gave both sun and shade. It was where the warriors would meet and talk and eat.

In the centre was a deep blue pool and many an evening the warriors would pass the time there once the day's activities were finished. Axatan loved that time of day. He liked listening to tales of battles or adventures in love and lust, until gradually the warriors slipped away to their rooms, either alone or arm in arm with some young soldier they had met in the market or on the lake. Then the Stable was silent except for the sounds of snoring or passion.

On the south side of the courtyard stood the refectory and recreation area, where military training took place, and the warriors kept themselves fit and supple. It was also where – Axatan smiled when he thought of it – 'Important Night Campaigns' took place after the sun had dropped below the horizon.

The fourth side of the courtyard contained the bathhouse and a doorway which led down to the ball court and gymnasium, and from there into the Great Courtyard itself, past the Palace and down into the marketplace.

Each week, after the temple ceremonies, the warriors would come to the bathhouse to relax, letting the warm waters soothe their muscles and allowing the sight of so many beautiful men to lead to not a little passion and adventure as the night closed in.

The sun was till low on the horizon, and Axatan knew that the Stable warriors would be sleeping late. He smiled at the thought of last night's 'manoeuvres'.

It had been the first night in the Stable for a young warrior called Janza.

He had arrived the previous week and, as was tradition, had been kept apart from the others until his initiation was completed. But once he had earned his warrior's cloak and spear, he had appeared in the Stable compound, looking a little lost and causing everyone to look up and take in the young beauty that stood in the doorway.

His body was muscled and tanned and had the easy grace of someone who had spent most of his life in the *chinampas* working the fields. His legs were solid and his stomach flat, and his loincloth showed off muscular thighs and a long, thick dick.

He was the type who would have been the most popular lad of his village, and Axatan could see him making the boys (and the girls) very happy in the fields. His strong arms, the proud muscles which rippled across his smooth torso and the slight sneer on his face marked him out as a man's man – the sort that fucks but never gets fucked. But, Axatan noticed, his arse was rounded and muscular, and that would be too much of a temptation for some of the warriors, who liked to fuck their way through the hot summer nights.

That night things had started quietly enough. The warriors were lazing around after the evening meal, swapping stories and boasting about past conquests, when Janza had slipped away towards his bedchamber.

It was getting dark, but Axatan noticed one of the other Stable boys – a lad named Huachan who had been a warrior for just a few months – creep away from the group and disappear through the curtained doorway of Janza's room.

He coughed and caught the eye of Quetzal, his best friend, ally and co-conspirator in any sexual adventure.

Quetzal looked up and Axatan nodded towards Janza's room.

His friend glanced round and grinned. His smile was always wicked, betraying his love of sex, games and tricks. Axatan loved to be with him. He loved his golden hair and his light skin, which showed that he came from the south. He also loved the ways they made love: the sight of his own dark cock against Quetzal's beautiful pale arse and the way the boy almost whimpered with pleasure as he ploughed his hard cock into his beautiful hole. Above all, he loved how anything they did together turned into a mad adventure.

Quetzal signalled to Tupac and Techuan, two of the Stable's strongest men, to join them. Tupac and Techuan were older than Axatan and Quetzal. They had been in the Stable three years when Axatan had joined, and they had a ferocious reputation. Both of them loved to fuck arse and both were excellent allies in any sexual adventure.

The four of them crept towards Janza's room.

'Huachan thinks he can have the new boy to himself,' Quetzal was saying, 'but I think we all have a right to the first fruit of the tree.'

He grinned and Techuan nodded in agreement, grasping the bulge in his breeches.

They stood outside Janza's door and held their breath.

From behind the thick curtain they could hear soft moans. Quetzal lifted the heavy cloth and they saw Huachan, naked and on his knees, with Janza's cock in his mouth. His eyes were shut and he was lost in pleasure as he sucked Janza's thick shaft, which seemed to be stretching the young warrior's mouth to bursting point.

Janza also had his eyes closed. He stood next to the bed, also naked, the thin line of hair which ran down from his chest leading the eye to his cock and Huachan's eager mouth. He was stroking Huachan's hair and pushing forward his hips so that his cock slid deep in and out of the boy's mouth. The deeper it went, the more Huachan groaned with pleasure. He was playing with himself and his own cock was rock hard against his belly.

Quetzal couldn't stop grinning. He squeezed Axatan's hand and Axatan felt his own cock begin to grow in his breeches. The two warriors were lost in their own passion and they never noticed the four others creep into the room.

Quetzal went first, and if the two were surprised to see him they didn't show it. He pulled off his loincloth and positioned himself so that he was standing next to Janza, his already-hard cock swinging in front of Huachan's mouth.

Huachan looked up and in an instant moved on to Quetzal's cock, sucking it greedily while he wanked Janza's massive dick. He pulled on Quetzal's balls and moved his mouth back and forth between the two shafts of heavy flesh in front of his face, so that he was sucking both of them, one after the other.

Quetzal had turned to Janza and was playing with his nipples, pulling them between his fingers and making the country boy writhe with pleasure.

Not to be left out, Tupac and Techuan both stripped off and positioned themselves next to Quetzal so that Huachan now had to move between four huge cocks, keeping them wet and sucking them all. Precome started to appear at the four cockholes level with his eyes, and his mouth turned raw with the need to service the four men standing above him. He never let his hand stray from his own dick, wanking himself frantically as he tried to take more and more flesh in his mouth.

Axatan kept his distance. He knew he would take part soon, but was enjoying watching his friend in the middle of all these beautiful men. Quetzal was on his knees now, sucking Janza, and Tupac had moved behind Huachan and was letting his cock play up and down the boy's crack.

Janza was ecstatic. As Quetzal sucked him, Techuan held him

in a wrestling lock and thrust his tongue down his throat, letting his rough stubble scrape over the boy's face. Janza was putting up a mock struggle and Techuan held him tighter like a prisoner in battle. By his groans, Axatan knew that Janza was enjoying every moment of it.

They paused and Techuan pushed Janza down on to the bed. In an instant, Quetzal had jumped up and was lowering his arse down on to the new boy's face.

'Now we'll make your tongue do some work,' he said. He grinned at Janza, who grinned back, his deep, brown eyes on fire with lust.

Janza sighed as his tongue flicked up into Quetzal's smooth crack. He licked all over the hairless skin and up into the soft, pink flesh of his arsehole. Quetzal writhed, grasping Janza's head and pushing him up into his arse. His cock was twitching and a drop of precome slid down on to Janza's chest.

Meanwhile, Techuan positioned himself between Janza's legs and with his strong warrior's hands pushed his knees apart to reveal the dark crack of his arse. He bent down and in one movement pushed his tongue deep into Janza's crack. The country boy thrashed around the bed. His tongue was in Quetzal's arse and his cock was rearing up off his belly as Techuan's tongue made its way past the thick, black hairs and deep into his soft arsehole.

On the other side of the bed, Huachan was on his knees, devouring and deep-throating Tupac's cock. The huge warrior swung his hips back and forth, fucking the young lad's face. Axatan looked on. It was a beautiful sight and he knew that soon he too would join in.

Techuan wet a finger and pressed it on to Janza's hole. The country boy groaned and Techuan pushed inside him, letting the muscle relax before pushing a second finger in and opening Janza up for what was to come.

This was Axatan's moment. He stepped over to the bed and climbed up, straddling Janza's stomach so that he could wrap his arms around Quetzal's strong torso and rub his dick up and down his lover's crack. Quetzal turned and kissed him full on the lips.

With one hand he stroked Axatan's hair. With the other he guided his cock underneath him so that Janza could lick Axatan's dick while simultaneously rimming Quetzal's arse.

Janza's dick lifted up off his belly in excitement and jerked around as Techuan's fingers reached inside him. The precome which had been lubricating his cockhead ran down his shaft and into the dark hairs which surrounded the base of his cock. Axatan could see that Janza was beside himself with pleasure.

Quetzal stood up and pushed his cock deep into Janza's mouth. The boy responded eagerly and took the long shaft deep into his throat as Techuan poured oil on to his long, thick cock and rested the head against Janza's open arsehole.

Tupac and Huachan moved to the other end of the bed and held Janza still so that Quetzal could tease him with his cock, pulling it right out of his mouth and then hammering it in again to the back of his throat, one moment brushing it against his lips and the next plunging it deep down inside him.

Techuan took a deep breath and started to push his massive cock into Janza's hole. The country boy yelled out with pleasure as the huge shaft plunged inside him. Tupac and Huachan were wanking their cocks over Janza's face and Quetzal was fucking his mouth as the huge warrior's dick slid deeper and deeper inside him.

Axatan grabbed the oil and began working his fingers into Quetzal's arse, making him grunt like an animal and arch his body towards his friend's rough hand.

Quetzal rode up and down on Axatan's fingers, pushing his cock deeper into Janza's mouth with each movement, and when he was ready he pushed Axatan's fingers away and sat back on to his friend's hard cock.

For Axatan, the feeling was like a thousand mouths sucking on his dick as he pushed his weapon deeper into Quetzal's arse. He closed his eyes as he felt Quetzal push down on to him and take his long, thick shaft inside him.

Quetzal was getting more and more excited and began to fuck Janza's smooth face faster and harder. Axatan responded by pounding his cock deeper and deeper into his arse. He could feel the come rising in his cock and knew that he was close to climaxing inside him. He put his arms around Quetzal and held him tight as he rammed his cock all the way inside. As he let out a cry of delight, he felt his friend shudder with pleasure as his dick filled him from within.

Tupac and Huachan were both beating on their cocks furiously as Quetzal leant forward and took the massive head of Tupac's dick into his mouth. Axatan was fucking his friend harder now. He was determined to bring him to orgasm first and he felt Quetzal's breathing get faster as his cock pushed up and down inside him. He looked around to see Techuan holding Janza's legs high in the air, pounding his arse like an animal. Meanwhile, Huachan leant forward and started to lick Tupac's balls as they slid in and out of Quetzal's mouth.

The five of them were working in unison now: Quetzal's cock in Janza's mouth, Tupac being sucked by Quetzal while Huachan licked Quetzal's balls, Axatan fucking Quetzal's arse and Techuan ramming into Janza's like he was a dog on the street.

It was Tupac who came first. The huge warrior let out a shudder of pleasure as his hot spunk flew out over Quetzal's face and chest and dripped down on to Huachan and Janza's faces below. The impact made Huachan shout with pleasure as his own come spurted up on to Tupac's legs, covering them with hot seed. Quetzal pushed hard into Janza's mouth and howled as his seed pumped into the boy's mouth, flowing over the sides and pouring down on to his neck and throat. Quetzal's coming made his arsehole tighten round Axatan's dick and Axatan found himself pumping his come inside him, trembling with joy as he held tight on to his lover's broad back and shoulders. Finally, Techuan filled the room with a roar as he came, covering Janza's arse with come and making the country boy arch his back and let his hot, white seed fly high into the air.

They collapsed in a heap, laughing and kissing. They wiped the come away from eyes and mouths and hands, relishing the soft reverie that follows sex and the company of each other's spent bodies.

It was Quetzal who spoke first.

'When I first saw you here,' he said to Janza, 'I thought you were an arrogant fool who would be the cause of much trouble. But now...' He laughed, wiping away some drops of come which were running down his chest. 'I *know* you are an arrogant fool, so whatever trouble you cause I want to be part of it. Welcome, my friend. You will enjoy your life here in the Stable.'

The others laughed in agreement and Janza smiled broadly, looking round at his new friends and wiping the sweat away from his forehead.

'You have given me a good welcome,' he said. 'I hope I can pay you back.'

'Oh, you will!' said Techuan, rising up off the bed and gripping Janza round the waist. 'And you can start now.'

He lifted Janza high off the bed and carried him screaming out into the courtyard.

'I think Janza has been claimed for the night,' said Quetzal, with a boyish grin. 'What are the odds that he will have some difficulty walking tomorrow?'

The three friends laughed and headed out of Janza's room to the bathhouse, and then to bed. It had been a good night.

It was late morning and still the Stable slept.

Axatan made his way over to Quetzal's bedchamber to see if his friend was awake yet. It was nearly time for the morning reveille and Axatan wanted to see him before everyone was up. He pulled back the curtain and glanced in.

Quetzal was still asleep. The golden hairs on his chest were glistening in the sunlight and Axatan immediately felt a pang of love as he looked at him lying there. Quetzal had come to the Stable a year before and Axatan and he had instantly become friends, sharing meals, adventures and sexual partners. They had scarcely spent a day apart. Axatan smiled. If he loved anyone it was Quetzal. And he knew how to make the boy happy.

Quetzal stretched and opened his eyes. He looked over and saw Axatan staring at him. Axatan glanced away, a little embarrassed, but Quetzal threw him one of his impish grins and beckoned him in.

'You had a good time last night,' he said, rubbing the sleep from his eyes. His face lit up. 'And so did I.'

Axatan grinned.

'I think you might find some time to take Janza on one of your outings to the countryside,' he continued.

Axatan blushed. He was well known for taking new warriors away from the city for a night in order to get to know them a little more privately. He certainly wouldn't pass up the opportunity to spend some time alone with Janza — but he had also enjoyed watching Quetzal the previous night.

'That's true, but I think three might be better than two.'

Quetzal smiled and pushed down the sheet so that Axatan could see he had a morning hard-on. The hair round his dick was golden, like that on his chest, and his cock was firm and straight. Axatan loved it when the two of them lay next to each other, rubbing their cocks together and letting their balls touch as they kissed in a deep embrace.

He stripped off and climbed into Quetzal's bed, breathing in the heat of his body as he put his arms around him and felt his smooth skin against his own.

Although they were almost the same age, Axatan was less of a boy and more of a man. He had grown quickly and his body was strong and coarse. It was because of this that he loved Quetzal's smooth softness. The boy was strong and he could fight any foe in battle, but in bed he seemed to melt as you embraced him.

They kissed, their tongues caressing as their cocks pressed hard against each other. Axatan moved his hand between Quetzal's legs and stroked the underside of his balls. Quetzal arched up and opened his legs so that Axatan could move deeper, flicking his fingers around Quetzal's balls, then over his thighs and down the taut skin of his crack towards his hole.

Quetzal reached up to lick Axatan's nipples, biting down on

them so that shocks of pleasure shot through Axatan's body and down into his cock. They were under the sheets now and Axatan positioned himself so that he was above Quetzal, looking down on his lover and slowly brushing his cock against his balls.

'You will always be my favourite.'

Quetzal smiled up at him. 'I love you,' he said.

For a moment the words tore at Axatan's heart as they looked into each other's eyes, and then he bent down to kiss Quetzal on the lips. They each stroked their cocks, breathing in unison and feeling the warmth flow between them.

Axatan drank in the beauty of his friend, marvelling at the time they had spent together, the hundreds of times they had made love, and the adventures they had had . . .

They had met a year before. Quetzal had arrived with a softness which could only come from growing up in the country. His skin was smooth and his muscles toned from the outdoor work he had done. He was trying to look tough, but Axatan could see that his head was full of confusion. This was someone who had spent most of his life with animals out in the fields. He was wearing just a white loincloth and what Axatan first noticed about him was the line of golden hair which ran from his belly button down towards his cock, hair which matched the golden locks which hung down to his shoulders.

Quetzal quickly found his room and was unpacking his bag and laying out the belongings on his bed when Axatan pulled back the curtain. Quetzal smiled at him and shyly beckoned him in. The curtain swung shut and the two of them looked at each other across the tiny room.

It was Axatan who moved first. He knelt on the floor and wrapped his arms around Quetzal's smooth torso, leaning his head against his flat stomach and feeling his heat.

He kissed his belly button and then began to work his tongue down the thin line of golden hair. Quetzal's cock began to swell in his loincloth and Axatan pulled at the soft fabric with his teeth, letting it fall away so that Quetzal's cock sprang up in front of his face. It was long and proud, the same light colour as the rest of his body, and it was surrounded by golden hair.

He could feel his own cock start to get hard as he nuzzled his lips against Quetzal's cockhead. His balls had a sprinkling of the same blond hairs that ran down from his belly button. Axatan kissed them and then started licking underneath his sack. Quetzal gasped and tensed the muscles in his legs, pushing his balls towards Axatan's face. Axatan licked a little harder, sometimes taking the skin in his teeth and nipping gently. Quetzal moaned as Axatan pulled on the sac with his teeth.

Quetzal's cock was rock hard in front of Axatan's face and the boy was lost in pleasure. Axatan opened his lips and took both of Quetzal's balls into his mouth. They tasted clean. He sucked gently and felt Quetzal's hands grab the back of his head in ecstasy. His tongue felt for the vein at the base of Quetzal's cock, swollen and ridged with pleasure, and he sucked on the boy's smooth balls and licked at the base of his cock.

He paused and looked up at Quetzal, who was smiling with his eyes closed. He saw his nipples standing out hard on his chest, his flat stomach, his tanned forearms and the black hair under his armpit – and he knew they would be friends. Quetzal's cock was in front of his face and tiny spurts of precome dropped on to his chest. He smiled to himself and felt Quetzal's body erupt as he took the cockhead into his mouth and sucked just behind the ridge, his tongue flicking over the hole. Quetzal pushed forward and Axatan felt the boy's cock slide deeper into his mouth, touching his tongue and the roof of his mouth and the soft lining with its hot taste of skin.

Quetzal pushed harder and Axatan found his own cock as Quetzal began to face-fuck him, making a rhythm in and out of Axatan's mouth. Axatan wanked himself harder and let his tongue flick over the head and shaft of the cock inside him. He was close to coming and he could feel that Quetzal was too. He squeezed harder with his lips, making Quetzal cry out and grab his hair in wild fury. The boy pumped harder and Axatan could taste his precome on the back of his throat.

His own cock was thick in his hand and he started to wank more furiously as Quetzal pushed his head away and shot his come all over Axatan's face and chest. It seemed it would never stop and the air filled with its sweet smell. Then Axatan came himself, shooting his come up into the air and over the legs of his new friend. Quetzal. Fresh from the country. Quetzal with the beautiful cock. Axatan smiled, his balls tightening, his cock still spitting the last drops of come.

'Welcome,' he said. 'Welcome to the Stable.'

That was a year ago. Now they hardly spent any time apart. This man meant everything to him – his body, his mind, his love of life. Axatan leant forward and kissed him full on the lips, and their tongues met, exploring each other's mouths.

The silence was beautiful. They wanked together, relishing the love between them.

Quetzal closed his eyes and Axatan watched as he lost himself in the pleasure of the moment. He remembered their first time together again; exploring each other's taut bodies, feeling for the places where each loved to be stroked or licked. He thought of the many occasions when they had just melted into each other's arms and drifted off to sleep, safe from the world outside and secure in their love and friendship.

He reached down and stroked Quetzal's face. The boy turned and took his fingers in his mouth, sucking them as he wanked his own cock. Axatan was wanking too and he felt the come rising in his shaft as he let his foreskin slide up and down over his smooth, wet cockhead.

They kissed again and Quetzal's breathing quickened. He cried out softly, locking eyes with Axatan as his body rose up off the bed and he came, his hot seed spurting from his cock in a gentle arc and running down his shaft over his taut belly. Axatan took a moment to breathe in the scent of his lover's come and then came himself, silently but strongly, shooting his sperm out over Quetzal's cock and balls and covering him with soft, white come.

They held each other tightly, dozing as the spunk began to dry between them, cementing their friendship and love. They dreamt morning dreams, inhaling each other's breath and savouring their love for each other, until the plaintive cry of the conch-shell trumpet broke through their reverie to announce the start of the day.

Two

For Juan, it was yet another lazy morning. So far, the expedition had been a waste of time. The voyage over had been long and boring (though some of the activities below decks had livened things up) and now they were here, all they did was build fortifications, forage for supplies and go swimming.

They had taken one of the savages captive and it was his job to give him food and water. The two men had spent a lot of time together, communicating through gestures at first, then teaching each other words from their language until Juan began to prefer his company to that of his comrades.

But it was still a long way from his dreams.

He remembered the day the soldiers had come to his village, how he'd heard their tales of gold and adventure, and how he knew he had to get away.

He and Pablo were in the fields when his little sister ran out to say that there was going to be a fiesta. A band of soldiers had arrived and Juan's father, as mayor, was arranging a feast for them.

The three of them had run back and found the village in a flurry of activity. The men were building a table in front of the bodega and the women were loading it up with trays of meats and vegetables and fruits. Antonio, the innkeeper, was rolling out barrels of wine and the priest was clucking around giving orders which everyone was ignoring.

Juan was eighteen years old and he'd spent most of his life in the fields, working or lazing in the sun, waiting for something to happen. He knew the village was too small for a man like him, but the nearest city was a week's journey away and there were stories of people going there, breaking some rule you didn't know about and disappearing into the castle's dungeons for ever.

He looked on at the preparations. His father was going to make a speech. He had that self-important look about him and was pacing up and down gesticulating. His mother was running around giving orders which contradicted the priest's, but it didn't really matter because everyone was ignoring her as well.

He loved his parents and he really loved his little sister, but he needed adventure and he knew he would soon find a way out.

He would find his fortune, he was sure. And then he would come back and take them all away from their tiny house and tiny world and they would go and live together in the city.

The sun was beginning to set when the soldiers finally arrived. Miguel-Angel's band started to play and the villagers all applauded as the six men self-consciously took their seats and the feast began.

They were tall, dark men, used to travelling and sleeping rough, and they had the gaunt look of men who sometimes went days without food.

Juan watched them ravenously gobbling up what was put in front of them. They seemed absorbed in the plates in front of them, oblivious to the celebrations going on around them. All, that is, apart from one.

He sat slightly away from the others and he looked younger and stronger, as if he had just joined them or came from a more rugged stock, letting him withstand the rigours of being on the road more easily.

Juan's father was trying to make his speech but he was finding it hard to be heard above the noise. The five soldiers were ignoring him, and the sixth, the younger man, was looking not at

Juan's father but at Juan, his eyes glinting with interest and invitation.

Juan looked behind him, sure that the soldier was looking at someone else, but all he could see were the fields disappearing into the distance.

He felt nervous and looked away, but he couldn't stop his eyes looking up again towards the feast. The soldier's deep stare pushed into him as if he was trying to get inside his body.

Juan's stomach filled with butterflies and to his horror he felt his prick stirring in his breeches. He crossed his legs and looked to see if anyone had noticed the bulge growing there, but the villagers were absorbed in the banquet and the only person looking in his direction was the young, handsome soldier.

Then he did something he would never before have dreamt of doing. He opened his legs slightly so that the man could see the outline of his cock in his breeches. He had no idea what he was doing; only that his body seemed to know what it wanted ahead of his mind.

The soldier stood and began to walk up the street, away from the square and towards the barn where the village kept its provisions. Juan was overcome with embarrassment. He had showed off his cock and this man had walked away in disgust. How could he live with himself now? The soldier was sure to tell everyone, and he would run out of town like the old man Ramón who had done that thing to Julio.

But then he noticed that the soldier was glancing back at him, and even from that distance he could see that his eyes were shining not with hatred but desire.

He stood up and found his feet acting on their own accord, taking him round the back of the bodega and out towards the barn. His heart was pounding with fear.

The man had opened one of the side doors of the barn and disappeared inside. Juan glanced behind him. The villagers were singing and dancing and no one had seen him leave. His dick was rock hard now, straining at the cloth of his breeches. He had never felt anything like it.

He pushed open the door. The barn was dark and it smelt of meats and cheeses. He could just make out some bales of hay stacked up in one corner and a couple of barrels, but otherwise it seemed empty.

The door closed behind him and the sound of the fiesta disappeared into the distance. He stepped forward into the dark.

He heard him first: a small cough and the sound of breathing. Then he began to make him out – the soldier, tall and broad, leaning against the far wall.

He had his shirt open and Juan could make out a mat of dark hair running down over his strong chest. The buckle of his thick belt glinted in the half light and to Juan's amazement his dark, thick cock hung loosely out of his breeches.

It was the first time he had seen another man's cock. He'd been swimming plenty of times in the river with the other boys of the village, and sometimes he'd lain in bed at night dreaming about Miguel's thick flesh which swung so temptingly between his muscled thighs. But this was different. This was a man's cock. And it was hanging there, ready and waiting for him.

Juan stepped forward, his throat tight with nerves. He reached out and took hold of the man's dick, surprised at its warmth and relishing the feel of its weight and power. It sprang up as he squeezed it and he was amazed to feel the blood pump through the shaft, making it swell and stiffen. The soldier put his hands on Juan's face and kissed him softly and Juan could feel the stubble scraping against his chin. The man tasted of wine and sweat and he suddenly wanted to lose himself inside him, and be with him for ever.

They pulled apart and the soldier gently but firmly turned him towards the wall.

Juan closed his eyes as he felt the man's hands unbuckle his belt and pull his breeches down round his ankles. His blood was racing with excitement and his cock was standing straight up against his belly. The air felt cool on his arse and made the little black hairs on his buttocks stand on end. He was being pushed hard against the rough wood.

He gasped as the soldier gently stroked his buttocks, letting his fingers play up and down his crack. This was a feeling like no other. He found himself pushing his arse back on to the man's fingers, spreading his legs and letting his balls swing free. The soldier's hands moved between his legs and touched his balls, and spasms of pleasure shot through him, making him shiver with excitement. Then, to his astonishment, the man got down on the floor and began to lick his tongue up into his arsehole.

The feeling was red hot and Juan pushed back, pulling his cheeks apart with his hands so the soldier could push his tongue further into him. He couldn't believe the man was doing this. He was licking his arsehole and the feeling was incredible. He felt dirty but thrilled and his cock was spasming in excitement as the man pushed his tongue further and further inside him. Juan reached for his own dick and started to wank himself, wanting to come but also wanting to hold back. When the man stood up and slowly slid his finger up into his arse he abandoned himself to a wave of feelings which were new and confusing and more thrilling than anything he had ever experienced.

He knew now what he had wanted for years and he grunted with pleasure as the man pushed in a second finger and then a third. Juan felt his arsehole being stretched and opened up. The feeling was one of pain and pleasure all mixed together and in an instant he understood what he had desired all his life. He wanted this man inside him, taking him to be his own and filling him completely; making him into a man. He reached out and grabbed hold of the soldier's cock.

It was hot, thick and hard and Juan felt like an animal grasping it and drawing in its beautiful strength through his fingers. The soldier paused and looked Juan straight in the eye.

'Are you sure?'

These were the first words he had spoken but Juan didn't reply. Instead, he turned and opened the man's shirt and started to lick and suck on his nipples, pushing him back on to the bales of hay and straddling his torso so that the man's cock brushed against his crack.

He took a breath and pushed his hole down on to the soldier's cock, biting his tongue to stop himself crying out as it pushed into him, stretching open his hole. It hurt for just an instant and then his whole body seemed to open up and let the soldier in. The feeling was unbelievable and he pushed down further, gripping his cock and fucking himself on the soldier's hard, thick meat.

He reached round behind and took the soldier's balls between his fingers. He began to twist and pull on them, making the man writhe in pleasure as he worked his arse up and down his cock. The soldier's hands were on Juan's hips now and he pounded his cock inside him as Juan watched his own sweat drip down and splash on to the man's solid torso.

The soldier closed his eyes and his breathing got faster as Juan started to ride him like a horse, letting the man's cock almost slip out of his arse and then sitting down hard on it, making him cry out with pleasure. He had one hand round his own dick now, working it up and down as he felt the man's shaft pound up his arse.

He knew he was going to come soon and he pushed himself down on to the man's cock once more before lifting himself high up above the soldier so that his shaft slid beautifully from his arse. The soldier cried out and took his thick shaft in his hand, wanking himself while gazing up at Juan, who was standing above him.

Juan wanked his own cock and crouched down so that the soldier could push his fingers up his open arse.

The feeling was indescribable and Juan found that he had started to come before he even noticed, his seed spurting from his cockhole and splashing down on to the thick hairs of the man's chest.

He wanked his cock harder and let the last drops of come run down his shaft. Then the soldier came too, splashing his hot spunk up over Juan's balls and making him come yet more until his balls were empty and they were both covered in hot, white spunk.

They collapsed in a heap, Juan's head on the man's chest. The soldier put his arm around him and Juan closed his eyes.

In the distance, the villagers continued their party, but Juan just smiled. He had found his way out of the village.

He had left the next day, crossing the fields with his new friends until they reached Cadiz and parted company. A ship was preparing to sail for the New World and Juan knew he had to be on it. He lied about his age and got himself on board. The captain was Señor Hernán Cortés and he held a warrant from their Imperial Majesties. They were ready to seek their fame and fortune in uncharted seas.

As he dug what seemed to be the hundredth latrine since they had arrived, Juan smirked. So much for fame and fortune! All he'd seen so far had been sentry duties in the camp and several good fucks from the older guys. He knew he was destined for better things. He was strong and could hold his own in a fight as well as the next man, but here all they did was wait and talk, talk and wait.

'Have you heard?' It was Sanchez, the camp clown and tireless gossip. 'They have found the city of gold.'

Juan didn't bother to reply. Sanchez's stories were usually far from the truth.

'Honestly. We're really close.' He pointed vaguely into the jungle that grew all around them, threatening to push them back into the sea. 'But we won't be seeing it.'

'Why not?' Juan feigned disinterest, but his heart was beating with excitement. A city of gold would be the answer to his prayers.

'They're looking for an advance party to spring a surprise attack. But rumour has it that the savages have darts tipped with poison which runs through your blood like molten metal. It doesn't kill you but paralyses you. You feel everything but can't move. Then they leave you out in the jungle to be eaten alive. The insects in there are as big as a man's hand and they have teeth which can chew into your face. The only mercy is when one of them finally eats through your ribcage and devours your heart.' He crossed himself. 'I like gold, but you won't find me volunteering.'

Juan shuddered. The jungle was a frightening place, but here was a chance for glory. They were sure to ask for volunteers at the afternoon parade. He would make sure he was chosen. He looked at Sanchez. They had been good friends since they had boarded the ship together at Cadiz.

'Do you want to go for a swim? It's getting hot.'

'Not for me, *amigo*. I'm going to see what's going on in the mess hall and then get a kip. Who says life in the navy is hard?' He scampered back up towards the camp.

Juan turned towards the sea.

The water was sparkling and the sun made little golden crests of the waves as they lapped up on to the beach. Juan felt his heart lift. Here was the chance to make his fortune. As one of the advance party he was sure to be given a bigger share of the gold. He would return home a hero and take his family out of the village and into Sevilla. They would live in a palace and servants would do all the work. He would make his sister a queen.

He ran down to the shore where you could see the fish in the crystal water. As a boy, he'd never seen the sea because the nearest port had been more than a day's journey away. But he'd heard about it from the merchants who brought salt fish to the village. The first time he'd seen it for real had been when he joined up with the conquistadors and set sail for the New World. And then he'd been sick for a week.

Now the sea was his friend. When he felt homesick or frustrated he'd strip off and dive in, feeling the cool water against his skin. It was like another mother for him.

He left his clothes on the beach and plunged into the water. The currents were strong and he let them carry him out across the coral and through the schools of tiny fish. He liked to see the brown of his body against the blue of the water. It was as if he was a sea creature, at home among the fish and bright shells on the sea bed.

The water between his legs made his balls tingle and he felt his cock harden, caressed by the millions of little currents. He let his hand brush against it – who said wanking was bad? – and swam back to the beach so that he could lie in the shallows, the water lapping between his legs.

He squeezed his nipples, slowly turning them and brushing them with the edge of his nail so that they stood up firm on his chest. His cock was hard, lying flat on his stomach, and he lifted his groin so that the water swept into his crack.

Juan closed his eyes. The sun was beating down on his dick and he felt himself being carried away, taken to a pure, white tent where he was laid on a bed and invisible hands squeezed his nipples and stroked his chest. A man was standing between his legs, strong and muscular, and he opened his legs wider to let the man in and fill him with his strength.

The water rushed up over his balls as his hands went down to his groin, running up and down his thighs and into the crack of his arse. He pushed a finger against his hole, wet and cold from the seawater, and with his other hand he pulled gently on his balls, massaging them between his fingers and thumb. He pushed the finger in and arched his body as he felt his arse relax and open, eager for more. He put in another finger and then a third, feeling the water rush inside his arse as he started to fuck himself with his fingers.

He grabbed his cock and pushed up into his fist, tightening his arse as he jerked himself off, feeling the waves crash against his legs. He closed his eyes and saw the man again. His strong chest, his muscled stomach, his cock sliding in and out of Juan's arse.

He wanked harder and pushed his fingers further into his arse. The come was rising in his cock and he bit into his lip.

'Fuck me.'

The voice echoed in his head as he saw the man pound his cock up into his arse, his strong muscles sending shockwaves up through his body.

'Fuck your boy.'

He lifted his arse into the air, taking the man deeper inside him, feeling him open him up.

'Oh, fuck me.'

The cock was ramming him now and he felt the come rising in his shaft.

He went wild, beating on his cock and thrusting his crotch into the air as he came, his balls pulling up into his groin and his dick covering him with white come which mixed in with the seawater and settled on his chest and stomach.

He lay back, lost in his dreams.

In the distance another man came too, looking down on the Spaniard at the water's edge. His face was sad as he pulled his cassock down and turned back to the camp for the midday mass.

Three

The Stable warriors were already filing out into the Great Courtyard when Quetzal and Axatan emerged from Quetzal's room.

It was time for morning parade and they pushed past friends and comrades to get to their allotted places before the conch shell was sounded again. The Aztec day had begun.

Around them, warriors were in various uniforms of their office. Some were wearing the magnificent jaguar skins which marked them out as swift infantry runners, others the armband and bright feathers of the hunter. But most wore the simple blue mantle and breeches – Stable standard issue.

Quetzal felt his finger. He was wearing the ring of an Eagle Warrior, the mark that he had passed the first stage of his initiation into the highest Aztec rank. He and Axatan had been training for months and their teachers were pleased. Now the day of their initiation was almost upon them.

He glanced at Axatan. He too possessed an Eagle Warrior ring, but it had adorned his finger since childhood.

Axatan rarely spoke about his background, only saying that a teacher put it on his finger in the House of Instruction in his neighbourhood. He had been too young to understand, and it was as if he had been born with the sign of the Eagle Warrior already upon him.

Now they were both on the cusp of their destiny.

The Prince was strolling among them. He towered above them, a giant of a man. His head was crowned with thick, black hair which was cut only once a year and hung in great swathes down on to his shoulders.

His broad chest, which rippled with strength won in battle, was adorned by a single diagonal leather strap carrying the golden symbols of his office. Around his waist he wore the golden belt of Tlaloc, from which hung jade skulls symbolising the power of the dead.

On his legs were deep blue breeches which showed off his muscular thighs covered with thick hair. Instead of sandals, he wore heavy black boots.

He was carrying a whip and his face was completely covered by the black mask of Tezcatlipoca, his eyes like black stones behind its grim face.

The conch shell sounded again. The time had come for the temple ritual and the Prince wandered among his men with greater determination, selecting the four warriors who would serve him in the dark rites of Tezcatlipoca, the most powerful of gods.

Under Montezuma, Tezcatlipoca was honoured not in the open, as the other gods were, but in a small temple which he had built himself deep down inside the Great Pyramid, below the twin towers of Tlaloc and Huitzilopochtli.

Tezcatlipoca was the god of divination, and the misty glimpses of the future which he offered to his priests were used to foresee the fate of the empire. The Prince had a passionate belief in his power and he personally took part in the rituals honouring him every morning.

He walked up to Huachan and tapped him on the chest. The boy dropped to his knees.

'Come, prepare yourself.'

The invitation was ritualistic and well known and Huachan,

who had taken part in the rituals before, nodded solemnly to his friends before running to the bathhouse to begin the rites of purification.

The Prince's next choice was Xenoc, a strong warrior who said little, and Quetzal watched as he strode to the bathhouse to begin his preparations.

He himself had taken part in the ceremony only once. It involved long rituals in a dark, airless chamber and Quetzal was always glad when the four participants had been selected so that he could run off and have the morning to himself.

Huachan and Xenoc were to be the lead priests in the ceremony. To serve them, the Prince would also select two youths from among the initiates. These were young warriors in the prime of their strength and beauty who were supplicating to become part of the Stable. Their teachers, grey and wise, stood by them, reminding them in low voices of the ritual and the etiquette of this, the most important of the Aztec daily rituals.

The Prince let his eye wander across their anxious faces. These young men had come from all parts of the empire to serve in the Stable and this was one route to preferment.

They were lithe and beautiful and in the prime of their strength. Supplication could take years and Quetzal recognised some faces from when he too stood in the Great Courtyard, hoping to be chosen and taken into the Stable.

Axatan, he knew, had come to the Palace as a warrior, already rough-hewn in the arts of war, and hammered on the gates until they had let him in. He, on the other hand, had learned his skills at the feet of noblemen and priests and, although he was a good warrior, he knew he had neither the stamina nor the cat-like intuition of Axatan. In battle they always fought together, their skills complementing each other, but Axatan always winning the day.

Montezuma was surveying the rows of young supplicants in front of him. At last, he pointed to two brothers who were standing together, their eyes as dark as their hair, their bodies hard from the regime of the House of Supplication.

The two youths looked back at him with proud defiance, determined to show themselves strong in the eyes of their Prince. They were wearing only white loincloths and, as befitted people not yet warriors, their feet were bare.

'These are they.'

The Prince's voice boomed out from behind the mask and the old men busied themselves around them, bustling them off in the direction of the bathhouse and the first stage on their journey to becoming Stable warriors.

The conch shell sounded again and the parade was over.

The warriors began to disperse, some heading for military exercises, others with business in the town. Quetzal turned to Axatan and pointed to the sky.

'It's a beautiful day,' he said. 'Let's go swimming.'

He expected Axatan to beam with pleasure. He loved swimming and their days on the lake were always fun. But his face was serious.

'What about being on standby in case the *telpolli* decide to attack?'

Quetzal blushed. The warriors had been ordered to stay constantly on alert. But things had been so quiet that life had gradually got back to normal and the order had been slowly forgotten.

In a skirmish at the beginning of the year, an Aztec warrior had been taken captive and all attempts to find him had failed. That was when people began to talk about ghosts or spirits from the dead.

'Well, I thought . . .' he stuttered. 'What with the *telpolli* being so quiet . . . we could . . . yes, you're right, of course.'

'I can't believe you wanted to swim at a time like this,' said Axatan, his face dark with anger.

Quetzal was afraid. He had never seen his friend like this.

He was nodding in agreement when Axatan burst out laughing.

'By Tlaloc, I could not keep a straight face any longer. Do you really think I would say no to a day on the lake for the sake of these pale-faced fools who are roaming the countryside?'

'But what if they are ghosts?'

'Look, my friend, if they are ghosts they are coming back to haunt those who haven't buried them properly. They will want nothing with us.' He smiled. 'Race you to the quayside. Last one there gets fucked by Techuan.'

They ran through the market where the traders were already busy doing business. They pushed through the dealers in gold and precious stones, confined to the area below the palace walls to protect them from thieves. They saw the bright, feathered cloaks laid out on display and the slaves chained to posts next to their sellers. There were piles of chocolate and maize as well as beans, vegetables and herbs, and then the sellers of fowl and little birds, animal skins and leather.

Axatan loved the market and kept stopping to taste something or feel the quality of a cloak or pair of sandals. It was as if the whole world came to the city to show off what it could produce.

Quetzal was getting annoyed.

'Come on!' he shouted. 'We haven't got all day.'

He pushed his way through the crowds and eventually they were standing on the quayside looking out across the sparkling blue water.

'Beautiful,' said Axatan, his smile showing off straight, white teeth against his brown skin.

'Incredible,' said Quetzal. 'Come. We need a canoe.'

A little further down the quay, a fisherman was sitting idly in the bottom of his boat. His catch had been unloaded and he was taking a moment to bask in the sun.

Quetzal reached into the bag he had brought with him and threw him a quill filled with gold dust.

'How much to the other side of the lake?'

The fisherman grinned. He recognised the uniform of the Stable and knew what it stood for.

'What do you have on offer?' He rubbed his crotch, but Quetzal spat.

'Gold, and that's all.'

The fisherman smirked, keeping his hand on his crotch for a moment, and then lazily leant over to untie his boat.

'All right. Where are you headed?'

'Across to the southern coves.'

'It'll be my pleasure.' He grinned a smile almost as white as Axatan's and made an extravagant bow.

Quetzal threw his bag in ahead of him and stepped into the boat. It was wet and smelt of fish, but it would get them there and then the day would be theirs. Axatan clambered aboard behind him and the narrow canoe headed out into the blue waves.

Axatan watched his friend. Quetzal was lost in thought. About the *telpolli* or the Eagle initiation they would both be facing in a few days' time? Both were unsettling. Both deserved to be forgotten about when swimming was in the offing.

He shivered as the boat sailed through the shadow of the city walls. Tenochtitlan had always seemed invincible. In the middle of a deep lake, the only routes in and out of the city were wooden causeways which stretched north, south and west on to the distant shores. The causeways were heavily guarded and could even be dismantled if necessary, making the city almost impregnable.

But now they faced another enemy. The *telpolli* didn't seem to be of this world. Either, as some said, they had come back to restore Quetzalcoatl, the great ancestor of the Aztecs, to his throne, or they were forces of the night ready to bring the time of the Fifth Sun to an end. Either way, Axatan doubted the wooden causeways would keep them away. They would have to trust to the will of the gods.

Quetzal and the fisherman had been chatting, but they fell silent as the huge walls floated by above them. Axatan closed his eyes and offered up a prayer for their own safety and that of the city.

The fisherman rowed on and Quetzal directed him towards the shore where high cliffs created a series of deep blue coves inaccessible from land.

'Land us near the trees,' he said, giving the man another quill filled with gold.

The fisherman steered the boat towards an empty beach where the pure blue water lapped up on yellow sand.

Quetzal jumped out first, throwing his bag in front of him and stripping off his clothes as he waded to the shore.

Axatan watched him. He was beautiful, his smooth muscles perfectly outlined by his soft, pale skin and his long, golden hair coming down to his shoulders. He looked like a spirit from another world.

Were they lovers or friends? They slept together, cherishing the moments of peace that each gave the other. But they also craved excitement and for that, Axatan wondered, did they have to look elsewhere?

In a few days' time, the Eagle initiation would admit them both to the highest rank of the Aztec nobility. It would mark for both of them the end of their youth. Would it also mark the time when they would part and seek their fortunes alone? He did not know.

Queztal had reached the beach and Axatan got up and followed, throwing his clothes on to the sand before he dived deep under the surface, relishing the coolness of the lake. He splashed about for a few moments, losing himself in the simplicity of the water, and then waded ashore and flopped down to sleep. He could forget the *telpolli*, the Eagle Warriors, their future. This was a day for forgetting. This would be a good day.

Quetzal let his eyes wander over his friend's body. His skin was a deep, dark brown. His hair was the black of burnt wood and his limbs were like those of a wild animal, powerful and ready for the chase. His cock lay lazily, thick and heavy, in the bush of dark hair round his groin. His hands were delicate like a girl's, but Quetzal knew they could break bones.

Quetzal loved him. He loved the fact that his eyes gleamed like jade, that his teeth were like pure crystal. Above all, he loved the fact that everything about him suggested strength: his strong limbs, his flat belly, the muscular shape of his chest. Even his grin was the grin of someone who went through life succeeding.

'What are you thinking?'

The sound shocked him. He thought Axatan was asleep.

'I was thinking about the *telpolli*,' he said quickly. 'Do you think the Prince is right, hesitating like he does?' Quetzal could only say this in private and to his friend. Doubting the Prince was blasphemy and punishable by death. But much of the city was asking the same thing. Did Montezuma know what to do about the invaders?

'I think he's right,' said Axatan.

A bird circled overhead.

'I was also thinking about something else.'

'Mm?' Axatan smiled at the sky.

'I was thinking about you and me. I mean, when we're in bed. How I like it when we make love.' He flicked some sand on to Axatan's leg. 'How maybe I'd like some more.'

Axatan grinned. 'Haven't you had enough of that this morning? I'm an old man compared to you youngsters.'

But Quetzal could see his dick was stirring and he leant forward and took it gently in his mouth.

Axatan groaned and guided his head down further on to his shaft, but Quetzal pushed his hand away.

'I thought you were too old to make love twice in the day, Granddad! Now you are going to have to work for it.' He leapt up and ran down into the water.

They splashed into the blue waves. Quetzal dived down under the surface and glided there, feeling the cool currents against his skin.

He jumped as Axatan grabbed his leg and pulled him down. Quetzal kicked out to get him off, but Axatan kept his grip until he had put his hands between his legs and turned him round so they were facing each other in the water.

They kissed and Quetzal closed his eyes so that all he could hear was the water lapping against the shore and the sound of their breathing. Axatan's tongue pushed inside him and he let himself be taken over by the beautiful strength of his lover.

He reached up and stroked Axatan's face. The stubble on his cheek felt good against his soft skin, and he felt a burst of joy that this man was his friend, holding him in his arms and making him feel safe.

He put his arms around Axatan, feeling the strong muscles of his back, and let himself be carried up into the shallower water where he laid him down in the surf. He knew he would happily give himself up to this man for ever.

He looked up. Axatan was towering above him, his body magnificent as the water ran off his taut skin, highlighting the easy strength of his limbs. His cock was half erect and Quetzal knelt down in front of it, sensing its weight and power in front of his face. They fell silent and Quetzal reached up and stroked the inside of Axatan's thigh, playing with the hairs that ran up into his groin.

He leant forward and gently put his lips around the end of his dick, holding it there for a moment and savouring the smell of musk and lake water that filled his mouth.

Axatan groaned and his cock hardened slightly, the end sliding out of his foreskin and over Quetzal's tongue. Quetzal bent forward, taking a little more of the shaft into his mouth and opening his lips wider as it swelled up and hardened in his mouth.

He started to move back and forth, teasing the end of Axatan's cock by flicking his tongue over the hole and licking under his foreskin, around the ridge of his head. He could taste saltiness as precome started to drip from Axatan's cockhead on to his tongue, and he could feel his own cock getting hard in the water as he leant forward and took the whole beautiful shaft into his mouth.

It was hot and smooth and strong, and Quetzal ran his teeth softly up and down it, licking the underside and squeezing round the head with his lips. He gently squeezed his friend's balls, making Axatan cry out and push his cock in deeper.

Quetzal reached down to his own dick and started pumping it under the water as Axatan began to grind his hips and slowly fuck his lover's face. Quetzal relaxed and Axatan's cock slid easily in and out of his throat, filling his mouth with the taste of salt and skin and come, and sending Quetzal's own cock into spasms of pleasure.

The water was licking up and down Quetzal's crack and he pushed his arse back so that his hole was splashed by the waves. Axatan's hands were all over him now and Quetzal could feel the spunk rising in his shaft. He gripped tighter on Axatan's balls, pulling them downward and plunging his head hard down on to his cock so that the head was in his throat and his face was buried in Axatan's groin.

Axatan pushed harder and Quetzal could feel the come rising in his friend's cock, making the vein bulge on the underside of his shaft. He could sense him bracing himself, and then in one movement, great spurts of come were flying out over Quetzal's face and chest and arms.

The light-skinned boy opened himself up to the sweet deluge. The salt taste filled his nose and mouth and he cried out with pleasure as his own come flew up through the water, making a milky slick on the lake's surface.

They fell forward into the water and dived down into the deep blue.

As they surfaced they kissed again, and Quetzal looked into Axatan's eyes as he stroked his face and held him in his arms.

'You'll always be safe with me,' Axatan said. 'Remember? The pact of friendship.'

Quetzal nodded. 'The pact of friendship.'

The waves lapped against the shore and the sun beat down on their shoulders. And they stood there in each other's arms, rocking gently in the waves.

Huachan lined up with the others. They had been cleaned and adorned in the ritual cloaks of warrior priesthood. Their hair was tied back in warrior knots and on their arms they wore the jewelled insignia of Tezcatlipoca. He knew what to expect and a sense of eagerness came upon him as he looked at the two supplicants who were to be initiated into the temple rituals that day.

The temple guards pushed open the heavy doors which led to the temple of the dark. From there they would make their way under the twin towers of Tlaloc and Huitzilopochtli until they arrived in a chamber directly below the killing stone.

During the ceremony, a captive would be tied to the stone table which stood between the fiery braziers of the sun, and his heart would be torn out of his chest and thrown into the flames.

At the same time, in the chamber below, Montezuma, Prince of the Aztecs, would introduce two more servants to the cult of Tezcatlipoca, leading a sexual ritual to please the darker forces of the universe.

They made their way down the dark corridor in silence. In front, the two youths led the way, stripped bare. They had been shaved and their cocks and balls swung smooth and fleshy between their legs.

Behind them, Huachan and Xenoc carried the ritual incense burners, and behind them the Priests of Tezcatlipoca had begun their low chant. The Prince brought up the rear.

They stepped into a dark, stone-lined room lit only by a single torch burning on the wall.

The doors swung shut and the Prince entered behind them. He was wearing the black mask of Tezcatlipoca and a dark leather harness. He had removed his breeches and a dark leather thong was pulled tight around his cock and balls. His chest and stomach were covered with short black hairs and his long, thick dick swung out from his body, half erect and revealing his heavy balls below. He was still carrying the whip.

He commanded the two boys to kneel. They looked at each other and Huachan recognised the excitement and trepidation in their faces. He and Xenoc looked on as the initiates prostrated themselves in front of their Prince, their cocks already hard against their smooth stomachs and their arses bare and ready to be used.

The priests continued their chanting and the smell of incense filled the room.

'Men of the Stable.' The Prince's voice echoed from the low stone roof. 'We come to worship our lord and master Tezcatlipoca, omnipotent god, god of time, dark mirror to the future. Prostrate yourselves.'

Huachan and Xenoc fell face down on to the floor as a crash of cymbals marked the beginning of the ceremony.

The two supplicants knelt and bowed their heads. The Prince moved into the trance and the god's spirit began to take hold of his body.

He grew in stature until it seemed that the tiny room could not hold him. Where once the Prince had stood, now stood Tezcatlipoca, eager and hungry for the day's offering.

The two boys edged forward and took the end of his cock into their mouths. They flicked their tongues around the ridge of his cockhead and licked up and down his shaft, pulling on his balls with their hands.

The Prince's cock began to grow and they lapped up and down it, worshipping its majesty and tasting its taut power.

The Prince groaned and ran the end of his whip between the two boys' buttocks, making them moan with supplication. Huachan remembered his own initiation into the cult of Tezcatlipoca. His arse had been beaten almost raw as the Prince became the angry god, punishing him in the name of a wicked nation and whipping the evil out of him. He watched as Montezuma ran his crop over the boys' firm buttocks and felt his own cock begin to harden.

'Show off to me.'

The Prince's command echoed around the room.

The two initiates lifted their arses in the air and Huachan licked his lips as he saw the thin line of hair running down their cracks and their smooth balls hanging free between their legs. He knew what was to come.

The Prince gave the sign and Huachan and Xenoc positioned themselves behind the two young men.

Huachan looked down on the youths below him, and he could see that they were full of lust and desire, ready to give themselves up in the worship of this dark god. They were slavering over his cock like dogs; devouring him with their lips. They rubbed their faces up and down his shaft as he grasped them by the hair and guided their tongues over his cock, down between his legs and into the darkness below his balls.

Next the Prince took two leather collars and put them round the boys' necks. He joined them with rope and used them as his slaves, pulling their heads one way and another and guiding their willing tongues to his balls, his cock, his legs, his nipples ... wherever he needed to feel the hot heat of their desire.

Huachan pulled off his breeches and let his cock spring out. His shaft was short and thick and the head was pushing through his dark foreskin. He wanked on it slowly and then began to rub it up and down the crack of the young initiate in front of him. Xenoc followed suit, pulling his breeches up and letting his long, pale cock push out in front of him. The boys continued to service the Prince as they lifted their arses in the air and showed the two warriors their tight, pink rings.

The Prince was lost in a frenzy of pleasure, using their mouths and pulling on their collars as if they were an extension of his own body.

Huachan let the sweat drip from the young warrior's arse on to his cock and used it to make the shaft smooth and shiny.

He pushed his cockhead against the boy's tight ring and, as the priests' incantations echoed through the chamber, pushed down into the young warrior's flesh. The boy cried out in pleasure and his ring opened up to admit the thick shaft of Huachan's cock.

Xenoc had also penetrated the smooth arse in front of him and now the boys were bucking on their leashes, desperate for more of the warrior flesh inside them and eager to taste the Prince's precome, which was dripping off the end of his cock. Huachan and Xenoc pounded their arses with their thick weapons.

The priests chanted louder and the Prince raised his voice in supplication. A deep growling echoed around the room and the air was filled with the smell of burning. The god was truly with them. The two boys were lost now. Positioned on all fours, they were filled from both ends with the thick cocks of warrior men, and Huachan knew it was time to release them.

He pushed down hard into the warrior in front of him while

Xenoc did the same, burying his thick shaft in the eager hole. The youths bucked in unison and shouted cries of joy as they came together and their seed spilled out on to the floor.

The growl turned into a roar as the room was filled with the smell of come and sweat and Huachan and Xenoc pulled out and let their seed spurt over the young warriors' smooth balls and arses. Finally, the Prince pulled on his cock and covered their faces with the hot seed of Tezcatlipoca.

The priests ended their chanting and Huachan smiled at Xenoc, both warriors remembering their own initiations in this chamber and feeling for the two boys who lay exhausted on the stone floor.

No one was prepared for the explosion which rattled the incense burners and sent plaster falling from the ceiling. A rumbling rose up from the floor below them and the stones began to fall in the entrance to the chamber.

Huachan and Xenoc grabbed the two youths and dragged them towards the door. The priests were running up the passage towards daylight and Huachan shouted to them to keep the door open.

They ran harder as stones and rock fell around them. The Prince was running too, shouting to them to hurry. Another explosion boomed through the air and the whole pyramid seemed to shake in its foundations.

At last they reached the doorway and emerged, coughing, into the Great Courtyard and the bright glare of the sun. Everywhere, people were running back and forth. Screams filled the air. They looked over to where the noise was coming from to see flames leaping up around the ramparts. The marketplace was on fire.

Quetzal was lost in his dreams, dozing in Axatan's arms, when the fisherman rounded the corner, shouting in their direction.

'Get in the boat! Quick! Get in the boat! The city is under attack!'

Four

The attack was coming from the north of the city. As the fisherman paddled towards the south causeway, Axatan and Quetzal could hear the little explosions which came from the *telpolli's* firesticks. Strange stones giving off fire flew through the air and landed in the water, and on all sides fishermen and merchants were paddling frantically towards the city walls.

They scrambled out of the boat and up across the wooden duckboards to the south gate. On the ramparts, the defence warriors were massing. Some threw spears in the direction of the enemy but even the strongest could only get as far as the shore. The archers did better but the *telpolli* attack seemed to be coming from a thicket of trees deep in the jungle and none of the Aztec weapons were reaching them.

They ran through the marketplace towards the Palace. Some of the stalls were on fire and a row of soldiers were passing buckets of water from the canal to put it out. Everywhere, people were running for cover, but it seemed that most of the fiery stones were landing outside the city walls.

Above the market, a winding path led up towards the Palace and the stone battlements were already blackened by the fire.

Axatan bounded up first. Quetzal paused to look down on the burning marketplace.

'Hurry up.' Axatan beckoned to him from the steps. 'They'll close the gate and we'll be stuck outside.'

Quetzal took one last look at the burning stalls. He thought of the gods throwing down fire on the city and shuddered. If that was Quetzalcoatl attacking from the jungle he would have no time for resistance when he finally entered the city.

A fire stone came flying through the air. People scattered as its terrible heat rained down on them but then fear was turned to laughter as it landed straight in the canal. Maybe the gods were on their side after all.

In the Great Courtyard, the palace warriors were lining up ready for battle. Tupac and Techuan strode mightily back and forth in their jaguar-skin regalia, encouraging the younger warriors and exhorting anyone who would listen to bravery and skill. The Prince was speaking with his generals in a small huddle in one corner and the ratings were whispering excitedly among themselves.

'Ah, we have reinforcements!'

It was Tupac striding towards them. Quetzal laughed but he could see the anxiety in his eyes.

'They're making these strange fire stones fly out of the jungle.' Tupac pointed over the battlements to where a rain of fire was still coming towards them, the stones mostly falling into the water. 'Our plan, if our good generals can make a plan between them –' He smirked in the direction of the Prince and his commanders '– is to provoke them from the rear and draw them into the marshy ravine where they have no chance against our men.'

He looked at his two friends.

'Of course, it is the Stable who will be "provoking" the attack.'

Axatan smirked but Quetzal's heart beat faster. This was a chance for heroism or death. If Quetzalcoatl and his ghostly army had returned to reclaim the city he lost in the time of the First Sun, what chance did even the most skilled warrior have?

Alternatively, if they could lure the army into the marshy ground, they would be returning that evening to a victors' welcome.

They walked in silence to their quarters and donned their battledress; Axatan from head to toe in jaguar skin, armed with a jade shield and spear thrower, Quetzal more lightly armed, carrying a bow and arrow. He left his sandals by the bed. In the jungle, bare feet could speak to the ground and find their own way home.

The warriors numbered around 200 men, with the men of the Stable at their head. They were an impressive sight. Many-coloured feathers fluttered in the wind, calling on the gods of the sky to help them in battle. Obsidian-tipped spears glinted in the sun and shields scowled with the ferocious death masks of Huitzilopochtli and Tezcatlipoca.

The air was heavy with anticipation.

Montezuma held up his hand.

'Brave warriors of Tlaloc and Huitzilopochtli. Tenochtitlan, our city, is being attacked. Our priests have prayed to the gods. We have sacrificed to Our Mother Earth. Now we must venture into battle.

'All of you have battled for us before. No one will forget our campaigns in the north. But these are different foes. These are men from another world.

'There are rumours that they come as gods to us. But our priests refute this. There are rumours that they are spirits of the dead come to punish us for our wrongdoings. But I refute this. I have met them. They are men who have never followed the ways of the gods. They are weak and use their magic to hide their failings.

'Today they have arrogantly made an assault on our city. Today we will go out and crush them.'

The warriors cheered.

'Open the gates,' the Prince commanded. 'We march to victory.'

The great wooden doors which led to the northern causeway were swung open. Fire stones were falling all around them, splashing in the water with a hiss. Quetzal touched the gates as they passed through. By tradition they would remain open as long as the battle raged, ready to welcome home the victorious or the dead. He turned to Axatan, who looked serious and distant.

'My friend.' Axatan turned and Quetzal could see worry in his eyes. 'We have been victorious in battle before,' said Quetzal, 'and I pray that we are victorious today. But, should the gods and chance have different plans for us, I will tell you now that I love you with all my heart. Wherever you go I will follow. Help me to keep you protected.'

Axatan held his friend's head in his hand and smiled.

'We will return tonight,' he said, 'and I will always protect you and take your protection. In life and death, we are here for each other.'

They embraced like men of battle and joined the others marching across the causeway towards the lake and the *telpolli* army. As they passed through the gates, Axatan reached out and took Quetzal's hand.

The green canopy of the jungle closed above them and shut out the sun, welcoming them to another world. The plan was for the Stable warriors to separate, surround the *telpolli* camp and await the signal to attack.

Axatan and Quetzal scrambled higher into the hills. Like all Aztecs, as children they had been led out into the jungle blindfolded and made to find their way home. They had learnt how to read the signs of nature; to allow the jungle to talk to them and yield up its secrets. They had spent nights listening to the jungle creatures and learning their language. They had come to love the jungle and respect its ways.

They were following the line of an old stream which took them high into the hillside. In the distance they could hear the *telpolli*. Their strange shouts mixed with the regular thud of the fire stones being launched into the air.

Every so often, a sound behind them would make them freeze in their tracks. The jungle was full of dangers. Animals dwelt there who held the angry spirits of souls murdered in their homes and never avenged. Evil spirits inhabited trees and streams, ready to grab the unsuspecting traveller and steal him away into their sad world for ever.

Quetzal looked up at Axatan in front of him, picking his way among the rocks that lined the stream's bed, his tongue sticking out of his mouth in concentration. He felt safe.

Axatan had reached the top of the hill and was looking down into the valley when Quetzal caught up with him.

'Look, down there. You can see them.' He was pointing into a thicket of palm trees which surrounded a small piece of water.

They were men, but their skin was the colour of chocolate mixed with milk. They reminded Quetzal of the merchant who came with spices into the market, telling tales of faraway lands. They wore dark clothes like the temple priests at the Time of Sweeping, and they seemed to have no weapons anywhere on their body.

Quetzal looked down on them. If these were the forces of Quetzalcoatl they had returned without nobility or grandeur. These men looked more like ants than mighty warriors.

In the centre of the camp was a huge machine which made the fire stones fly up over the trees and towards the city. In the distance they could see the lake and the city itself, its gates open to welcome them back as victors. The stones were still falling in the water.

The wind blew in the trees. Quetzal turned to his companion.

'I thought they would be taller. Those guards that came back made them sound like monsters.'

Axatan nodded.

He stared down into the strangers' encampment, his brow furrowed with thought.

'They're not tall,' he said, 'but they are dangerous. That machine could destroy the city and we wouldn't be there to defend it. We need to take them soon.'

He looked around them. On each side, pairs of Aztec warriors were preparing for the assault. Janza and Huachan were crouching perfectly still, camouflaged against the jungle background. Further away, Tupac and Techuan stood like statues. All the Stable warriors were fanned out above the enemy camp, silent and motionless. They were men used to hunting birds and animals; expert in the art of waiting.

They crouched down and Quetzal turned his arrows in his hand, their tips coated in poison, ready to paralyse a victim at a hundred paces. The signal to attack would be the release of the Hupan birds from the cage the commanders carried with them. The Hupans were homing birds and would fly high above their heads back to the city, noticed only by those who were looking for them.

They never saw the *telpolli* soldier until he was almost on top of them. Axatan was the first to turn and he let out a cry of alarm as the man bore down from the jungle behind them, his sword flashing through the air.

The angry blade crashed down beside them, slicing though the wooden branches and sending leaves flying into the air. Quetzal leapt to the side as Axatan swung round with his club and hit the stranger in the stomach. The soldier buckled and Quetzal drew his hunting knife, ready to despatch him for good.

'Attack! We are being attacked!'

Axatan's voice cut through the jungle as the *telpollo* drew himself up again and swung his sword deep into Quetzal's arm. The pain was intense and Quetzal cried out, lunging his knife forward towards his attacker, but he had already disappeared into the deep green of the trees behind them. Quetzal was left, venting his anger at the trees.

The blood poured red from his arm and he found himself becoming transfixed by it as he watched it drip on to the jungle floor. He thought of the priests who cut themselves every day. He thought of the children sacrificed on Mount Tlaloc during the Great Vigil, feeding their blood to Our Mother Earth. He watched his own blood sacrifice, which would flow straight to the Humming Bird fields to feed the spirits of the dead.

He could hear a dull noise in his ears. Someone was calling to him from a great distance.

'Hurry!' they were saying. 'Hurry!'

It was getting louder and now Axatan was shaking him and shouting in his ear.

'Run! They will send reinforcements and we have to get back to the others.'

Quetzal looked up. He was caked with blood and a deep throbbing pain was running through his left arm.

He bit on his tongue.

'I am all right, Axatan. Let's move.'

He directed all his strength into his legs and hauled himself along the path.

Behind them they could hear trumpet calls and strange shouts. The *telpolli* had seen them and were pushing their way through the undergrowth. The strange pale creatures stood out against the green of the jungle, like ants on the floor of the banqueting hall. He wanted to crush them there and then. But he held back from shouting. They were already heading for the marshy ground.

At the brow of the hill, they found the rest of the Aztecs watching the *telpolli* advance. They pushed their way through the ranks of their comrades until they found Techuan.

He looked at Quetzal's arm.

'What have you done?' he asked, smirking. 'Did the stranger bite you?'

Quetzal spat on the ground. 'It was a surprise attack,' he snarled. 'We fought him off, which is more than you did, but they are returning. Don't just stand there! Get me something to bandage this with.'

Axatan stood around awkwardly as Techuan tore a strip from his cape and tied it tightly round Quetzal's arm. Tupac joined them.

'It seems your little interlude was the perfect decoy. They are heading exactly where we want them – towards the gorge of Huitpolli. The ground there is soft and they will begin to get stuck. That will be our signal to attack.'

He glanced at Quetzal's arm.

'You be careful,' he said, looking him straight in the eye. 'A lot of people would miss you if you failed to return from this battle.'

Quetzal felt a pang of remorse that he had been so hard on his friend, but inside he was devastated that he was the first casualty of the battle. The wound was less serious than it looked but the news that they had let a *telpollo* creep up on them wouldn't be so easy to forget.

It took almost an hour for the *telpolli* column to reach the gorge, and by then the warriors could see that they were tired and thirsty. The soldiers were throwing down their baggage in the heat and even left weapons behind them as they scrambled through the harsh undergrowth.

The advance party had only seen 30 or so men in the *telpolli* encampment, but they had assumed that the rest of the army was somewhere nearby. Now it was becoming clear that this was the full contingent, the rest remaining in their encampment in the east.

The Aztecs' excitement began to grow. What had started as a defensive manoeuvre now looked like turning into total victory. Not only would they defeat the *telpolli* in their first engagement, they would also bring them back as captives for the killing stone.

Warriors started to swing their spears and grunt the war songs of their ancestors under their breath. Below them the *telpolli* continued to march into the gorge, like flies into a spider's web. The warriors smiled to themselves, watching them from above. The gods were looking favourably on them today.

They heard the birds before they saw them. The high-pitched squawks and flutter of wings rang out over their heads as the golden creatures soared high towards the sun and home to Tenochtitlan.

As one, the Aztecs leapt from their hiding places and rushed down the hillside, shouting their war cries and screaming at the tops of their voices.

The *telpolli* looked up, surprised and confused. They began to run in every direction, but the Aztecs had positioned themselves on all sides. At last, the *telpolli* were facing their destiny.

Juan looked up. From where there had been once just the strange, tall trees of the jungle, there were suddenly hordes of savages screaming down upon them, covered in feathers and swinging blade-encrusted clubs around their heads.

'*Dio Mio*. Run!'

It was the platoon commander, the one who liked to fuck him after parade. His face was as white as a sheet and his mouth was wide open with shock. He was already running in the opposite direction.

Now the savages were in the ravine itself. He saw some of the men fighting back, but the air had made their gunpowder wet.

The savages ran down the hillside, making a terrible screaming noise as they hurled themselves at the Spanish. A group of them had surrounded Ferdinand, the old mercenary from the north, and he was punching out, ducking the onslaught of their clubs and trying to scramble back into the jungle.

Everywhere was chaos. The Spanish had been caught virtually unarmed and were seriously outnumbered. There was no option but to run.

Ahead, he could just make out a path leading back into the trees. The jungle would give him some cover and from there he would be able to make for the setting sun and hopefully back to the camp.

He took one last look behind him and leapt into the green night.

All was silence. Above him the branches stretched as far as he could see. A bird fluttered from one tree to another, screeching with its strange call. He could still hear the sounds of battle but here it was as if armies had never existed. This was a secret world.

He crossed himself.

The trees had blocked out most of the sun and the jungle was shrouded in darkness. He walked on, tripping over the roots which lined the floor. A bird was making a cawing sound somewhere above him and now the buzz of thousands of insects filled the air.

He shivered. Despite the heat he was strangely cold. He broke into a run. He thought he saw people lurking behind trees, like ghosts in the underworld. Faces stared at him from the branches and he heard whispering voices call out his name.

He turned around, but instead of the path he had just come from all he saw was green. The trees seemed to crowd in on him. A stump looked familiar, as did a broken branch hanging from a trunk. But then so did that branch over there, and that one and that one. He couldn't see the sun. It was as if the green shadows had eaten it up and were now coming for him.

Ahead of him was a patch of white. At first it looked like a stone, gleaming on the dark floor, but as he got closer he saw teeth and eyes and realised with horror that it was a human skull.

He looked behind him. Another skull stared at him from the soft earth, and then a third and a fourth, until he realised that the ground beneath his feet was littered with the bones of the dead.

Then he screamed. His voice rose up inside him, gasping for air in his dry throat, trying to free itself from the sickness in his stomach. The sound rang around the jungle and sent birds flying high into the air from the tree tops and animals scuttling for cover in the dense undergrowth. He knew the savages would be after him.

It was his feet which moved first, carrying his body with them as if they had a mind of their own, taking him deeper and deeper into the jungle. He was screaming still and the branches tore at his clothes as he ran, catching at his legs, reaching out for him as if the jungle was trying to slow him down. Faces laughed at him from behind the trees. Spirits flew through the air calling his name. He had no idea where he was going. All he knew was that he had to get away from those skulls.

The attack had not been a success. The *telpolli*, seeing the Aztecs coming down the mountain, had not stopped to engage in battle as they should have done. Instead, they had run like women into the jungle. The astonished Aztecs had flooded down into the valley to find their enemy disappearing in front of their eyes. They had captured one or two men but most had vanished into the dense green of the trees.

They had made fools of them all.

Standing in the middle of the gorge, the Prince divided his army up into small search parties.

'These cowards will not get away!' he bellowed, picking up a stranger's bag. 'After them and take them alive! The killing stone will run bright with their blood tonight.'

He beckoned them to follow him – Tupac, Axatan, Techuan and Quetzal, plus Janza and some others from the city brigades – and pushed south into the jungle towards the lakeside. They were quick on their feet and knew the sounds of the jungle well. Every twenty paces, they stopped and listened to the air, imploring the gods of the jungle to tell them where their prey was and promising them gifts after their victory. And the gods did not desert them.

The scream echoed through the jungle.

Montezuma paused. He had always said that the jungle was like a huge spider's web. Treat it carefully and you could slip through the holes undetected. Rush, and you would soon be caught in its threads, the whole area feeling the vibrations of your fear.

The second scream rang through the jungle from the west, filling them at once with bloodlust and excitement. Their quarry was close at hand.

'It came from the killing fields,' said the Prince, and the others nodded in agreement. 'The hunt is on.'

Quetzal was in the frontline and as they picked up speed, the cut in his arm filled him with pain. But he was not going to withdraw. Since he was a child he had been a good hunter and he knew this stage of the chase well.

'He senses us,' he said to Axatan, 'but he doesn't know we are here yet.'

Axatan nodded and the warriors fell into single file, their breathing silent and their blood running with the thrill of the chase.

It was Techuan who spoke.

'There he is.'

In the distance they saw a dark figure scrambling through the undergrowth.

'He is running towards the river. Our prey is in sight.'

He took a poison dart from his quiver, but Montezuma stopped him.

'I want these people captured not killed,' he said. 'They will be a gift to Tezcatlipoca for protecting our kingdom. Put your poison away and treat him like a chicken you wish to sell in the market. He must be captured in prime condition.'

The tiny figure was scrambling up a small bank about a hundred paces ahead of them when the Prince gave the order to attack. He was renowned for the speed of his chase and as a youth had earned himself the name Jaguar King for running three days' journey in just a day and a night. Many said that he was the offspring of a god, and he certainly seemed to move with a supernatural ease through the rough terrain of the jungle.

Quetzal and Axatan followed him. They were the warrior's runners. What Techuan had in strength they had in speed. The trees were whizzing past them as they flew towards the dark figure in the distance. The Prince was focused on his target, his expression at the same time fierce and calm, like a hunting bird who can see nothing but his prey.

They were closing in now and they could see that the figure was struggling. The Prince reached to his belt and took off a coil of rope tipped with golden weights. Quetzal knew the *telpollo*'s time was numbered. He balanced the weapon in his hand and waited until there was a small clearing between them and the stranger. And then he seized his prey.

Juan ran as fast as he could. He was pushing the trees out of the way, leaping over roots and running anywhere to get away from the skulls. All he needed was a small place of refuge – some water and shelter for the night. He never noticed the rope flying through the air until it caught him round the stomach and brought him crashing to the floor.

The Aztecs could see the surprise on the *telpollo*'s face as the rope swung him round and brought him down into the sharp undergrowth. He scrambled around for a while and then rolled over, looking up at them with defiant eyes and tugging on the Prince's lasso.

The warriors surrounded him, catching their breath as they

looked down at the specimen on the floor. He was younger than all of them, his eyes shining with defiance.

Montezuma spat.

'Is this the best the *telpolli* can do? A mere boy? They send boys to fight against the might of Tenochtitlan, of the kingdom of the Mexica? Come, I will show you what a boy can expect when he fights with men.'

He grabbed him by the shoulder and lifted him up off the ground, pushing him towards a tree at the edge of the clearing.

'Tie him to the trunk.'

The moment of danger had passed. The *telpollo* was not going to hurt them. He stood there, gazing around him as the warriors caught up, ready to witness what the Prince called his 'special pleasure'. Now was the time for fun.

Techuan threw some rope to Janza and the two of them forced the youth's arms round the trunk of the tree and tied them high above his head. His face was pressed against the bark and he let out a little groan when his legs were spread open and his knees and ankles tied firmly to the trunk.

The Prince stepped forward.

'Strip him.'

The stranger's clothes were in shreds and Janza pulled them easily from his muscled body.

Quetzal let his eyes run up and down the beautiful contours of his back and arse.

The boy was young; perhaps a little older than the boys in the House of Supplication. He was pale, but his body already showed the strength of the finest warrior and Quetzal wondered if he had been one of the *telpolli* champions. His chest and arms were covered with thick black hair which ran down into his groin. The hair on his head was cut short but still showed the same dark richness as that on his body. His legs were muscular and hairy, too, like those of a gazelle. He looked like a child of the forest.

Quetzal could feel himself getting hard and tried to cover up the growing bulge in his breeches. He tuned to Axatan and saw that he too was staring at the youth, his eyes distant and enigmatic.

The Prince had undone his cape and was running his hand over the captive's hairy legs and arse. He was smiling and his cock was rising up from his groin. Quetzal felt his own cock stir again.

The Prince ran his hand up and down the boy's crack, teasing him and flicking his finger over and around his pink hole. The captive's cock was hard, pushing up against the bark of the tree, its pink head pushing out of his foreskin. He pushed his arse back towards the Prince, beginning to play a game which as yet had no rules.

The Prince lifted his hand and let a heavy slap come down on the captive's buttocks. A red mark glowed on the young *telpollo*'s arse, and the young warrior allowed himself a smile.

The Prince spat on his hand and rubbed his saliva up and down the thick shaft of his cock. His eyes were drilling into the back of the *telpollo*'s neck and he positioned himself so that his cock rested against the boy's crack, sliding up and down the hairy crack, lubricated by its own precome.

Quetzal reached for his own cock. He felt strange being excited by this man who was his enemy. He tried to banish the thoughts of pleasure from his head, but his mind teemed with desire and he longed to take the boy back to the Stable and discover the secrets of his pale-skinned body for himself.

The Prince took hold of the boy's hips and pushed his cock forward, letting his cockhead slip inside the captive's soft, pink ring. The *telpollo* cried out for an instant and his cock reared up against the tree, then the Prince's dark flesh slid up past the pale skin of the captive's arse.

The young man pushed his hips back to take more of the Prince's cock inside him. A smile played around his mouth as he moved his arse in time with the Prince's fucking.

The Prince thrust forward again and the captive pushed back, twisting his hips so that he was sliding the Prince's cock in and out of him like a huge dildo. Quetzal could see that it was turning into a war of wills.

The other warriors were wanking themselves, looking on at this battle of desire. The boy's cock pushed against the bark of the tree as the Prince fucked him and a glistening white trail ran down the trunk and on to the roots on the jungle floor.

Montezuma growled as he grasped the boy's hair and thrust his cock deep into his arse.

'You will see who is Prince here,' he said, as he slammed down into the boy's hole. But the *telpollo* pushed back, his muscles tensing as he took the massive weapon inside him.

The two were rutting like animals now, lost in desire and wild abandon. The warriors around them were still pulling on their cocks, and some were already coming, filling the air with the scent of their seed.

Techuan was wanking himself hard and, fixing his eyes on the magnificent pair, let out a bellow that ripped through the trees and sent his come flying through the air so that it landed on the *telpollo*'s buttocks.

The others crowded round as the captive and the Prince worked themselves to a climax. Tupac came and then Huachan, covering the boy's legs with their white seed.

It was as if the Prince and the captive were in another world. All around them, come was splashing down on to their bodies, but they were aware only of each other, their sweat dripping on to the jungle floor, the Prince's cock slamming in and out of the captive's muscular arse.

At last, Montezuma gave one last thrust and came with a roar, his spunk pumping into the boy's arse, filling him with his strength. At the same time, the youth thrust back on to the Prince's come-covered cock and let his spunk spurt up the tree trunk, covering it with white seed. Quetzal wanked harder and let his seed flow on to the ground, his balls contracting. The young captive slumped down in his ropes, exhausted, with the come of four Aztec warriors drying on his skin.

Montezuma smiled.

'This one will not perish immediately. Bind him and bring him to the Palace.'

Five

Juan had been blindfolded when they entered the city. His hands were tied behind his back and a thick leather collar had been put around his neck. One of the warriors led him on a rope, still naked from the punishment he had received against the tree, as if he was a stray dog.

He remembered taking one last look at the high walls, the savages looking down at him from the battlements and the sun going down over the hills across the lake before the darkness when they pulled the rag over his eyes and pushed him through the gates which led into the city.

The noise was incredible. People were shouting on every side and hands reached out to prod him and push him around. He could feel their hatred through the darkness of the cloth and his heart pounded with fear for his life.

He flinched as something wet and heavy hit him in the chest. The crowd gave out a great laugh. They were throwing vegetables; calling to each other to see who could score a direct hit. He was beginning to stink.

More objects came, pelting him from either side, and his guards seemed to take pleasure in tugging his rope one way or another as if to position him better for the onslaught of rubbish which was raining through the air.

They had talked about being taken captive. The savage the Spaniards had captured, Huitacan, had been treated well and Juan had spent time with him, learning about what went on in their city. Huitacan had said they were peace loving, but rumours had gone round the camp that the Aztecs ate their victims after tearing their hearts out for their savage gods. He hoped it wasn't true.

At last, the noise began to recede. They were climbing stone steps, rising higher and higher, and gradually the sound of the rabble below became fainter and fainter, to be replaced only by the soft, sad breathing of the hot wind in his ears.

'Stay.'

The voice was barely a whisper. He wondered who was with him in this strange place. He shivered slightly in the breeze, his cock and balls contracting in the late-afternoon cool. He felt tired and helpless in his nakedness. If they were to kill him here, they should at least afford him the honour of his uniform.

A sharp slap stung across his buttocks and he felt himself being pushed forward and down a single step. His blindfold was removed and the sound of the wind disappeared as an iron door closed quietly behind him.

He blinked. The room was lit by a single oil lamp hanging from the ceiling. It measured about twenty paces square and was lined with stone. In the centre stood a large wooden scaffold about the height of a man. A wooden trunk lay against one wall. Otherwise, the place was bare.

He looked around for some means of escape but the iron door was shut tight.

'Welcome again.'

He recognised him immediately. In the shadows stood the man who had fucked him in the jungle. His body shone in the dim light, his muscles broad and strong like a wild beast. He was dressed only in a pair of breeches and his cock was outlined against the soft fabric. He was holding a whip.

Juan stood silent.

'By rights you should be dead by now. Our captives are freshly slaughtered from the battlefield and you are no more important than the waves of men who fall before the might of Tenochtitlan.

'But you have within you an arrogance which is attractive. In the jungle you refused to be bowed by me. Here, men dare not meet my gaze without my permission. There, you fought back when I tied you to the tree. You refused to surrender your spirit. I am interested in another bout. Let's see how long your pride will stand.'

He cracked the whip across Juan's thighs and Juan winced as the pain rose up into his stomach.

'Come.'

The Prince led him towards the wooden frame. Juan felt himself mesmerised by this strange man, all thoughts of resistance melting away in his heart. His ropes were undone and he automatically raised his hands above his head so that they could be tied to the cross beam of the scaffold – leaving him hanging there like a piece of meat at the market.

The Prince tied ropes around his ankles and attached them to metal rings which were embedded in the floor. He walked around to face Juan and looked straight into his eyes.

'You came here to destroy this land and everyone who lives in it,' he said, running his hands down the thick hair which covered Juan's chest and stomach. 'You came to raze this palace to the ground. You came to make us all your slaves, to exert your domination to the very edges of the empire. Now you are my slave and I will see to it that you always remain that way.'

He stroked the handle of the whip up the inside of Juan's thigh. The fine leather point made the black hairs on his leg stand up and sweat break out all over his body. The Prince kept him fixed with those dark eyes as the whip roamed higher and higher, seeking out the tender skin of his balls and brushing against the smooth flesh of his cock.

He was getting hard. He willed his prick to go down but the more the whip explored his body, the more his cock engorged with blood and rose out of its bed of thick black hair, as if crying out to take the full force of its beating.

He closed his eyes. The whip was sliding along the underside of his cock now, flicking at the vein which swelled the length of his shaft. He let out a tiny groan and the Prince responded by flicking the hard leather up on to the underside of his cock, making it rear up with the cruel pleasure of its bite.

The second stroke flicked against his balls and made him cry out. The feeling was one of intense pleasure, as if his body had been set on fire and his come was going to hose out of his cock and cover them both with the sweet smell of lust.

He bit on his lip to stop himself crying out.

The whip found his cock again, this time harder, biting across the thick head. He thrust his hips forward as if to beg for more and opened his eyes to face up to his adversary and show him his strength and desire.

But the Prince was behind him now and out of nowhere the fourth stroke came down hard on his buttocks, the slap echoing across the stone walls.

This time Juan could not remain silent.

A burning sensation rose up through his legs and filled him with both pain and pleasure. A cry – of pain? of lust? – rang out around the stone chamber. All he wanted was to give himself over to this man's desire; to make his body a receptacle for the Prince to fill as he wished.

The Prince brought the crop down again and Juan pushed his buttocks back to take the blows of his new master. The thrashing landed across his arse and legs, flicking against the inside of his thighs and catching the tender skin of his balls.

His mind was screaming with a thousand questions, but he knew he had only one desire – to serve this man for ever.

'You are strong.' The Prince's voice seemed distant, as if he had taken Juan inside him and was speaking from another world. 'But you also understand. Only complete submission will allow you to achieve your desires.'

He opened the wooden trunk. Inside, surrounded by soft fabric, was a dark, wooden club, about the length of a man's arm and the same thickness at the base, tapering at the other end to a soft, rounded point.

The Prince ran his fingers across the hairs of Juan's crack. Juan remembered the tree and the moment when the man's cock had finally penetrated him to the hilt, filling him with its solid flesh and opening up completely from inside. Then he had known they were destined to be one, to feed each other in their lust. It was as if the savage leader had unlocked a secret of Juan's heart: the need to be filled and used, to be pulled open and left exposed for all to see. He knew then that he would be the thrall of this man; that this was his destined master.

Juan pushed his arse back to open his cheeks and the Prince scratched his nail lightly over the boy's pink arsehole. The sensation was thrilling and he pushed back further to open himself up and beg the Prince to enter him.

The man reached down and Juan watched him take a small pot of oil from the chest and hold it over the oil lamp. They remained silent, as if the enmity between them had evaporated and they now worked to a common cause.

The Prince rolled the oil around over the flame and then poured the warm nectar down into Juan's crack. Juan gasped as the soft heat ran across his arsehole, making it first contract and then open up as if it were breathing in the liquid fire.

The Prince's fingers quickly found their way. Juan's arse opened to welcome then inside him as his master worked his fingers into his arse, massaging his ring before exploring the dark depths inside and making Juan writhe with pleasure on the scaffold.

He breathed out long and hard as the Prince probed within him. He had let himself be taken over by this man. The Aztec had been right. He had started as his enemy. Now he wanted to put himself completely in his power.

The Prince's fingers pushed further inside him, opening his hole and stretching him open.

Juan let great floods of air fill his lungs as the Prince pushed silently deeper, making his arse throb with pleasure as the thick force pushed him open from the inside.

The Prince held him there for a moment and then, with a final thrust which sent the air rushing from Juan's lungs, pulled his fingers out and left his arse open and begging to be filled again.

He looked around. The sweat was pouring from both their bodies and in the light of the oil lamp their muscles shone like beasts of the forest. Slave and master, man and boy. Juan knew they were finding a bond which would be almost impossible to break.

The Prince took up the club and brushed the end of it against his hole.

'You will take this to make you a greater man. Succumb to the force and you will find your strength.'

The words echoed in his head. He would take the dildo. He would worship this man and obey his wishes. He wanted to pledge himself to him for ever.

The hard wood slid inside, opening him further than the Prince's fingers had done and impaling him on its merciless force.

The Prince had thrown off his breeches and was wanking himself in lust as he twisted the dildo around Juan's arse. Juan's cock lay flat against his belly, precome trickling down the shaft as he pumped back on to the dildo with his hips, fucking himself on its magnificent force.

They were both close to coming, their breathing rapid and full of passion. The Prince's face was in front of him now and Juan leant forward and touched his lips to his master's. The Prince's tongue pushed between his teeth and deep into his mouth. They were writhing together as one, lost in their passion for each other, as the kiss became deeper and the Prince pushed the dildo further into Juan's arse.

Their cocks touched and Juan's precome oozed over the Prince's swollen cockhead.

Juan writhed in the pleasure of the moment.

'Take me, my lord,' he whispered. 'Take me and use me. I am yours.'

The Prince had heard what he needed to hear and he pushed the dildo hard inside him as a shower of come flew high out of Juan's cock and up on to the Prince's chest and stomach.

Keeping his grip on the young captive, the Prince beat at his own cock.

He looked him dead in the eye and spoke what Juan knew was the truth.

'You are made to serve.'

And then he came, covering the boy's dark hairs in white seed, which splashed over his cock and balls and legs and on to the dusty, stone floor.

They held there for a moment until Juan closed his eyes and all became blackness.

The last thing he remembered was the iron door opening and two of the guards arriving to free him from the biting ropes.

Axatan surveyed his team.

They were assembled in the ball court in the shadow of the Great Towers where the gods Tlaloc and Huitzilopochtli had their earthly residence. Despite the *telpolli* attack, the priests had decided to continue the rites of Xilonen, the maize god, and they had called a sacred ball game for the final hours of the day.

The ball court stood 100 paces long by 50 wide and was flanked by high walls. A single door gave entry from one side but otherwise the court was completely enclosed.

The rules were simple. Two teams of five men each lined up opposite each other. The aim was to hit your opponents with a hard rubber ball. You could only touch the ball with your hands and if the ball hit any other part of your body you were out. The only other rule was that the ball had to bounce once off the floor or walls after it had been thrown, before it became 'alive' and could capture opponents. This stopped players hurling it straight at their opponents.

The Stable had built on these rules with the blessing of the priests. Taking on the practice of the battlefield, the Stable rules were that anyone hit by the ball became the 'captive' of the person who had thrown it and was theirs for a day and night.

Special bars had been set up at either end of the court for captives to be chained to once they were out. And after the game, the captives would be dragged away by their respective masters for suitable 'punishment'. Needless to say, on the nights after a ball game, the Stable often echoed with the sounds of passion.

The warriors were lined up against five fishermen from the town. They were brawny youths, eager for victory, and fully aware of the penalties and pleasures of being caught. Their eyes glinted with an appetite for the night to come. Their captives would be taken down to the quayside where the fishermen's parties had a reputation for being rough with no holds barred. Some of the Stable warriors had swapped jokes about deliberately being hit by the ball so that they could find themselves guests of honour at the feast, but Axatan had silenced them with a stare. He expected his men to play to win.

On the outside flanks were Techuan and Quetzal – fast runners who were skilled at winning points and players from the opposition. In the centre, Janza and Tupac were already marking the men they saw as dangerous. Axatan himself held back, ready to pounce as the enemy came towards him and determined to win the one he wanted.

The fishermen's captain was a muscular, squat lad called Techpolli. Axatan knew him from the days when they would hang around in the marketplace together, stealing fruit from the stalls and playing practical jokes on the unsuspecting traders.

He strolled up to Axatan.

'So you think you and your soft bunch of boys are going to get the better of us today?' he leered. He grinned and Axatan saw that one of his front teeth was missing – almost certainly the result of some brawl in the town. He was glad he was no longer part of that life.

He grinned back.

'It wasn't so difficult last time, Techpolli.' He grabbed the fisherman's cock through his breeches. 'I seem to remember that we had you tied to a bench and servicing all the Stable warriors before the game had begun.'

Techpolli blushed, but he kept his eyes locked on Axatan's and Axatan could feel his cock swelling a little in his hand.

'You didn't seem to mind it so much,' he continued. 'In fact, some people are saying that you deliberately got caught by the ball.'

'Is that what they're saying, eh? Well, I wouldn't be surprised if it's young Axatan the warrior who accidentally on purpose gets knocked out in an early round today. I've heard he likes a little arse play before supper and, from what people are saying, the bigger the better.'

He slapped Axatan hard on the arse.

'And from what I've heard, I'm going to be first in the queue.'

The trumpet sounded for the first round and Techpolli sauntered back to his team.

Axatan watched him. He had always been a handsome boy and their swimming trips to the lake had often ended with them pleasuring each other among the rocks.

He knew that Techpolli hadn't meant to be caught last year. He usually liked to be in charge, not someone's slave, but once he had been tied to the bench the sight of his taut body bucking up and down, servicing those warrior cocks, showed that he was enjoying his defeat.

The four other fishermen were dark and forbidding. But he could already see a glint in their eyes which revealed they were looking forward to the night ahead, whichever side won the game.

Topaz, the clerk of the palace, entered with the small rubber ball that would decide everyone's fate for the rest of the day. Axatan had persuaded him to take time off from his relentless listing of palace stocks to referee their ball game this afternoon.

'Men of Tenochtitlan,' he said, with a barely concealed leer. 'You know the rules. You may only touch the ball with your hands. The ball must always bounce at least once before it is touched by another player. If any part of your body except your hands touches the ball you become the slave of the man who threw it.'

He looked round at the men ready to play. On either side of the centre line, five muscular youths stood tense and ready for action, dressed only in the tight breeches of sportsmen. He knew that whatever the outcome, there would be no sleep in the Stable quarters tonight.

'And my word is final.'

He threw the ball high into the air and ten pairs of eyes watched its ascent. It had to bounce once and then it was anyone's.

The ball landed next to Techuan on the right flank, who threw it immediately to Janza on the other side. The fishermen held back, waiting for their chance to intercept it and take control of the ball.

Janza grinned at them, twisting the ball in his fingers before hurling it towards a young fisherman who was lurking towards the back of the court.

'Hey, dreamer!'

It was Techpolli, bawling at his team mate. The boy looked, saw the ball coming and did a sort of back flip to get out of its way, which made everyone fall about laughing. He blushed and picked up the ball which had come to rest in the corner.

'A close one,' he shouted to Janza, 'but not close enough.' He swung the ball up against the high wall and it deflected dangerously close to where Janza was still basking in his glory. He leapt out of the way and Axatan moved in with a low flick which sent the ball hurtling towards Techpolli.

The fisher captain sidestepped it neatly and glanced at his adversary. Axatan knew he had received the message: he was going to be Axatan's tonight and there was nothing Techpolli could do about it.

The first person to fall was Karab, an olive-skinned youth, whose tactic had been to taunt Janza until the warrior was tied up in a blazing fury.

He was incredibly fast on his feet and would run right up to Janza when he had the ball, then skittle away again before the warrior could bounce the ball towards him.

'Janza! Janza!' he shouted, grinning, as he streaked up and down the court. 'You suck cock in the marketplace. Janza, Janza, everyone knows your arse.'

The others laughed. Janza had only just come to the Stable but during his time in the House of Supplication he was known to walk the streets of the city at night, taking strangers down alleyways and showing them the magic of his tongue. He pretended he didn't do it, but most people knew that he liked the dark, anonymous encounters of the night, and once Techuan had stumbled across him with some market boy's cock up his arse and another's ploughing in and out of his mouth. Janza had paused for a moment, grinned at Techuan, then carried on as if nothing had happened.

In general, however, Janza liked to pretend he lived a life of virtue, and he sped towards Karab, flicking the ball across the ground and towards the fisherman's feet. Karab leapt high in the air.

'Cock sucker, cock sucker, you can't catch me!' He pulled down his breeches and flashed his arse at Janza, who in a flash caught the ball again and spun it off the side wall until it flew towards Karab's arse and knocked him flying.

Everyone fell about laughing and Topaz blew his horn to indicate a catch.

Karab picked himself up and brushed the dirt off his front. He eyed Janza up and down, letting his eyes rest on the Stable warrior's crotch, and sauntered to where the Stable captives were tied to a bar to await the end of the game.

Now the fishermen knew they had to play for real. They were a man down and the Stable warriors were skilled players.

The Stable warriors fanned out across the court, slowly passing the ball from one to another. The fishermen looked nervous. If you weren't in control of the ball, all you could do was jump out of the way when it came towards you. They sprung up and down on their feet, unsure where the attack would come from, eyes flitting between Axatan and Techuan on the right flank and Janza, Quetzal and Tupac on the left.

The first onslaught came from Tupac. He caught the ball and began a slow walk towards the opposing half of the court, flicking the ball off the wall and back into his hands.

The fishermen were uneasy. They needed the ball back in their half of the court but Tupac's intentions were unclear.

It was Techpolli who acted first.

He ran right up to Tupac with the aim of grabbing the ball away from him and returning the attack. Tupac flicked the ball to the wall and Techpolli leapt in and managed to close his fingers around it just as it bounced.

He threw it hard to the floor so that it would bounce back and hit Tupac, but Tupac sidestepped it and instead it flew high in the air.

They all watched its path until Axatan positioned himself where it would land. In one movement, he caught the ball and threw it to the wall. It bounced straight on to Techpolli's back.

The brawny youth glared at Axatan as the ball ran lamely to the edge of the court, but he said nothing and swaggered to the captives' bar with a confidence that promised a hard time for Axatan as the night continued.

From then the fishermen suffered defeat after defeat. Their captain and Karab chained up as captives, the others could hardly avoid being caught by the onslaught of the Stable attack and soon there were five defiant but lustful fishermen tied by their wrists to the Stable's bar.

Topaz announced the victory and Axatan wiped the sweat off his body with an old cloth and strolled casually towards Techpolli.

'Well, my old friend. They'll be saying you got caught deliberately again.'

Techpolli looked him up and down, taking in the strong muscles which rippled under Axatan's soft, dark skin.

'Perhaps I did, warrior man.' He flashed him a grin and their days together at the lake rushed into Axatan's mind. 'Perhaps I did.'

He untied his captive and led him up towards the Stable quarters. Behind them, Tupac and Janza were squabbling about who had won the fifth fisherman, but Axatan was unconcerned. He had his prize and he was going to enjoy it privately.

There was no need to keep Techpolli's hands tied and Axatan

let the ropes drop to the floor as the curtain which covered the door to his bedchamber fell shut.

The two friends grasped each other in a long, fond embrace. Axatan closed his eyes and remembered the love he had felt for Techpolli when they spent their days together before Axatan had joined the Stable ('a woman's life', Techpolli had called it) and Techpolli had gone to work on his father's fishing boats.

He ran his hands down Techpolli's back, feeling the rugged skin, hardened by days out on the lake and turned black by the sun.

He let his fingers run through Techpolli's hair, enjoying its roughness, then ran his hand down the fisherman's cheek until their lips met. They closed their eyes and lost themselves in exploring each other, reawakening old dreams and lost memories.

Techpolli groaned and ran his hands up and down Axatan's strong back.

Axatan could feel them both getting hard under their breeches and he pushed forward his crotch so that their cocks were rubbing against each other, loving each other's hardness and letting their bodies anticipate the pleasures to come.

Techpolli brushed his tongue against Axatan's neck and pushed him down on to the bed.

The warrior stretched out and sank into the soft bedding as the other man knelt over him and began to flick his tongue over his neck and shoulders.

He gasped and let Techpolli take him back to those days at the lake. His body sprang up and begged for more.

'Stay still.'

It was the first time either of them had spoken since they left the ball court and Axatan understood its significance. Techpolli was his prize, but the fisherman needed Axatan to give up control if he was to pleasure him as he wanted.

He lay back and Techpolli pulled his breeches off him and threw them to the other side of the room.

A breeze played round his balls and he lay there, enjoying the feeling as if a second tongue were flicking over his cock and balls while Techpolli began to work on his nipples.

The man's tongue was expert. He took one of Axatan's nipples into his mouth and caressed it with his lips, kissing it so that it grew in its tiny hardness to stand erect off the smooth contours of Axatan's chest.

'You have always been my god,' he said. 'I long for the time I can worship you again.'

Axatan was surprised at this and he opened his mouth to respond, but Techpolli shut it with a firm hand.

'Silence, warrior. Just take.'

He ran his tongue over Axatan's chest, brushing just to the left of his nipple and sending shivers of excitement through Axatan's body.

'Now I am your slave I can pleasure you how I want.'

He began to work on the nipple itself, licking it softly so that his tongue just brushed the end.

Axatan felt it growing in Techpolli's mouth and in his mind's eye he saw himself spurting milk out of it like a beautiful mother feeding his friend of old.

Techpolli's tongue became more insistent and Axatan knew what he wanted.

'Go on,' he said. 'Suck it.'

Techpolli took his nipple in his mouth and his lips curled round the soft, red flesh. Axatan shut his eyes and let the fisherman take him to a land of pleasure. Techpolli had found Axatan's other nipple with his hand and was brushing it and squeezing it between his fingers, pulling on it gently so that the warrior thrashed back and forth.

Axatan saw them at the lake, Techpolli beautiful and naked as he rose up out of the water, his cock dripping wet and big even then. Axatan would take him in his mouth and taste the lake in his friend's prick, before Techpolli would push him away, eager to get his lips round Axatan's cock and make him come over his face.

Techpolli was letting his tongue slide lower, licking at the thin line of black hair which led down towards Axatan's hard cock. Axatan tensed his stomach and felt his friend's tongue find its way into his belly button.

He wondered what Techpolli's life had been like since they parted all those years ago. Did he enjoy his life on the lake? Did his father still beat him, like he used to when he had drunk too much *pulque*? Had he done his time in the army, earning his captives to sacrifice on the killing stone? Why had be lost touch with this man?

Techpolli's tongue had worked its way down into the bush of wiry hair that lay at the base of Axatan's prick. He was slowly licking in the fold of flesh that lay between his balls and thigh.

Axatan glanced up and saw that Techpolli had taken off his breeches and was playing with himself.

His cock was magnificent, rising up from his hard body like a mighty club, revealing heavy balls swinging below. His stomach was ribbed with the hard muscle of a man of work and his chest was firm and strong. Axatan sat up a little further and let his eye run down the broad expanse of Techpolli's back to the two domes of his arse rising into the air.

They were smooth, with a little line of hair running down the crack, and Axatan knew he wanted to run his tongue between them and taste the dark secrets of his body.

Techpolli pushed him back down on to the bed and began to lick his balls.

Axatan's breathing began to become irregular. The feeling of the fisherman's tongue on his balls was almost unbearable, sending spasms of pleasure up the shaft of his cock and through his body to his nipples, which seemed to cry out for more attention.

He opened his legs slightly to let Techpolli go deeper and cried out loud as the man's tongue found the flesh which ran between his balls and his arse. His licking was hot and Axatan arched up his crotch so that Techpolli could explore deeper and deeper with his mouth.

The first finger slid in almost unnoticed. Techpolli was licking Axatan's arsehole, making it warm and wet and causing him to writhe around on the bed, when he pushed his finger in beside his tongue.

Axatan gasped as he felt his friend begin to open him up and explore the soft, pink passage of his arse.

'Lie back.'

Techpolli's voice came through the air like a beautiful present. This man was going to take Axatan to the place of his ultimate desire.

He pushed a second finger up inside him and moved up the bed so that he could slide his tongue deep into Axatan's mouth.

They lay there kissing, Techpolli's tongue taking Axatan over, filling him with love and pleasure, while his fingers pulled open his arsehole and found their way to the hard knot of pleasure inside Axatan's arse.

Axatan would have given up everything now to stay with this man.

Their breathing came together as they kissed, Axatan breathing in as Techpolli breathed out, tasting the boy from his youth who had become this man.

Techpolli's cock lay flat against Axatan's stomach and Axatan reached down and began to stroke his fingers up and down the shaft.

Techpolli groaned and Axatan let his fingers slide round the ridge of his shaft, pushing the foreskin back and feeling the smooth silkiness of his cockhead. He squeezed and a tiny drop of precome flowed out on to the skin under his fingers. He rubbed it round the ridge of Techpolli's cock and let his thumb brush up and down on the sensitive skin.

Techpolli squirmed in pleasure and let himself be rolled over on the bed so that Axatan was now kissing him and playing with his cock. Techpolli's fingers had slipped gently out of the warrior's arse, giving himself up to the true victor from the ball court.

Axatan turned him over so that he was lying on his front and let his eyes take in his arse. He ran his hands over the smooth cheeks and his fingers brushed up the line of hair in his crack. Techpolli groaned and pushed his arse higher in the air.

Axatan reached between his legs and took hold of his balls. They were big and heavy like the fruit of the avocado tree and he could feel that they were full of come waiting to be released.

He squeezed them and Techpolli sighed with pleasure.

Axatan bent forward.

His eyes were fixed on the dark beauty of Techpolli's crack. He wanted so much to taste the man's sweat which glistened in his arse hair. He wanted to lick inside his cheeks and find the pink beauty of his hole. He wanted to taste the musk on his tongue.

He licked his lips and let his tongue run gently over the hair between Techpolli's crack.

The fisherman could barely stifle his groans.

'Oh, yes, Axatan, please, take me.'

Axatan closed his eyes and savoured the taste of the salty sweat on his friend's arse. He breathed in and relished the man scent which filled his nostrils and made his cock swell with anticipation. Techpolli pushed his arse on to the warrior's face and Axatan felt his tongue slide down the walls of his crack, taking in the dark scents of his manhood until he found it pushed against the tight, pink flesh of his hole.

He flicked his tongue against the ring of muscle and Techpolli let out a long, anguished groan.

Axatan pushed his tongue forward until the whole of his friend's body shuddered and the ring opened up to welcome him to its dark world of pleasure.

He pushed inside and tasted the dark musk on his tongue. The ring swelled open around him, pulling him in and helping him find the magic spot of pleasure where he could take his friend to ecstasy. He flicked his tongue hard on the inside of the tight muscle, at the same time taking a tiny fold of flesh between his teeth and sucking the deep secret out of his arse.

Techpolli was playing with his cock, frantically rubbing it up and down.

'Oh yes, Axatan, oh yes . . .'

He writhed around the bed and Axatan sucked harder as if he wanted to eat his friend from the inside.

He reached up and let a single finger slide past his lips and into Techpolli's hole. The flesh inside was soft and warm. He let his finger explore the smooth cavities of Techpolli's arse, following his first finger with a second so that he could open up the ring further and let his tongue flick round the inner softness of his hole.

The smell was intoxicating. He breathed in the beautiful musky scent, filling his head with it and taking himself back to the fields and pleasures of his youth.

He sat up. Techpolli was stretched out on the bed, his hard body throbbing with the pleasure Axatan was giving him with his fingers. Axatan smiled. He knelt next to the fisherman's face and rubbed his cock against his lips.

Techpolli needed no prompting.

He took first the cockhead and then Axatan's whole shaft inside his mouth, reaching up with his hands so that he could guide him in more easily.

Axatan pushed a third finger into Techpolli's arse and began to move his hand in and out, stretching his hole and making Techpolli pant with throbbing pleasure and swallow Axatan's cock deeper into his throat.

Another finger. Axatan loved this. His hand was brushing against the soft flesh of Techpolli's arse, feeling him deep inside and bringing him pleasure. He had never pushed his whole hand inside someone before, but Techpolli seemed to be begging him to take them both to new extremes.

He pushed in his thumb and Techpolli cried out, thrusting his arse back on to Axatan's hand and burying his head in the warrior's crotch, the full length of his shaft deep inside him.

Axatan pushed deeper.

He could see Techpolli's arse stretched around the knuckle of his hand. His own eyes were wide with amazement at the two of them finding union in this way.

Techpolli let Axatan's cock slip from his mouth. He looked up, his eyes alive with fire.

'Fuck me, Axatan.'

Axatan reached underneath him and felt his prick. It was rock hard against his stomach and the head was smooth and wet with precome.

'Like the old days, Axatan. Fuck me like the old days.'

Axatan pulled his fingers out slowly and let his beautiful arsehole close tight again.

He rested his cock against Techpolli's hole and began a slow rhythmic movement with his hips, teasing his hole and making his friend beg for more.

He reached round to rub Techpolli's cock, using the precome to moisten the shaft and awake the seed in his huge balls.

He pushed forward to let the head of his cock slip in. Techpolli's cock jumped in his hand and his lips let out a tiny moan.

He pushed further and his mind was filled with images of their youth together – fishing on the lake, walking on the hills, running around the marketplace looking for trouble. And, of course, their lust for each other; exploring each other's bodies and their first experiments in wanking off and making each other come.

He let his cock slide in some more.

And now he was fucking him again, but this time in very different circumstances. He was a Palace warrior and Techpolli was just a fisherman. In any other place, they would never meet, but now their bodies had brought them together again and the old feelings of friendship and loyalty were flooding back.

His shaft pushed deeper into Techpolli and his friend spasmed with the sensation, bucking his arse and pulling hard on his cock.

Axatan pushed in deeper still until his whole cock was buried in his friend's arse. He put his hands on Techpolli's hips and began to pump him with the slow, strong rhythm of a warrior.

'Oh, yes!' cried out Techpolli. 'Oh, Axatan, my master.'

Their breathing quickened and Techpolli wanked harder on his cock, pulling himself to climax. Axatan's balls were crashing down on to Techpolli's arse. He was grunting now, savouring the pleasure of Techpolli's hole as it sucked the seed up his shaft, setting his balls on fire.

He pulled himself higher and pounded his cock into the young fisherman.

'Techpolli, take this, for you, and me, for our times together, for our youth at the lake.' He clenched his teeth and squeezed his eyes shut, picturing the two of them at the lake, in the water, on the sand, in the marketplace, in the jungle. He squeezed his balls to give him a few seconds more, but Techpolli thrust back on to him and he felt his seed pump into his arse, filling it up and spilling out on to the floor.

Techpolli cried out and worked his cock faster.

'Ah, Axatan!' he cried out, as an arc of white come flew from his cock, splashing everything with hot, man-scented come, until the two of them collapsed into a sleepy, pleasurable embrace that filled them with dreams of memories lost.

They lay there for what seemed like hours and Axatan fell asleep, holding his friend in his arms. He dreamt of their time at the lake, of Quetzal and the Stable, of growing up in the fields, of his mother and father.

He dreamt that his father was also Quetzal. He was fucking him, laughing loudly and mocking his efforts to take his giant cock in his tiny arse. His cackling got deeper and deeper, forming itself into words. He was calling him from far away. The gods had carried him off to be their plaything and he was calling for his help. An eagle flew by so close to the ground that all the people in the field had to lie flat on their faces. It was him, his eagle claws scraping across the grass, seas and mountaintops, until he soared to the sky and flipped over and fell back down to the water which rushed up to receive him in her arms, holding him and squeezing him until the last drop of life had come out of him like the blood on the sacrificial altar and his spirit had drained away again into the earth.

He awoke with a start.

The sun was setting and the room was filled with a deep purple light. Techpolli had gone.

Six

He was in the middle of a large stone room, a chain round his neck fastened to the floor. At the far end, four other captives knelt in a row, their hands tied behind their backs and their cocks hard against their bellies. They were sucking the cocks of four warriors who stood in front of them and joked with each other, exhorting the men before them to speed up or slow down as they licked up and down their shafts.

It was an amazing sight – eight handsome men pleasuring and being pleasured – and he felt himself getting excited again, his cock becoming engorged with blood.

The guards who had released him from the scaffold in the Prince's quarters had obviously brought him here but he could remember nothing of the journey or how he got to be kneeling with a chain round his neck.

Around him stood probably twenty of the enemy soldiers. They were naked except for their strange jewellery of shells and gleaming gold, and they eyed him with a predatory lust. Others sat around the side of the room on benches, playing with themselves while watching the two scenes develop in front of them. Their eyes flicked from the group of eight at one end to Juan and his captors at the other, drinking in the passion of these strong warriors who would stop at nothing to attain their desires.

The warriors circled him, taking in his body, which gleamed with sweat, devouring his cock and balls and arse with their eyes. He met their gaze, challenging them to make a move and enter into the game of mutual pleasuring which was sure to follow.

One of the warriors, a tall, broad man with a dark, mean expression, broke ranks and walked straight up to him. He was half erect and stood so that his thick cock hung directly in front of Juan's mouth.

The warrior was stern and silent, looking down on him with the same eyes the Prince had had. Juan felt himself yearn for the pleasures of submission, the voice in his head begging to be taken and used. He leant forward and kissed the man's thigh. It was hard and wet with sweat. A hand held the back of his neck, stroking his hair, and a finger brushed against his lips. He looked up again. The warrior was smiling at him. He could feel the heat of the man's cock next to his cheek and closed his eyes to relish the promise of man. For a moment they froze in that instant, master and servant, pleasurer and the pleasured, and then Juan felt the moist softness of the man's cockhead push against his lips.

He opened his mouth and let the silky shaft slide in. It tasted of manhood and he let his tongue slide up and down the shaft, savouring the sweet pleasure of serving another man and bringing him to climax with the softness of his mouth.

He reached down and started to play with his own cock, letting the foreskin slide back and forth over his cockhead and send waves of pleasure down into his balls.

The others had stopped their circling and had fixed their gaze on him. He was their toy now and he knew he would be servicing each of them before the night was out – twenty warrior cocks ploughing his mouth and filling him with their seed. His heart raced with excitement and desire.

He tightened his lips around the man's cock and let his tongue work its way into his slit. He loved to feel the little flap of skin part under his tongue. The warrior grunted in approval and pulled back so that just the head lay between Juan's lips, the ridge brushing against his teeth.

He sighed with ecstasy. Above him, the warrior was groaning deeply, holding on to his hair to guide his mouth up and down his massive shaft.

He reached up and took the warrior's balls between his fingers. His ball bag was thick with black hair and he twisted it gently in his hand. The warrior cried out and a tiny drop of precome slid into the back of Juan's throat.

He let the man's cock fall from his lips and brushed his tongue across his balls. The man groaned again and he took one of his balls into his mouth, caressing it with his tongue. The warrior was playing with his cock, rubbing it up and down against Juan's face.

The others were drawing closer now and the air was becoming thick with desire. He reached out and took another cock in his hand. It was thicker than the one in his mouth and he ran his fingers up and down the shaft, feeling its weight and mass. The warrior stepped closer and now he had two cocks in front of his face. He licked at the second, savouring the difference in taste and smell, and then began to pass his mouth from one to another.

The two warriors were kissing and he paused for a moment to watch their faces merge; stubble against stubble, tongue finding tongue, in a union of manhood.

A third man approached and Juan took his cock in his hand, working up and down the shaft while his lips moved between the two cocks in front of him. Now hands appeared out of nowhere, stroking his chest and back, feeling his nipples and exploring the soft skin between his balls and his arse.

His own cock was hard now and another soldier lay down flat on the floor and started to lick at it, slurping and grunting as he flicked his tongue round Juan's cockhead.

All around him, men were exploring each other's bodies. Some had their eyes fixed on him; others were watching longingly as the four captives moved from soldier to soldier, offering them their tongues and arses for the men's desires. One young lad was on all fours with two cocks in his mouth and another up his arse.

Another was splayed out on the floor playing with himself as a group of soldiers surrounded him, wanking their cocks and ready to cover him with spunk from head to toe.

He closed his eyes. The room was full of sex; of men pleasuring men. He sucked at cocks all around him. Hands were brushing across his chest, pulling on his nipples and making them hard. Others were stroking along his crack, making him arch his arse out towards them, begging them to enter him and discover the silky beauty of his hole.

And then one of them spat on to his arsehole and pushed a finger straight in.

Juan reared up with the force of the entry. He looked behind him. The warrior was tall and broad with great slabs of muscle spanning his chest. His hair was short and his face was dark and closed.

The man pushed in another finger and then a third, all the time wanking his own cock, which stood enormous and weaponlike in front of him. Juan was ready to be fucked and he reached behind him, licking his lips as he guided the warrior's cock between his cheeks.

The man was huge and Juan gasped for air as he pushed at his ring, forcing it open and driving his cock deep inside.

The other warriors looked on as the two of them quickly found a rhythm; pushing his cock inside Juan and then pulling it all the way back, holding for a moment and then plunging it deep down inside him again.

Juan opened himself up to the man so that he could fuck him harder, and he closed his eyes to relish the warrior's thick shaft pounding deep inside him. He had been fucked many times before, but the sheer size of this man made him grunt with pleasure as the hard flesh stretched him to his limits. He took hold of his own cock and began to wank himself as the warrior used him for his desire.

And then, out of nowhere, a punch landed on the side of his face. He knelt up in shock. The man had hit him, and the pain was tearing through his head. He twisted to pull himself away, but the man grabbed him by the hair and raised his hand to hit him again. Juan looked around in fear. The other warriors were just looking on. The chain round his neck was firmly secured to the floor. The warrior's face was twisted with hate and there was no means of escape.

A kick landed in his side and he doubled up on the floor, trying to protect his head with his hands as blows rained down on him.

The pain was spreading through his body and his head was screaming with fear. His only chance was to kick out and catch the man off balance. He pulled in his legs and then in a single movement twisted on to his back and kicked hard into the man's groin.

But all his feet met was air.

The warrior was lurching sideways, stretching his hands out to find his balance, but not making it before his head hit the wall with a sickening crunch.

The other warriors were still standing open mouthed. He tried to speak but the words just came out in a jumble and the last thing he noticed was their astonished faces before he fainted and the black mist of oblivion filled his head.

Axatan had entered the recreation room, still angry that Techpolli had left so early. Wasn't he supposed to be his captive? Who had really been the master and who the slave? He felt wounded and confused and was in no mood to join in with the other fishermen taken captive during the ball game.

The sight which greeted him made him stop dead. The new *telpolli* captive was there, being fucked by Tojo. He looked beautiful as the warrior's huge cock pounded his arse, his young muscles tensing each time Tojo's shaft pushed inside him. The boy was pleasuring himself, his cock fat with lust.

Axatan stepped forward to watch and found himself becoming excited by the sight, his cock growing in his breeches and his thoughts now focused on the beautiful boy who had come out of the jungle.

And then things began to go wrong. Tojo's face turned suddenly from desire to hatred and the next thing Axatan knew he was punching down hard on the boy's face, making a thin line of blood run from his mouth. Axatan looked on, astonished. Tojo growled and kicked the boy in the stomach and the *telpollo* curled up on the floor, trying to protect his head.

Axatan stepped forward. He was going to put an end to this.

'Enough now, Tojo.' His voice was firm but his throat was dry with anxiety. Tojo was bigger than any of them and no one wanted to pick a fight with the man whose strength was heralded throughout the empire.

Tojo looked up, his eyes mean and spiteful.

'"Enough now, Tojo",' he said in a high-pitched woman's voice which became a roar. 'Enough is when Tojo chooses.'

He spat on the floor and raised his hand to deliver another punch.

Axatan felt the anger rushing through him. He swung his fist round and it crunched into Tojo's face, sending him staggering towards the wall. Tojo was flaying around and Axatan stepped forward to deliver another punch to his stomach when the warrior seemed to keel over, falling backward and hitting his head against the hard stone of the wall. He looked surprised and then fell to the floor unconscious.

The others stood staring at him. Axatan looked from one face to another – his comrades in arms, his friends of many years. Would they have stood there and seen a captive killed? Or were they going to intervene if he hadn't done so?

The question hung in the air. Some of the warriors met his gaze, staring back with what he thought was shame. Others looked down at the floor in embarrassment. They knew Tojo had broken a strict warrior code and they knew that they were as guilty as he was for not interceding.

Quetzal opened his mouth to speak but Axatan silenced him with a glare. This was no time for words.

He bent down and unchained the *telpollo*, then put his cape round the boy's shivering body.

He picked him up and carried him to his bedchamber.

He was just passing through the curtained doorway when the voice echoed behind him.

'Axatan, you have overreached yourself. This will not be forgotten.'

He turned to see Tojo staring at him, slumped against the wall, nursing his jaw. His eyes were hot with fury.

Quetzal waited until the two figures had disappeared through the doorway and then began to walk slowly towards Axatan's bedchamber.

He felt embarrassed but also worried. To hit another warrior was a serious matter. He knew why Axatan had done it, he knew too that he had been too frightened of Tojo to intervene himself. But what would be remembered now was that Axatan had punched an Aztec to protect a *telpollo*. It was a reputation Axatan would find hard to live down.

The fishermen had taken their clothes and left. The other warriors had shuffled away in silence, as if someone had opened a shutter and let the daylight in on their games of the night. Tojo had stormed off to his bedchamber. No one had spoken.

Quetzal reached Axatan's room, drew back the curtain and stepped inside.

The boy was stretched out on the bed, sleeping. Against the pale sheets he looked soft and harmless, and Quetzal found it hard to imagine him plotting the overthrow of the city, ready to massacre its inhabitants with his strange weapons.

Axatan had covered him with his cape and was wiping the blood from around his mouth. Quetzal watched for a moment and was shocked when his friend bent down and kissed the captive on his forehead. He felt embarrassed and wanted to slip away, but Axatan looked up and caught him standing there, his expressionless eyes hiding the thoughts that were in his head.

'Come in.'

Quetzal hesitated. Axatan was smiling but his eyes betrayed a deep sadness.

'Axatan, I . . .' The words were dying on his tongue. He

wanted to say so much, but found he could say nothing. Axatan looked at him and for the first time he saw him not just as a friend but as a man. His mouth was dry with nerves.

'Axatan, I think what you did was right. I should have done the same myself but I was afraid. No one expected this to happen. We were having fun.'

He looked at the boy.

By the next full moon, he would have joined the line of victims making their way up the temple steps to the killing stone. A flint knife would cut through that soft chest, and his heart, still beating, would be fed to the hungry earth.

It would be an honourable death but still a chill ran through his blood.

Axatan stepped up to him and put his hands on his shoulders. He kissed him gently on the forehead.

'None of us knows how we will act. Do not chastise yourself, my friend. Courage works in strange ways.' He looked him in the eyes. 'Now leave me. I have an errand to undertake. I need to see somebody.'

Quetzal kissed his friend and stepped out into the Great Courtyard. As the setting sun caught him in the eyes, he glanced back into the bedchamber. Axatan was sitting on the bed, staring at the sleeping boy.

The clerk was being annoying.

'You know the protocol. Of course you cannot see the Prince unless the Prince summons you first. Even you, Axatan. It is the law and I *for one* will uphold the law.'

They were standing in the entrance hall to the Royal Palace.

Axatan had put on his finest ceremonial costume and courtiers and commoners alike bowed as he swept across the jade-inlaid floor to the entrance to the Prince's private quarters. But the clerk was not yielding.

He glared at the little man. Axatan had become a man on the battlefields of the empire while this man knew no finer wars than the gossipy intrigue of Palace life. He wanted to punch him like he had punched Tojo. The blood was still racing in his heart, but he knew he had to restrain himself. He grunted, bowed sarcastically and started to walk back across the jade floor.

A voice called out from the other side of the hall.

'Axatan!'

He turned and saw one of the serving girls beckon him from a small doorway which had been cut into the wall. He recognised her as one of the women who baked *tamales* in the courtyard in the mornings. He strolled over.

'Hello, pretty one. Are you a Palace messenger now?'

'Enough of the pretty one. You want to see the Prince?'

Axatan nodded.

'Then give me your ring and I will leave it in his chamber as a sign that you are out here. If he wishes to see you, he will send a message.'

It was a chance, he thought. Axatan took off his ring, showing an Eagle Warrior proud and ready for battle. He had owned it since he was a boy, and every day had dreamt of being an Eagle Warrior himself. Now he was on the threshold of achieving his ambition.

The woman took it and disappeared into the private quarters. Axatan looked up and saw the clerk frowning at him. He turned away.

The wait seemed an eternity and he was beginning to think he had been fooled when the little door behind the clerk opened and a courtier came out into the hall.

'Axatan, Stable warrior, Prince of the Aztecs, come forth.'

He turned and looked towards the open door. The clerk was glaring at him, but now Axatan was too nervous to make a joke of it. He walked through the doorway and into the Sun Prince's quarters.

He had never seen these rooms – most of the Palace was out of bounds to all but the highest of the Prince's staff – and he gazed on their beauty in awe. On the walls hung cloths of pure gold. Jade masks hung from the ceiling, looking like sacrificial heads taken from the skull rack which stood at the foot of the Great

Temple. A fountain filled the room with the cool scent of eucalyptus, and the setting sun sent shadows playing across the walls.

He looked out of the window.

Far below him he could see the Stable warriors playing together in the Great Courtyard. He could make out Techuan and Quetzal and wondered how many times the Prince himself had stood there, watching their every move.

He could see his own room among the whitewashed blocks that made up the Stable quarters and thought of the *telpollo* sleeping there, rescued from the violence of Tojo. But for what? To be sacrificed on the altar of Huitzilopochtli? To have his heart torn from him? He frowned. The future was uncertain. This was why he was here.

Further down, the marketplace still teemed with people who seemed to have no care in the world but earning their living and buying for their family. Beyond them, disappearing into the distance, the lake shimmered with blues and pinks and on the horizon the great volcanoes of the west rose against the setting sun.

'An impressive sight.'

He turned and found himself looking deep into the dark eyes of the Prince. It was the first time he had seen him unmasked.

Axatan fell to his knees and bowed his head to the floor.

'Stand up. Here you may set aside the ceremony of the outside world. Here you are my guest.' The Prince smiled, his eyes drilling into Axatan's head. 'Come. Follow me.'

The Prince led him through a small doorway into a larger room. By contrast with the antechamber this was almost completely bare. The walls had been whitewashed and a single tapestry hung above a plain wooden chest. It showed the ancient kings Tizoc and Ahuitzol, great Aztec rulers, on either side of an earth altar. Axatan knew the story well. Tizoc had come back from the dead to hand over power to his successor Ahuitzol. He did this by making Ahuitzol cut his ear and spill his blood on the floor. Tizoc then did the same and in the mingling of their life spirits the power of kingship was transferred through blood offering to the hungry mouth of Our Mother Earth. The ceremony had been repeated at every coronation to this day.

'It is an important story.' The Prince was standing behind Axatan. 'Our Mother Earth is hungry for our life. She gives us life and we must pay her back. Even great princes must offer themselves to the earth. Do you know why Our Mother Earth is shown with her mouth wide open? Because she is like a hungry baby, never satisfied, always with a gnawing in her stomach, the pain of hunger, the threat of starvation. That is why we must give her blood. That is why we must feed her captives. Otherwise she will eat us.' He turned to the window and looked out towards the west. 'In the night, her long, sharp teeth will rise up out of the ground and tear our flesh from our bones as we scream for mercy. And there will be no mercy. The sun will not rise again and we will all be eaten by the mother who gave us life.'

He paused. The sun had gone down and the room was filled with the sad light of dusk. The Prince clapped his hands and a servant girl entered with a small tray of oil lamps, their flames low and smoky.

She ran around the room, placing them in little niches in the wall, and now Axatan could see more furniture: a long, low table, a small couch and a large floor mat covered with cushions.

'Come and sit.'

The Prince gestured to the mat. He himself lay back on the couch and gazed at the ceiling.

'Yes, we must feed her, or we all will die. Even our young *telpollo* captive.'

Axatan's heart stopped. He had told no one of his feelings for the *telpollo*. He did not even understand them himself. But why else was he here? Why else if not to plead for the life of the *telpollo* captive?

'He is a beautiful animal,' the Prince continued. 'And I believe he stirs your loins. I saw how you looked at him in the jungle. And your behaviour today confirms what I suspected.'

He held up Axatan's ring in his fingers. It glinted in the light of the oil lamps. Axatan felt himself frozen to the mat.

'An Eagle Warrior is the finest of the Aztec army. You are not an Eagle Warrior yet, yet you choose an emblem that shows your aspirations and not your achievements. It is a dangerous course. You can always be struck down with disappointment, and disappointment will eat you from inside.'

He lay back and stared at the ceiling.

'You have excelled yourself on the battlefield and soon you will excel yourself in the rank of Eagle Warrior. Your ring will come true. But do you know what else awaits you? You are strong and ambitious and you understand the secrets of people's hearts. The others in the Stable see you as a leader. Only you could punch another warrior and not cause a riot. Only you could take a captive – which I have given to the whole Stable to be their plaything – back to your own private chambers. Only you could run up to the very inner court of my Palace and demand an audience with the Sun Prince himself.'

He sat up. His face remained tranquil but his deep black eyes were eating into Axatan's body.

'You do not know yet where your destiny lies. You feel strong, but tiny doubts eat away at your confidence. You feel wise, but often the world puzzles you. You feel that life will give you everything, but you fear that all could disappear in one fell swoop. But what you do not know is that you are destined for greatness.'

He held out his hand. Axatan felt his mouth go dry.

'Stand up and come to me.'

Axatan walked over to the couch. The Prince stood up and began to undress him, carefully laying his garments on the low wooden chest until he was standing there naked, his skin like chocolate in the orange light. He realised that he had no sense of embarrassment. Instead, the room seemed to be filled with a warm security which made him fell drowsy and adored. He felt like a child.

The Prince brushed his hand down the side of his face.

He was wearing an embroidered tunic which gleamed with

gold and jade. On his feet were sandals of soft leather. Around the muscles of his upper arm a beaded band showed his allegiance to the Warriors of Quetzalcoatl. His forearms were covered with thick, wiry hair.

Axatan had serviced this man many times in the temple, when he was wearing the sacred regalia of the Sun God. But he had never known him as a man.

The Prince let his hands run lightly down Axatan's chest. His fingers were soft but insistent and they pulled at his nipples, making them stand on end.

As the Prince's eyes drilled into him, Axatan found himself filling with desire to give himself up to him and be taken over by his strength and power. His cock was hard as rock.

The Prince squeezed one of his nipples and Axatan knew that the Prince could see deep into his very soul. He opened his mouth and the Prince ran a finger round his lips, probing him and making Axatan suck on it like he was a baby.

Another finger pushed into his mouth and then a third, and Axatan sucked on them, showing the Prince the softness of his mouth and promising him untold pleasures when his cock was where his fingers were, being sucked to new heights of ecstasy by his willing servant.

They kissed, the Prince pulling gently on Axatan's balls. He let them roll between his fingers and Axatan sucked all the more eagerly, savouring the waves of pleasure that swept through this body.

The Prince's hand was behind his head and his tongue inside Axatan's mouth, probing it, sliding over his teeth, caressing him from within. Axatan felt his body collapsing around him as he let himself be held by the Prince's strong arms, surrendering himself up to his deep kiss.

The Prince carried him as if he were weightless and laid him on the floor mat.

He let his hands run between his legs, stroking the underside of his balls and gently caressing the soft hair that ran down to his arse.

The Prince stripped off, and for a moment the two of them looked at each other, drinking in their nakedness.

In the half-light of the oil lamps, the Prince's body was even more sculpted, like a noble statue come alive, strong and magnificent. The hair on his chest and stomach made him look like a wild beast of the jungle.

Axatan let his eyes wander over the Prince's body, relishing its strength and feeling honoured to be the one who would worship it.

The Prince lifted Axatan's legs into the air and leant down to rub oil in Axatan's crack. Axatan closed his eyes, ready to receive his master.

The smooth flesh of the Prince's cock brushed against his hole and then started to push inside, opening the tight ring and making the two of them one.

Axatan called out in a voice he barely recognised.

'Take me and love me. You are my master and I am your slave.'

The Prince slid his cock into Axatan down to the hilt, fixing his eyes on him so that Axatan's mind was filled with those black eyes and that godlike face.

Their fucking was slow and passionate. Axatan was pinned to the floor, his own cock wet with precome without him even touching it. His mind raced with images: Quetzal, the battlefield, his friends in the Stable and the *telpollo*, always the *telpollo*, coming into his mind to haunt him with his sad beauty. He looked at the Prince, who was lost now in his lust. His chest was dripping with sweat and his muscles tensed each time he thrust his cock inside Axatan's arse. Axatan took hold of his own cock and shut his eyes, thinking of the Prince and the *telpollo* and the three of them pleasuring each other, trapped in a paradise of desire.

He felt the seed rising in his shaft and wanked himself hard, losing himself in the pleasure of the moment.

The Prince's breathing was harder now and he was pumping his cock in and out of Axatan's arse. Axatan wanked his cock all the more, but it was the Prince who came first, plunging down into Axatan's arse and letting his seed flow inside him like a mighty river. He roared, filling the room with a sound like thunder as Axatan's cock lifted up off his belly and sent a cascade of white come pouring down his chest and stomach, covering him with its sweet scent.

He looked up at the Prince, trying to capture his face and strong body in his mind for ever.

The Prince looked at him for a moment.

'The boy is yours,' he said. 'Do with him what you will. Between us is a deeper bond which cannot be broken.'

'My lord,' said Axatan.

The Prince paused for a moment.

He opened his mouth to speak, but then just looked sadly at Axatan and turned and left the room.

Seven

Juan awoke with a start.

In his dreams he was being chased by a wild animal. The ground was sticky and his feet were sinking into the mud. He had turned and seen his own face on the beast's head, opening its jaws wide and showing sharp, bloody teeth. He had screamed but his voice was empty and his mouth gave no sound.

He was covered in a cold, clammy sweat which made him shiver in the cool breeze which came in from the window.

He sat up and looked around him.

The room was sparse with whitewashed walls. In front of him, a small tapestry showed what looked like a hunting scene. There was a wooden chest and in the corner stood an oil lamp on a metal tripod.

Through the shutters the first rays of the sun were making shadows on the ceiling. All was silent except for the birdsong which would greet its arrival in the sky.

The doorway was covered with a heavy curtain, but he felt unsure about leaving this room. He pulled the bedcovers up to his neck and took stock of where he was. He remembered the warriors and being hit; he remembered deciding that his life was at an end and that he would die in the savages' camp. And he remembered his attacker suddenly flying into the wall. But then he remembered nothing.

He sat there for some time, hearing noises outside the door and strange voices calling to each other. He needed to piss, but somehow he dared not move from the bed. He was hungry.

The curtain across the door was pulled up and in stepped a young warrior. He was dark, his eyes a deep brown, his hair short, his face handsome but serious. He was probably around Juan's age, maybe a little older. He was wearing a blue and gold tunic and sandals. He let the drape drop behind him and crouched by the bed.

'I am Axatan.'

He spoke the same language that Juan had learnt from their savage captives in the camp. He'd been responsible for taking them food and water and had grown to like them, having spent time with them, listened to their stories of magical lands, heroes and gods and learnt their strange language.

The man was looking into his face. His eyes were dark and burnt with a soft fire as if they had seen both hatred and love. Juan looked back at him, ready to defy his captor, but all he saw was tenderness.

'I am Juan.'

The man looked at him for a second and then burst out laughing. Juan was stunned.

'Hu-an?' he said. 'Hu-an, Hu-an.'

He was laughing so much now that tears were coming to his eyes. Juan felt annoyed.

'I am sorry,' he said. 'In our language, Hu-an is the big, stupid animal that gives milk. You know?' He made a braying, roaring sound and burst out laughing again. Juan wanted to laugh but he didn't feel funny. And this man was mocking him, mocking a soldier of the Spanish King's navy. He stood up, his face set in a proud grimace which would show the savage that he was to be respected. But as the sheet fell to the floor he realised too late that he was naked and that his cock was still half hard from the night.

He grabbed the sheet and wrapped it round him, burning with embarrassment.

The man looked at him and smiled, unshocked by what he saw. Then he said, 'Your face. Is it good?'

Juan knew that a bruise had spread across the side of his face where the big warrior had hit him. He could feel that it was red and sore.

The savage stretched out his hand and stroked his fingers down it. His skin was cold and soothing and Juan found himself starting to relax.

'Who are you?' he said.

'I am a warrior here in the Stable. You are my prisoner. I have been given you by the Prince.' He let his fingers rest on Juan's face for a moment, scrutinising him with those deep, dark eyes.

'You had a lucky escape last night,' he said. 'Tojo is a violent man and he would have killed you if I had not arrived. He has no regard for prisoners.'

He spat on the ground, clearly angry.

'We have a code, a rule, which says that captives are to be treated with respect. Tojo was breaking that rule. Some warriors do not have enough respect.'

They sat there regarding each other in silence. Two men, Juan thought, from such different backgrounds, and yet he felt close to him. He did not feel in danger.

'Where were you born, Axatan?'

The name felt comfortable on his tongue.

The man looked at him for a moment and then said simply, 'Far away.'

They sat in silence again, the brilliant white of the sun's beams pushing through the slats on the shutters. Then Axatan stood.

'Come,' he said. 'I must show you to your quarters. You are one of the lucky ones. The Prince has decreed that you will live as part of the Stable until the gods have shown us your destiny. You will be comfortable, but you must understand not to leave the Stable except with me.'

His face was stern.

'If you are seen alone you will be killed.'

He turned and they stepped out into the bright sunlight. Juan had to shade his eyes from the light.

A long colonnade stretched out on either side of them, lined with doors hung with coloured drapes.

In front of them was a fountain, and across the courtyard were high doors covered in ornate gold and beautiful jewels. The sun was making the gold shine so bright you had to squint. Juan felt his heart sing. He had found the city of gold.

They walked along the colonnade and stopped at another doorway hung with a blue and red drape. Axatan lifted the heavy cloth and waved Juan in.

'These are your quarters.'

The room was exactly the same as the one they had just been in. A wooden trunk was pushed up against one wall. A low bed almost filled the floor and a stone lamp sat in a metal stand. The sun shone through wooden shutters. Juan stepped inside.

'I will bring you some food. You may find it strange that we do not lock you in a dungeon, but I assure you, this is still a prison and you will not be able to flee further than the boundaries courtyard.' He smiled. 'And I hope of course you will not want to.'

For a moment they stood there, holding the silence.

Then Axatan turned and said, 'Make yourself comfortable. I am going to get some food. This is now your home.' He stepped out into the sunlight, leaving the drape flapping in the breeze.

Juan lay down on the bed. He smiled to himself. His luck was in. He had found the city of gold and the fools had left him unguarded.

He would wait for the food – he needed strength – and then overpower this Axatan man, collect as much gold as he could carry and find a route back to the others. They would welcome him as a hero and at last the great Spanish assault on El Dorado would begin.

Axatan returned, carrying a tray. He had brought little *bocadillos* which he called *tamales*, and a sweet, yellow wine which made Juan's head hum. They ate together, keeping silent, until all the food was finished. Then Axatan spoke.

'You asked me where I come from,' he said. 'Well, I will tell you.'

They talked until nightfall, the sounds of the warriors coming and going outside the door, the conch-shell calls from the city walls marking the passing of the hours. They swapped stories of life in the army, of growing up in the country, of their dreams and ideals. They talked excitedly about the adventures they had had. Juan was amazed that Axatan had never seen the sea and he stared in wonder when Juan described how many hundreds of men had sailed from Spain. Juan was thrilled. At last he felt important. He loved it when Axatan begged him for more stories of growing up in Spain. And in turn he sat rapt as Axatan told him about the spirits in the jungle, the Aztec gods and strange creatures who were half man, half animal.

They laughed together, drinking the sweet wine, their stories intermingling as they lost track of one and began another. Their smiles and their laughter became more frequent and eventually the moon's sad light streamed in through the shutters, reminding them of the day which had gone.

And then they stopped and sat quietly, savouring the sweet taste of new friendship and the soft sadness of a day coming to its end.

At last, Axatan stood.

'I will leave you now,' he said, 'but I will return tomorrow.'

He smiled at Juan.

'You are welcome here. Welcome to the Stable.'

Juan watched him leave and sat for a while, reflecting on all that had happened since he had been captured, until the oil lamp burnt out and he curled up on the small bed and went to sleep.

The weeks passed and Juan became more and more part of the Stable. He got to know which warriors to trust and which to avoid. He learnt to avoid Tojo, the warrior who had attacked him on that first night. Stories were still going round that Tojo was looking for revenge. And above all, his friendship with Axatan grew and blossomed.

Axatan visited him every day, sometimes bringing him gifts of a little jade box or some feathers from a brightly coloured bird. He came in the evening, talking until late, asking him questions about his village, his brothers and sisters, his friends. And every time, when the moon was high in the night sky, he would stand up and smile and say he had to go. And every time Juan would ask him to stay a little longer. And he would, until finally he would head out into the night, the gently flapping drape the only sign that he had been at all.

And then suddenly he appeared one morning, long before the Stable was awake.

'I have brought you breakfast,' he said. 'I have been out with the fishermen all night and I have caught a fish just for you. The women in the square cooked it for me on their fire. It is just right.'

He opened a small basket he had laid on the floor and the room was filled with the smell of food.

'I know it is early, but eat with me. It is our fish.' The words sent a flash of excitement through Juan's bones. *Our fish*. Had he too been feeling the bond that had grown between them, that had left Juan awake at night, yearning to lie next to this beautiful savage and hear their hearts beating in unison? He looked at Axatan, whose eyes were gleaming like gold. He had put a little fish into a *tamale* and was holding it out to him. He was grinning and the stubble on his chin framed pure white teeth.

Juan took the gift and put it in his mouth. It was hot, but it tasted fresh and good. Axatan had brought milk and Juan drank greedily, thirsty after the salty fish.

'You have milk all over your mouth,' said Axatan, smiling. 'Here, let me wipe it off.'

He leant forward and brushed his fingers over Juan's mouth. Juan closed his eyes, feeling him softly caress his face. He sighed and in an instant he felt Axatan's mouth on his, his tongue probing past his lips, exploring him with the desire that they had let build up for so long. He put his arms round him, feeling Axatan's strength and the tender muscles of his chest and back. He ran his hands up over Axatan's head, feeling his hair and caressing his face as their tongues met, their lips locked together in finally requited passion.

Axatan was stroking his face, letting his fingers graze across the stubble on his cheek then pulling back to look him in the eyes, his face a bewildering mixture of love and surprise and hurt.

Juan pulled him on top of him and their bodies met, rubbing together, hands feeling the contours of each other's chest, arms and legs. Their cocks were hard and they pushed against each other, exciting them more and making their breathing fill the air with gasps of passion.

Juan fumbled with the sheet, pushing it out of the way, and grappled with Axatan's breeches, eager to taste the nectar of the warrior's cock, but Axatan pulled away.

'Our passion is ruling our heads. I came here to speak with you and we are already caught in the spider's web of desire. Since you were taken captive I have thought of no one but you. I have tried to banish you from my mind, but I have found myself lying awake at night calling your name to the wind.'

He bit his lip and looked at the floor.

'I cannot tell you what your destiny is here. You know that our captives are killed. So far your life has been saved, but the Prince will soon decide your fate. All I can ask is for a gift you have in your power to give.'

He looked up, and Juan saw a boy, not a warrior.

'I love you and I am here to ask for your love.'

Tears welled up in Juan's eyes.

'Today is the feast of Huitzilopochtli and, as my captive, I must bathe you in the sacred baths. If you will come with me as a friend and not a captive, I will also use the ceremony to pledge my soul to yours as friends for ever.' He looked deep into Juan's face. 'Will you come?'

Juan's heart was pounding. He knew that his reply would seal his fate. Axatan was drawing closer and closer to him so that their destinies would become one. He looked him in the eyes and said, 'I will come.'

Axatan threw himself forward and embraced him with all the

strength of a warrior. They kissed, holding each other tight, pulling themselves closer as if their bodies could become one.

Finally Axatan pulled away and spoke.

'I am glad.'

They walked to the bathhouse, deep in thought. Two massive doors covered with jade towered above them. Set into one was a smaller door which Axatan pushed open. They stepped through.

They were in a vast hall. A huge domed roof loomed above them, cut with tiny holes which let in thin shafts of light. Laid into the floor were three large pools of water, the one nearest to them giving off billows of steam into the air. The walls were decorated with friezes of warriors doing battle with great monsters which came out of the earth. Around three sides of the hall ran a low bench.

Axatan was gesturing around the room. 'Bathing is an important ritual,' he said. 'It binds us to the gods. These three pools are not only for cleansing. They also represent each of the great gifts the gods have given to the world of men.'

He carried on. 'The first bath is hot because it represents fire. We cannot live without fire and when you enter it you must thank the gods for the gift of the sun's heat. The second –' He pointed at the middle pool '– is as cold as the lake. When you enter it you must thank the gods for the gift of the lake which Our Mother Earth has given us to feed us. Without the lake the sun's heat will destroy us. Without the sun, the lake will rise up and carry us away.

'The third bath is the temperature of blood. It is the bath of our life and body here on earth. When you enter it you must thank the gods for the gift of our bodies.'

Juan looked at the baths. He had given away his life to this stranger. He had thrown away the world he had come from and now he was being told to worship heathen gods.

Axatan took off his tunic and laid it on one of the benches that lined the walls of the bathhouse. Juan let his eyes roam over his new friend's body. His legs were strong and toned and covered with wiry black hair. The same hair formed a thin black line which ran down from his stomach to his cock. His nipples were pink and small against the darkness of his skin and Juan found the spit welling up in his mouth as he imagined himself licking on them and taking them between his teeth. His buttocks were firm and covered with a sprinkling of hair and Juan saw himself kissing and caressing them and licking in the crack. His cock, which lay sleepily in the nest of his balls and cock hair, was soft and thick, its smooth head just beginning to slide past his foreskin.

Axatan looked up and caught him staring at him. Juan blushed, but Axatan smiled and pointed to the bench.

'Strip off. It is time to bathe.'

Juan let his breeches drop to the floor. He was fascinated by this man whose commands seemed to come so easily but whose kiss had been so tender. His cock was already swelling. In the bedchamber he had been impatient for his body. Now he wanted to take time and understand the feelings which were flowing between them.

The water was hotter than a thousand ovens and Juan instantly found himself covered with sweat.

Axatan jumped in and dived under the surface – staying there for so long that Juan thought he might have drowned – before bursting up with a great splash, red and grinning.

'Can you feel it?' he laughed. 'It is the beauty of the sun.'

Juan could feel it too much. He thought his body was going to melt away and he scrambled out and plunged head first into the second pool.

No two things could have been so different. Where the heat had burned him, the cold cut through his skin and grasped his heart with icy hands. He tried to draw breath but found his throat blocked with the fearsome cold which gripped him from head to toe.

Axatan was standing on the side, laughing at him.

'It is a big change, is it not? Not everyone jumps straight in like you did.'

He eased himself into the water and stood perfectly still while the icy ripples lapped round his neck.

'This bath hardens your body for the trials of the earth. Some warriors spend days in it preparing themselves for battle. It is said that you can learn how to make your heart stop beating so that your enemy will never find you in the jungle.' He looked at Juan. 'I have never managed that, but I will.'

Juan could barely manage another minute in this icy water and he climbed out, shivering in the cold air before stepping into the third bath – the bath the temperature of blood.

It was as if a thousand fingers were massaging his body, soothing him and holding him in perfect ecstasy. He lay back and the water lapped across his chest. This was paradise. The water had become silk and was brushing across his soft skin, sending waves of pleasure running through his body. He shut his eyes, letting the ripples play across his chest and shoulders. He barely heard Axatan slipping in beside him.

The Aztec's hand brushed against his thigh and sent a shiver of excitement through his body. He kept his eyes closed but opened his legs slightly, letting Axatan run his fingers along his soft skin. He lay back as his new friend discovered the secrets of his body. The water was lapping at his chest, making his nipples hard, and he could feel the movement of the water rush past his balls.

He reached out and took hold of Axatan's cock. It was hard and felt magnificent in his hand. He knew at once that he wanted it in his mouth and dived down under the water, taking the shaft between his lips and wrapping his tongue round its silken majesty.

He rolled it around his mouth, sensing its weight in the water, and then came up for air and kissed Axatan on the lips before diving back down again, this time sucking just on the end of his cock and letting his fingers play around the Aztec's balls. Axatan's hand ran through his hair and as he came up for another breath, he pulled him towards him and pressed his lips to his.

They kissed for what seemed like hours. Tongues exploring each other's mouths and hands roaming over bodies, taking up what had been started in the bedchamber, each delighted to find a new place or feeling which would excite the other further.

The water rushed around them as Juan let his fingers run up

and down Axatan's arse. He felt for the precious ring of muscle that nestled there in his black hair and rubbed it gently with his finger. Axatan let out a long sigh of pleasure as he opened up to let him in, his hole relaxing and Juan's finger sliding softly into the smooth place within.

He took one of Axatan's nipples into his mouth. It was hard and smooth and as he ran his tongue across it he felt his chest rise up towards him, begging him to suck harder and to take him into his mouth. His finger pushed deeper into Axatan's arse, finding the little knot of pleasure behind his balls and making him close his eyes and groan with ecstasy.

In an instant, Juan saw all the men he had ever pleasured and been pleasured by in this way: the farm lad to whom he had shown the secret of bringing yourself to climax, the young soldier in the village barn, the men on the ship who had used him roughly, until they were alone with him and then shown him the highest tenderness and care. And now Axatan, a savage, but not a savage, his enemy, but not his enemy. His friend. His love.

He dived under the water again and let Axatan's cock slip deep into his mouth. His pushed another finger into Axatan's arse and with his thumb pulled down on his balls.

Axatan took his head in his hands and guided him up and down his cock. He was bucking back and forth like an animal on heat, letting his cock slide in and out of Juan's mouth.

Juan reached between his legs and started to wank himself in the warm water. He came up for air and then dived down, letting his tongue flick on the underside of Axatan's cockhead, unleashing the well of pleasure within.

With his other hand he began to wank up and down Axatan's thick shaft, pulling his foreskin back and feeling the vein on the underside of his shaft throb and thicken.

Axatan was thrashing round the bath in ecstasy and he pulled Juan clear of the water and kissed him roughly, squeezing their cocks together and wanking them both with his strong hands.

They kissed long and hard, firmly and urgently, while stroking their cocks harder and faster, letting their balls knock against each other. The water was seething around them and Axatan threw back his head and with a great cry of ecstasy let his come flow up into the water and over Juan's cock. Juan came too, his seed pumping out in great clouds of white which rose up to engulf them and place a seal on their newfound love.

They returned to Axatan's quarters arm in arm, hardly able to stop looking at each other, each grinning wildly. Juan had never felt so happy. As they pulled back the curtain they kissed again, ready to kindle and rekindle their passion as the day went on.

Neither saw Tojo waiting for them, crouching in the corner.

Quetzal awoke late.

His first thought was for Axatan, and their shared obsession with joining the Eagle Warriors.

It was an honour they had coveted for years. He thought of Axatan's ring and how proudly he showed it off – the mark of his ambition to rise to the Aztecs' highest rank. They had talked about it since they had joined the Stable and each had fought hard on the battlefield, taking captives and excelling themselves in bravery to capture their Prince's attention.

And then, just before Axatan's fateful confrontation with Tojo, they had received the order – to be ready at dawn in two weeks' time to be taken from the city and face the initiation rites. The teachers at the House of Instruction had told them about the ceremony, but even the Eagle Warriors they lived with and fought alongside were unable to divulge the secrets of the ceremony. All they knew was that they would be taken away blindfolded and subjected to the trials of passage. And now the initiation was tomorrow – but would Axatan's behaviour have jeopardised everything they had worked for?

He got up and opened the shutters. It was a beautiful sunny day, the perfect day for going out to the lake. He thought of waking Axatan and then decided against it. He was angry with him for his behaviour. And if he was looking after the *telpollo*, he could plan their own entertainment.

He dressed in a white tunic and breeches and put on his sandals.

Out in the courtyard he looked quickly into the bedchambers of Tupac, Techuan and Janza to see if they wanted to go with him. The first two were asleep still and Janza was nowhere to be found. Quetzal smiled to himself. There were many beds Janza might be in now. The boy had proved a popular addition to the Stable.

He let himself out of the back gate to the Stable, and walked through the city streets down to the quayside.

Preparations were already beginning for the Festival of the Sun and the marketplace was thronging with people from out of town. Women from the villages were selling the little cake figures which would be given to the children in each of the townships. Sweepers were cleaning the route of the sacred procession which would wind its way through the narrow streets of the city and up towards the Great Temple. And in the temple itself, Quetzal knew that the priests were sharpening the flint knives which would cut the hearts from 600 captives taken in battle, ready to be fed to the gods as sacrificial offerings. And the *telpollo* would be one of them.

Quetzal hated the blood sacrifices that were made on the killing stone. He knew that without them the sun would refuse to give its warmth and the earth would close up her supply of food. But at the Festival of the Sun the gods were at their greediest and more people were sacrificed on that single day than in the rest of the month around it.

He thought of last year. He had been officiating at the base of the temple and by the afternoon the temple steps had become a river of blood, flowing into the Great Courtyard and filling the city with the sickly-sweet smell of death. It was a duty he put up with rather than welcomed.

He jumped into a canoe and paid its owner to take him to the far shore. He felt better as the great white mass of the city receded behind him. The water was crystal clear and he looked down on the fish darting around beneath them, playing in the sunbeams which cut through the blue water. By the time they reached the shore he was happy again.

The water was inviting and he stood up, clambered on to a rock and dived into its clear blue depths.

The sounds of the day disappeared as he dived down through the silent depths towards the coloured pebbles on the bottom of the sea. He loved to swim this way. The gods of the water would always make sure he had enough air and they would yield up beautiful colours which would shine up and call to him like animated jewels. Water was good, he thought.

He swam for a while, rounding an outcrop of rock, and was ready to turn back when he made out two figures on the shore.

He ducked under the water and swam closer.

They were both naked and he laughed to himself when he realised that they were having sex. He kept low in the water and swam quietly towards the shore.

The man was young and lean – a fisherman, perhaps, or a farm lad from one of the villages. The girl was rounded and had skin the colour of light wood. She was lying back on some rocks and he was half lying, half standing over her, his arse rising and falling as they fucked.

Quetzal grinned and turned to swim back when a loud whistle echoed over the water. He turned around and saw that they were waving at him, beckoning him over.

He paused for a moment, wondering what to do, when the man smiled at him. He felt his heart leap with anticipation. He kicked out and swam to the shore.

The man was about his age and a little taller. He was smooth skinned and dark, probably from working outside all day. He had a huge erection. She was lighter and younger than him, with small, rounded breasts that came to a little point. They had stopped what they were doing and were both smiling in his direction.

It was the girl who spoke first.

'We saw you watching us.' She smiled and ran her tongue around her lips. 'Would you like to join in?'

Quetzal was taken aback. He wanted to say no but there was something about the two of them that rooted him to the spot. The man put his hand on his cock.

Quetzal felt his stomach tense, but he waded up on to the shore, the lake water running off his body and making his nipples stand out on end. They stood there for a moment, sizing each other up, and then the man stepped forward, knelt down and immediately took Quetzal's cock in his mouth.

His mouth felt warm and soft and by the way his tongue flicked around his shaft, Quetzal knew that he had done this before. He took hold of the man's head and let his cock slide deeper into his mouth so that it was pressing on the back of his throat.

The man groaned and started to wank his own cock as the woman looked on, making little noises of encouragement.

Quetzal thrust his hips forward so that his cockhead pushed deep into the man's mouth. The man raised his arse in the air and Quetzal saw that he had a dildo in him, its dark end sticking out of the man's hole.

He reached down and twisted the dildo slightly in the man's arsehole. The man cried out with pleasure and the woman winked at Quetzal and began to finger herself, rubbing her other hand over her breasts. Now Quetzal could see why they had invited him over. The man wanted to be fucked while he was fucking his betrothed. The idea filled him with excitement and he felt his cock grow harder in the boy's mouth.

Quetzal looked down. The pale skin of his cock was shining against the dark stubble round the man's mouth. He watched as he pushed it past his lips and then pulled right back again, teasing him so that his cockhead brushed against the man's tongue.

The man's eyes were closed and Quetzal knew that this was what he dreamt about. He let his fingers play around the man's face, slapping him lightly as his cock slid in and out of his mouth. The man groaned in appreciation and sucked harder on Quetzal's cock. And the more he sucked, the further Quetzal pushed the dildo into his arse.

The woman was losing herself as she let her fingers slide in and out of her hole. Quetzal watched as she thrashed around on the rocks, crying out in ecstasy. Then the man pulled quickly away from Quetzal's cock and pushed his cock deep into her again, letting the sweet juices ease its passage up into her belly.

Now Quetzal needed no prompting. He pulled the dildo from

the man's arse and plunged his cock into the moist hole. The man shouted out in jubilation and the force of Quetzal's entry pushed him down flat on to the woman, who in turn let out a scream of encouragement.

Quetzal was amazed. He pulled his hips back and then let his cock slap down into the man's arse, pinning him to the woman and making him beg for more.

The two of them were crying out in unison and Quetzal began to feel like one of those gods in the stories at the House of Instruction, pleasuring everyone around him and sating man and woman alike. It was a strange feeling, but a nice one. The man was grinding his cock into the woman and, as he twisted his hips, he squeezed on Quetzal's shaft inside him so that the seed was forced up from his balls.

Quetzal looked down at the broad brown back in front of him. He wanted to give this man pleasure and pass on the joy he was feeling to the woman lying on the rocks, so he doubled his efforts, punishing the man's arse with his cock and making him cry out as his flesh thrust inside him. The man shouted to him to fuck harder and Quetzal saw that he was losing himself to a whirlwind of lust and pleasure. The woman was crying out too as the force of two strong men came down on top of her, filling her with their might.

Then it happened. Hands grasped him by the hips and suddenly another cock was nuzzling against his arsehole and pushing its way inside. Quetzal couldn't believe it for a moment and looked round. The boy's double was standing behind him, grinning lustfully at him, running his tongue over pearl-white teeth. His thick shaft was glistening with oil and he was ready to thrust up inside him.

There was no mistaking it. This was the boy's older brother. The similarities were clear. He had been watching them and now he had come to claim his part of the pleasure.

Quetzal grinned back. His cock was still inside the younger sibling and he was in no state to refuse the advances of his brother. He flicked his fingers over the man's nipple and then turned back to where the first man was pounding his cock into the girl's moist hole.

The older brother took hold of Quetzal by the hips and pushed his cock inside. His shaft was like a fist pounding inside him and sent waves of pleasure through him and he found himself pushing back on it like a huge dildo, penetrating him and taking him to higher and higher levels of pleasure. He thrust his cock into the man in front of him, pressing down on the two lovers beneath him, and then with equal force pulled it out again, pushing back on to the cock behind him and filling himself with its massive length. The brother was expert, grunting like an animal as he thrust his prick up Quetzal's arse and twisting his hips so that Quetzal cried out with pleasure, impaled on this weapon of lust.

The woman was shouting at the top of her voice, her cries filling the air as she reached her climax, and the younger of the two men joined her with a mighty cry, pumping his come inside her and filling her with seed.

Quetzal could hold back no more and he let forth a river of come into the young lad, thrusting his cock deep inside him with each spurt of seed. At the same time, he closed his ring around his older brother's cock and felt him come too, the hot jets of his seed spurting into Quetzal's arse and filling him with the essence of his manhood.

His heart felt it was ready to explode.

They disentangled themselves and Quetzal got a good look at the man who had been fucking him.

He was solidly built, with the muscles of someone who worked in the fields. His face looked younger than his body and carried a cheeky grin. His eyes were sparkling blue.

Quetzal smiled and extended his hand in friendship. The younger brother and his girl jumped into the lake and began to frolic in the water. Quetzal stood his ground, drinking in his brother's deep blue eyes.

The man took his hand. 'I am Coatl,' he said.

'My name is Quetzal.'

They laughed at the coincidence, took a step forward and kissed.

Eight

Tojo came towards them like a jaguar thundering towards its prey. In his eyes they could see the fury of a man humiliated; a man set for revenge. He struck Axatan first, knocking him back against the wall and sending a punch into his stomach which made him double over in pain.

Juan backed into a corner, his eyes wide with panic, hastily looking around for a weapon. Axatan had slumped to the floor and the giant was pounding on his head with his fist.

'Traitor! Animal fucker! You are worthless. You are a savage.'

He kicked Axatan in the face, banging his head against the base of the wall.

Juan knew he had to act. But how? With this giant? He reached out across the bed and grabbed the metal tripod that supported the oil lamp.

He raised it high in the air, ready to bring it down on his head, but the sound of the lamp crashing to the floor caught the giant's attention and he turned around, his eyes hot with murder. He lunged towards Juan, who jumped up on the bed as the beast grabbed his legs, pulling him down towards him. But Juan managed to duck out of the way and with a burst of strength bring down the metal frame on the giant's head with a blood-curdling crunch.

Tojo screamed and held his hand up to where blood was already pouring from his cheek. He looked at Juan for a second, drilling into him with eyes of hate. Then, letting out a mighty roar, he charged towards him.

Juan glanced behind. He was already in a corner of the room and the only way was down. He ducked but the giant grabbed him by the back of his neck and sent him flying to the floor.

Now Tojo was on top of him, his hands squeezing round his neck. Juan kicked up, his throat screaming for air. He was losing consciousness. Everything around him was going dark and hazy. He pushed up one more time against the mountain on top of him and then all went silent. Tojo's face froze with shock and he slumped on to his side.

Axatan was standing above them holding a flint-blade club. His face was grim and tiny drops of blood fell from the blades on to the floor.

He stood there for a moment, surveying the two men. The body of the giant lay still, his eyes open but lifeless.

'He was a coward.' He turned over the giant's body with his foot. 'He had no right to be a part of the Stable.'

Juan blinked at him. 'That is the second time you have saved my life.'

Axatan looked grim. 'I did what anyone would do.' His face was grey. 'But now there will be trouble. An Aztec warrior has been killed. We must account for ourselves in front of the judges and clear our names.'

He began to pick up the broken pieces of the lamp.

'I did what anyone would do,' he was mumbling to himself. Juan reached out to touch him on the shoulder, but he pushed his hand away.

'I need to find Quetzal,' he said, running to the door. 'I need Quetzal!'

He pushed his way past the heavy curtain and out into the courtyard.

Juan sat for a moment, looking at the giant's lifeless body, the broken lamp and the little puddle of oil running down towards the door. The bed had been pushed away from the wall and behind it he saw a tiny metal object glinting in the sun.

It was Axatan's ring – the one with the strange warrior with the eagle head.

He kissed it and put it on his finger.

'I tell you, he must be killed.'

Topaz was storming up and down the mosaic floor of the courthouse, his portly bulk stretching out his advocate's tunic. It was evening and the Stable warriors had been summonsed to the court of justice.

'An Aztec warrior has been murdered in our own palace and all for the sake of a *telpollo*. Have we forgotten who our enemy is here?'

He turned and pointed at Juan.

'Look at him!' he screamed. 'He sits there as if he was our friend. But let us not forget that he came here to destroy our city. He says he is a friend. But did we have murder in our own palace before? Did Aztec slaughter Aztec before this scum came into our walls? And as for our so-called comrade . . .' He glared at Axatan who sat impassively in his warrior uniform. 'He is nothing but a *telpollo* lover. He has no right to exist in an Aztec city.'

He paused to look round the courtroom.

High on their bench sat the judges, splendid in their coloured-feather headdresses and masks of jaguar heads. Their faces were stony still. Their word was law.

Opposite them, in a huge iron cage, sat Juan and Axatan. Quetzal had been nowhere to be found and soon the news of Tojo's death had spread around the Palace. The sun was only at his zenith when the guards came to escort them to the courthouse. They had wanted to throw Juan straight into the dungeons, but Axatan had demanded that he stay with him.

'He is my prisoner,' he had said, 'on the authority of the Prince.'

The other Stable warriors had formed a circle enclosing the judges and the accused, each wearing the signs and symbols of his rank and office. Techuan, Tupac and Janza sat next to each other, their sad faces focused on their friend in the cage. Techuan was dressed in eagle feathers to mark his high rank as one of the Aztec elite. Janza wore a white loincloth and bead armband adorned with two coloured feathers, the marks of his slow but sure progression up the many ranks of Aztec nobility.

Topaz was speaking again.

'And so, most excellent highnesses, there is only one response to those who love our enemies: treat them as our enemies. We have no alternative but to condemn the accused to death. The gods have shown us the evil among us. They delivered this *telpollo* like the sign on a tree that shows the hunter where his prey has run. The traitor Axatan has been snared and I call for him and the *telpollo* to be wiped out for ever.'

He sat down and an uncomfortable silence filled the room. Juan looked on. His life had never been safe in this place, but now he knew he was facing death. He reached for Axatan's hand but the Aztec did not move. The judges rose and the court stood as they made their way to the private rooms at the back of the courthouse.

'What happens now?' Juan whispered to Axatan.

'They pray to Tezcatlipoca, the god of judgement, who will advise them on their course of action. He is above us and has already made up his mind.'

'But they have not heard that Tojo attacked us. How can they make up their mind?' argued Juan.

Axatan felt the anger mounting in his throat. 'Tezcatlipoca knows.'

'But they do not. I want to speak,' said Juan, his voice getting louder.

'It is all right. Tezcatlipoca knows.'

'No, it is not all right. They must hear our story!'

'No,' said Axatan, through clenched teeth. 'We are the accused. We must keep silent.'

Juan glared at him and walked to the front of the cage. 'You are a woman,' he said.

He rattled the bars. 'I demand to speak!' he shouted. His voice cut through the chilly air of the courthouse, echoing in the stone roof high above them. 'I demand to be heard.'

A thousand pairs of eyes turned to look at him. Some of the warriors were smiling in disbelief. Topaz's face was burning with fury. At the far end of the room, the three judges stopped and turned. Axatan buried his head in his hands. Juan shouted again.

'I demand to be heard!'

A sneering laugh was heard from somewhere in the room. The warriors were smiling at each other. Techuan and Janza were staring at him, their mouths wide open.

'Sit down.' It was Axatan, his voice strained with anxiety. 'You are making it worse.'

But Juan could not sit down.

'He attacked us...' he said. 'He came at us when we came back into the room.' His voice felt tiny all of a sudden, and wasn't helped by the growing laughter which swamped it. People were clapping their hands in mockery.

'We would have died if... It wasn't our fault...' The room was filled with raucous laughter. He tried to fight against it. 'We never meant... He was waiting for us behind the bed.' He was crying out now, but his words were lost in the noise of so much laughter. He felt as if he was trying to be heard against the roar of the mighty ocean.

The judges looked at him across the sea of mocking faces, their expressions inscrutable. Then they turned away, disappearing through an ornate doorway at the back of the courtroom.

Axatan was silent.

Quetzal was pacing up and down the courtyard. He had only heard about the court sitting when he had returned from the lake. The guard had refused him entry and now he was cursing himself, not knowing what was happening inside.

There was a noise from within and a boy came out of the door and ran across the square. Quetzal caught up with him and grabbed him by the scruff of his neck.

'What's happening in there?'

'The clerk called for them to be killed. And then the stupid *telpollo* started shouting at the judges. It was so funny. He was shouting at the judges. Now everyone's saying they will be burnt alive. Before they had a chance, but that stupid *telpollo* fucked it up.'

He laughed and Quetzal slapped him hard across the face.

The boy reeled back.

'What did you do that for?' he shouted.

But Quetzal was already striding across the courtyard back towards the courtroom door.

'Warriors of the Stable, rise for the most excellent judges of this court.'

Juan gripped on to the bars of the cage. The judges had changed their regalia and each now wore the mask of Tezcatlipoca, showing that they had supposedly met with the god and he was within them. Everybody bowed.

The judge in the middle spoke, his voice booming out of the mask like a terrible thunder.

'Warriors. What happened in the Stable quarters today has brought great shame on our city and empire. At a time when our city is being attacked by these strangers from the east, an Aztec warrior kills another to save the life of a *telpollo*. We have all sworn to protect our comrades even to the death and yet today we see before us a live *telpollo* and a dead Eagle Warrior who was mighty and courageous both on and off the battlefield.

'We have not had to deliberate for long. The god came to us quickly and told us his verdict. Axatan, we have heard the god. Your record as a warrior is stainless and we intend that it remains so. We believe you killed as if you were on the battlefield. Tojo had an honourable death. You are innocent of the charge and are free to go.'

A murmur spread around the court. Juan felt a wave of relief running through him. He turned to Axatan, tears streaming down his face.

'As for the *telpollo* . . .' He turned to Juan. 'You are a curse among us. You come here with your witchcraft and cast your spells on our warriors. We will purge you from our city. At dawn on the day of the Festival of the Sun, you will be dipped seven times into the fiery pit until your skin is burnt from your flesh and your bones are turned to ash.'

Juan's heart stopped and an icy panic crept through his veins. The warriors were clapping and shouting and the courtroom was becoming blurry. Hands grabbed him from behind, dragging him down the stone steps which led into the dungeons. He called out to Axatan, begging him to help him, but his friend never turned round. He kept on shouting, calling Axatan's name, until the passage turned a corner and the judges, the warriors and the courthouse all disappeared from view.

The mood that night in the Stable was grim. Tojo's body had been taken away and prepared for cremation. Some of the warriors who had laughed at Juan's outburst came up and offered their condolences to Axatan. Others kept their distance, realising that they had judged too soon and betrayed a noble comrade.

Quetzal and Axatan sat around the fire.

'He must not die. He must not die.' Axatan was poking at the wood with a stick, making the ashes flare up into the air and flames illuminate the worry on his face.

Quetzal remained silent.

'You remember when we first came to the Stable? What was the first thing that we learnt?'

Quetzal looked up. 'I don't know . . . the art of fighting? The way in which we rise up through the ranks?'

'No. What was the first thing they said to us when we came to the city?'

Quetzal reflected for a moment. 'That we were part of a noble family . . .' he said. 'That we were all indebted to each other.'

Axatan sprung to his feet. 'I have to go. I am going to demand the payment of a debt.'

Quetzal watched him cross the Great Courtyard. He said nothing as his eyes followed the tiny figure weaving its way through the colonnade of pillars until it had disappeared into the darkness of the sleeping city.

The dungeons were laid out on either side of a long, stone corridor and as the two guards pushed him onward he could see the faces of other prisoners, some fixed with hatred and anger, others like skulls, grey and beyond hope. Behind one door he could hear the sound of whipping and the anguished cries of a prisoner begging for mercy; from another the groans of man facing death echoed through the metal grating.

He found himself in a large circular room. The ceiling was domed and torches burning on the walls had covered it with black soot marks, filling the place with a flickering orange light. A stocky man stood in the shadows wearing a black mask and the bead armband of the Aztec forces. He was holding a whip.

At one end of the room, a large wooden board stood propped up against the wall. Two holes had been cut in each corner and the unmistakable colour of blood stained much of its surface.

Below it was a drain.

The door closed behind him and Juan saw for the first time the guards who had brought him down from the courtroom. They were clearly brothers. Both had smooth, lean bodies, paler than many of the Aztecs he had seen, and the same square chin and green, menacing eyes. Their hair was cut short and they wore it tied back into the knot which Juan now knew was the mark of warriors still in training.

The stocky man stepped forward and undid the ropes behind his back. He laughed when he saw the look of surprise on Juan's face.

'Don't think you are being given a chance, *telpollo*. There is no way out of this chamber except through the door you came in. My men are strong and even if you did manage to find your way into the corridor, you would be set upon immediately by the guards at the other end. This is my kingdom and you are now my subject. All that went on above ground is nothing down here. You obey me and only me, and if you please me you may even live to see the day of your execution. Strip him and tie him to the ropes.'

The two brothers moved quickly around him, tearing off his loincloth and pulling his sandals from his feet. A pair of ropes were lowered from the ceiling and tied to his wrists.

'Lift him up.'

The ropes became taut and his arms were pulled up over his head, stretching away from his body and making him stand on the tips of his toes.

'Stop there.'

He was held there swinging for a moment as the older brother spat straight in his face.

He was Juan's age, but harder and tougher. He wore a diagonal sash made of animal skin which held a bag on his hips. He was wearing an Eagle Warrior ring like the one Juan still had on his finger.

He thought of Axatan, and how he had betrayed him, and felt a sickness rising in his belly. These men were nothing but savages. How could he have thought otherwise?

The spittle slid down his cheek, warm and sticky against his chin. The man laughed but Juan locked eyes with him, staring back at his cruel face and challenging him to harm him if he dared.

The man slapped him on the face. Juan flinched, but he noticed that the slap was not hard; that the man was playing with him like a cat plays with a mouse. He kept his eyes fixed on his opponent's and began to understand. If he played their game he might find a way out.

The man undid his loincloth. His cock was thick and veined, like a gnarled truncheon ready to punish or reward. The man played with it for a moment, spitting on the end and rubbing his hand over his cockhead, and then he let forth a strong stream of piss over Juan's feet and up the insides of his legs.

The piss was hot against his skin and Juan was reminded of the Prince's words – 'You are made to serve' – and the thrill that had sent through his veins. Those words had given him the key to his freedom. Serve well and be rewarded. That was the secret. He found his cock growing between his legs as the hot liquid dripped on to the floor.

The man's brother looked on. Smaller and smoother than his sibling, he shared his angry looks. He too had cast aside his loincloth and was playing with his cock, making himself hard at the sight of Juan tied up and wet in front of him. The jailer stood impassive.

Juan's eyes returned to his opponent. The man's teeth were perfect white and he flicked his tongue across his lips as if contemplating a banquet. The jailer stepped forward and the younger man moved away, letting the end of his cock brush against Juan's thigh, the head still wet and cold. He gave the jailer a nod.

'*Telpollo*,' said the jailer, standing in front of him. 'My men are pleased, and so I can make you an offer. Once the court passes sentence, you become my property. No one really cares about you. Hundreds of captives will die during the Festival of the Sun. No one will notice if you are not among them. You are a handsome boy and you will do more good alive than dead.'

He brushed the end of his whip over Juan's cockhead.

'I am offering to bargain with you. If you please me, I will see to it that you are not among those who walk to their deaths in three days' time. I will change the records to show that you died in custody. Death is not quick in the fire pits. I have seen people lowered seven or eight times into the devouring flames, each time revived so that they are conscious of their fate. Their skin is hanging off their still-breathing bodies and their feeble voices cry out for mercy and a quick end.

'This I can spare you. But in return you will become part of my kingdom and my slave. And if you ever fail me, I will punish you in such a way that you will long for the mercy of the flames.'

Juan looked him in the eye. His throat was dry, but he knew this was his only chance of freedom.

'I will become your slave,' he said.

The man smiled and raised the whip above his head, bringing it down across Juan's naked body. The first stroke flowed like molten lead through his buttocks and legs, wrapping itself around his thigh and flicking up on to his balls. Juan bit his tongue to stop himself crying out and his dick reared up as the heat reached his cockhead and caused a small drop of precome to fall to the floor.

'I am pleased,' said the jailer. 'You understand how to serve.'

He let the whip come down again and Juan clenched his buttocks, feeling the heat spread through his arse and up inside him. His cock was rock hard and although his brain fought against the beating, his body cried out for more. Pain and pleasure. Pleasure and pain. These were the feelings that had led him to leave his village, to find fame elsewhere, to explore the dark side of the world. And these were the feelings which were transforming him now from a boy to a man and a foot soldier to a member of a higher fraternity.

He closed his eyes and the whip came down again, this time on the other side of his arse, wrapping itself round his leg and filling him with white heat. He thrust his arse backward, and stopped himself crying out. He wanted the man's whip and his cock. He wanted to be used by all of them; the object of their pleasure. He wanted not Axatan, that clean, noble creature who had so betrayed him, but the dark Prince who had used him so well and enslaved him to his desire. He knew he was locked into the dark forces of the night.

The whip came down on to his legs again, flicking up to sting the end of his cock. His balls stirred and he stretched out to give himself up to the hard caress of its life-giving strength.

The younger of the brothers stepped forward and knelt in front of him.

Juan looked down and as the whip came down once more, the boy reached up, opened his mouth and took his dick deep inside him. His brother looked on approvingly.

The sensation was overwhelming. The boy's hot tongue flicked around the head of his cock, probing his hole and letting his teeth brush over the ridge. At each crack of the whip, Juan felt his body being pushed forward, sliding his cock deeper into the young guard's mouth and filling them both with lust and desire.

The soldier reached up and pulled on his sack, rubbing his balls around his soft fingers. Juan pushed forward and the whip came down again, biting into him and burning through his flesh as if purifying him of his worldly life.

The older brother had moved behind him and he felt fingers open his arse cheeks and begin to explore the smooth skin around his hole. He closed his eyes. The sensation of the boy's mouth around his cock and the heat of the whipping through his body were turning him into an animal, wild with desire and ready to please these men in any way they wished.

Ropes were being attached to his ankles and he felt his legs pulled in opposite directions until he was hanging like a star from the ceiling.

A finger pushed inside him and then another, and another, rough against the softness of his skin. They were forcing him open, using his sweat to find their way inside, making him yield to their desires.

Now each man was hard and eager to satisfy his lust. Juan breathed deeply. Their ritual had become a competition. Who would come first? Their slave, trussed up and hung from the ceiling, or his captors, hungry to devour his body and cover him with their hot white seed?

He focused his mind on the soldier in front of him and began to thrust his cock into his mouth. The young Aztec writhed with pleasure. The boy shut his eyes as he took more and more cock into his mouth, making Juan's balls swing against his chin. Juan swung on the ropes, plunging his cock deep into the boy's throat as the guard felt between his legs and started pulling on his own shaft.

Juan pumped harder and the smooth boy moaned with pleasure, wanking himself hard, his breathing becoming faster, until he let forth a stream of white come, up on to Juan's balls and down over his legs.

He slumped aside and immediately his place was taken by his brother. The older man opened his mouth and ran his teeth along the length of Juan's cock, biting into the base and nibbling at the ridge of his cockhead.

Juan's cock sprang up with pleasure, inviting him to bite again into the firm flesh and pull on his foreskin with his teeth. The man gobbled hungrily. He had the same lusty glint in his eye as his brother.

Juan pushed deeper inside him as he felt a warm liquid run down his crack and over the smooth skin of his hole. He looked behind him. The jailer was rubbing oil on to his cock. He was thick like a horse, and slightly crooked, and Juan knew that he would have to work hard to take that massive shaft up inside him. He was thankful for the oil and writhed with pleasure as the man poked his fingers in and out of his hole.

In front of him, the older brother was gobbling furiously on his cock. Juan saw that he too was well hung and solid and he longed to take the man's cock into his mouth and suck him until he came.

And then the jailer took him by surprise. Instead of fucking him, he walked round behind the blond guard and in a single movement rammed his cock up inside him. The Aztec cried out and involuntarily pushed down on to Juan's cock so that it was buried deep in his throat.

Juan was transfixed, watching the man's massive flesh beating in and out of the soldier's arsehole. He had expected it to fill him and make him cry with pleasure, but instead he watched as the guard was pushed down deeper on to his cock every time his master fucked him.

With a crack, the jailer slapped his hand down hard on the Aztec's arse, leaving a red mark which spread through his buttocks, making him buck his arse against the force of his cock.

Juan thrust his cock deeper into the man's mouth, grinding it around so that his throat was filled with hot, sweaty flesh. Juan was concentrating so hard on the man in front of him that he never noticed the younger soldier get up until he felt his cockhead push against his arsehole. Now he too would be filled. He glanced round and pushed his arse backward, opening himself for him.

The boy had the same grin on his face and was running his tongue round his white teeth. He winked and in a single movement thrust his cock up into Juan's arse.

Juan felt his hole being stretched open as the hard flesh drove deep inside him. He bucked forward, almost throwing the man in front of him off balance and causing the jailer's horse dick to push even deeper inside the Aztec's arse.

The lad was fucking him like a dog, letting his thighs smack into Juan's arse and the shaft of his cock pound hard up inside him. His fingers were biting into Juan's nipples and his hand slapped down on the young captive's buttocks.

The four of them were fucking in unison, filling the air with grunts of pleasure. The room echoed with the sound of flesh against flesh and the deep moans of men abandoned to their lust.

The older brother came first, his cock spurting come into the air and filling the room with the potent scent of sex. The jailer thrust his cock deep inside him one more time and cried out in ecstasy as his thick shaft pumped his come inside the young arse in front of him. Juan felt the younger brother tense as his seed spurted up into his eager hole, making him finally come like a river himself into the hot mouth of the man in front of him.

They fell away from each other, the last drops of seed oozing from their cocks, and for the first time they heard the urgent knocking at the door.

The jailer looked up. 'Who is it?' he said gruffly.

'It is Topaz, Clerk of the Palace. Open up at once! I have a message from the Prince.'

Nine

The windows of the private quarters were dark when Axatan arrived at the walls of the Palace. There was no guard in front of the tall gates. All was silent.

He looked up at the tall building. There were three windows on each floor, each of them closed with a lattice shutter which showed only darkness within. To the left, a low wall ran round what Axatan knew to be the Prince's private garden. He took one last look up and down the street, found a foothold and climbed up and over into the soft foliage below.

He paused. He had landed in one of the flowerbeds. A tall, sweet-smelling bush gave him cover and the chance to assess his situation. In the distance, he could hear the sound of running water – a fountain, perhaps, or a stream that was fed by water from the lake. Nearby, a rustling noise suggested a bird or a small animal in the bushes. Other than that, the night was silent.

He kept against the wall. The moon was almost full and it filled the central part of the garden with a sad, grey light. He could see no stars – an unlucky omen – and he mumbled a hasty prayer to the goddess of the moon not to betray him.

The Palace buildings were in total darkness. A shuttered window looked out on to the garden and Axatan decided he would break in there. He crept round the walls of the outbuildings until he was directly below the sill. The moon was bathing him in her light and he jumped each time a shadow moved or what sounded like a ghostly footstep echoed out of the dark.

He took out his knife. It shone in the moonlight and for a moment he was reminded of the killing stone and the terrible honour of being slaughtered to the gods. He kissed it and thought of Juan, then pushed it up under the shutter so that it swung open on its hinges.

He jumped back in terror. Two red eyes were staring out at him, sending him tumbling across the grass and scrambling for cover in the bushes. He looked up, and they were still there, looking mournfully into the garden and fixing him with their gaze. He muttered prayers to all the gods. His heart was beating fast and his mouth was dry with fear. And then a cloud passed across the moon and they were gone.

Nothing would make him go back to that window. Nothing except for the thought of Juan, and how only he could intercede on the boy's behalf. He was here to do a duty to a friend; to the man he loved. The window was still dark. He recrossed the lawn and peered in. The room was empty.

He climbed inside and jumped down on to a pile of matting. This was some sort of storeroom. An oil lamp stood in the corner. He examined it closely and found that the wick was cold. No one had been in here recently.

At the far end, a drape half concealed an archway which led into blackness. He screwed up his eyes to see in with the sight of the hunter, but the dark revealed nothing. Another hanging covered much of the third wall. He pulled it back and had to thrust his hand in his mouth to stop himself screaming as he revealed a skull rack lined with the heads of sacrificial victims, all grinning out at him with their hollow eyes and evil, bony teeth.

He stepped back, letting the drape fall shut, and almost fell through the second doorway into the next chamber.

He stood stock still. As his eyes became used to the dark he began to make out a wooden chest and some mats against the wall. Above it hung a tapestry. Now he knew where he was. Only a day ago he had come here to speak for Juan. Now he was here again. On the same mission? He thought so. Or was he here because he wanted to place himself under the spell of his master again? To feel the hypnotic presence of one so powerful and so strong? His cock stirred as he remembered the dark passion of their love-making and the deep bond which sprang from each of them, sealing them in a pact for ever.

He had reached the other side of the room. A doorway led into the Prince's bedchamber. His mission was about to begin — to persuade the Prince to free Juan. He raised his hand to pull back the curtain.

'Axatan.'

His blood froze. The voice cut through him like a thousand flints, gripping his heart with an icy hand.

The room was filled with a chill wind. He shivered.

'Axatan, turn around.'

A flame roared up and the room was suddenly lit, as if with a thousand oil lamps. The Prince was sitting on his golden throne, wearing the sharp-fanged mask of Mixcoatl, cloud serpent, Lord of the Dead. By his side lay the twin sceptres of the underworld.

His eyes were on fire, burning through Axatan's skin and drilling into his soul. He seemed larger and more powerful, as if he were a beast in a man's body.

He waved his hand and there to his left, bound, gagged and tied face down to a stout wooden pole, lay Juan, a dildo pushed into his arse and the red weals of a beating angry across his back. His eyes were filled with terror.

'We have been waiting for you.' The voice filled the room like thunder. 'You are a brave man, forcing your way into my Royal Palace and scaling the wall into my private garden. And yet you have no idea what it is you meddle with. You seek knowledge, but there are darker forces here than you can contend with. You seek freedom for this boy, but you seem willing to lay down your life in his stead. Some would say you are mad. Others that you are driven by an evil spirit. What do you say, Axatan the brave? What is your response to those who attack you?'

Axatan stood frozen to the ground. Juan's eyes stared at him pleadingly. What had he been through? What had happened to him since he was dragged down into the dungeons?

He looked at the Prince. His body was gleaming with sweat. He was magnificent in his strength, awesome in his power. Axatan bowed his head and knelt in front of the throne.

'My lord, I . . .'

'Look at me.'

He met those eyes and stared hard into the Prince's soul, but all he saw was blackness.

'I watched you today in the courthouse. You took the sentence well but you refused to turn when the object of your desire needed you most. You know you could have interceded with the court. You know you are a respected warrior. What prevented you from speaking? What stopped you appealing to the judges on your friend's behalf? Was it pride? Or was it shame? Pride in being an Aztec. Shame in causing the death of a comrade to save the life of an animal.'

Axatan's heart stirred. 'He is no animal.'

'He is a beast and nothing more.'

The Prince was standing now, but his face had softened. 'But enough of our disagreements. You have come on an auspicious day. At dawn, you and the warrior Quetzal will face the trials of an Eagle Warrior. If you succeed, you take on the burden of the city's highest rank. If you fail, you will surely die and this piece of scum will have no one left to rescue him. Quetzal is in his chamber now preparing his spirit for what lies ahead. You are scrambling over walls to plea for the life of a rat.'

He paused and let out a deep sigh. For an instant, Axatan saw the man and not the god. How much, he thought, must he be troubled by the attacks on the city? How many prayers to the gods must he give up each day to save Tenochtitlan and its people? What was Juan but a *telpollo* spy, set on the destruction of all they held dear?

'Axatan, you are my favourite and I am ready to make you a bargain. If you succeed in the morning I will give this boy up to your care for ever. It will be your reward for overcoming the greatest trial an Aztec can face. You will be able to do with him as you like. If you fail, however –' He stretched the twin sceptres of the underworld out over Axatan's head '– you will both die.'

Axatan opened his mouth to speak but the Prince clapped his hands and the room was filled with darkness. A burst of air punched him in the stomach and sent him flying across the floor. He tore at his throat. The air was suffocating him as if he were deep under water, the last drops of life being squeezed out of his body. He closed his eyes and passed out.

When he awoke, the moon was still shining through the open window, but the throne had been pushed against the wall and the room was empty.

The guards were waiting for him when he entered the Stable compound. Quetzal was standing there barefoot and dressed only in a white loincloth. He was flanked by two Eagle Warriors he had not seen before – older men, marked with the wisdom of battle. Two more stood ready for Axatan.

He looked at his friend and realised how little he had been with him since Juan had been brought into the city. He tried to speak to him, but one of the warriors barred his way.

'Prepare yourself, Axatan. It is time.'

He went into his chamber. The oil stain on the floor reminded him of that terrible moment when Tojo had jumped on them and they had looked death in the face. Tojo had been cremated now; sent on his journey into the next world. He was at peace. Axatan's heart raced with anxiety. He was fighting for himself and Juan.

He stripped off and washed his face and hands in the little bowl of water next to the bed. On the chest was the simple white cloth he would wear for the initiation. He wrapped it round him, looked around his room and stepped out into the courtyard. The morning breeze made him shudder for a moment. In the east, the first rays of the sun were pushing over the mountain tops.

He looked at Quetzal, who returned his gaze with questioning eyes, and held out his hands for the guards. The last thing he saw was the rope being wound around his wrists before the blindfold was pulled over his eyes and he was plunged into a world of blackness and uneasy anticipation.

They walked for hours, the ground under his feet turning from stone to sand to wood and then to earth and grass as they marched further and further into the mountains. Axatan listened for sounds which would tell him where they were – the running of a stream or the lapping of the lake against the shore – but all he heard was the soft whistling of the wind and the occasional hollow cry of a vulture high above them.

At last they stopped, and he heard a knocking on what sounded like an iron door. The air was cold and he knew they had to be high in the mountains, but he had long lost any sense of direction.

The door opened and rough hands pushed him forward. The floor below him was made of stone and a damp heat hit him in the face as if he were in the bathhouse. Rough hands removed his ropes and a voice whispered in his ear.

'There is only one rule. Do not be fooled. Remain true to yourself.'

His blindfold fell to the floor and the door closed. They were alone.

The passage was just wide enough for the two of them to walk side by side. At intervals, a small oil lamp spluttered and smoked, barely illuminating the area immediately around it. In the distance, shouts and bangs echoed. The heat was almost unbearable.

Axatan looked at Quetzal. His friend looked strange to him, scared and anxious about the task ahead.

The passage led downward as far as the eye could see. Every so often, dark corridors led off to the right or left and in one of them Axatan made out the unmistakable form of a human skeleton still tied at the wrists and ankles with rope.

Axatan shivered. In the House of Instruction, his teacher had taken him aside one day, away from the other boys, and bent down to whisper something in his ear. His words had been faint and he had never understood them until now.

'Seek out the depths which will take you higher,' the old man had said. 'You will fly as a man, you will soar as an eagle.' He had then given Axatan the ring he had worn ever since – the ring of the Eagle Warrior. Where was it now? He had lost it in the fight with Tojo and never found it.

He glanced again towards Quetzal, wanting to speak, but the words froze in his throat. He had a fixed expression on his face, as if trying to see through the walls to what lay ahead of them on their unknown journey. He himself knew that what was to come was unknown but unavoidable. His heart was beating fast with a scared exhilaration.

He thought of the Prince's words. Pass the tests ahead and Juan would be his. His soul sang with the thought.

They reached a fork in the corridor and, as if guided by unseen hands, took separate routes. From now on they were to face the trials on their own.

He looked down the passage he had chosen. There was no light, just the same cries and shouts they had heard earlier and the same sense of foreboding and excitement that had brought him here in the first place.

He breathed deeply and stepped into the dark.

Immediately, hands were all over him, clawing at his flesh, pulling at his limbs and stroking him as if they were trying to eat him with their desire. He heard moans of pleasure or despair. He smelt sweat and blood and anxiety. And he tasted hope and disappointment in the air. He was being pulled down by the arms and hands which seemed to come out of the wall.

'The first step will be those who have failed.' His teacher's voice echoed in his head. 'You must ignore them.'

He pushed the hands away but yet more ran across his chest and stomach, pulling on his nipples and finding their way to his groin. He walked on, pushing them off until they began to fall away and become less insistent. Soon all that was left of them were the scratches on his body and the pregnant silence of disappointment echoing in his ears.

He turned a corner and stepped into an enormous cavern, the setting for the trials proper. The roof towered high above him, disappearing into dark invisibility. On the walls, torches gave off a smoky light. Against the wall, on pavements barely a shoulder's width wide, stood warriors, their torsos stripped and gleaming with sweat. In front of him, almost filling the room, was a huge circular pool of water.

A horn sounded, its plaintive cry disappearing into the blackness of the roof high above him. The first ceremony had begun.

'Axatan, warrior, Prince among Aztecs.' No one was speaking. The voice seemed to be coming directly out of the rock. 'In battle you have taken many captives. You have brought many gifts to the killing stone. Now you are offering yourself as a captive. You will make your own killing stone and throw yourself at the mercy of the gods.'

Two of the men approached him, stripped bare and magnificent in the shimmering light of the torches. Their nakedness showed off their strength. Great sheets of muscle rippled in their chests. Their arms could lift oxen and their legs could support the weight of the world. Their eyes viewed him with desire.

'Bind him.'

The guards pulled off his loincloth and wound a thin rope around the base of his cock and balls. He felt the blood gorge his cock and make it stand out from his body as they passed the rope up between his buttocks and around his wrists. Another rope was passed through the first and tied around his ankles, trussing him up like an animal captured in the hunt.

'The first trial is the trial of water. May you excel yourself and prove yourself worthy of an Aztec.'

They pushed him forward into the water and at the last minute he managed to gulp a lungful of air before his face hit the water and he sunk into the murky green depths.

He pulled at the ropes, holding his breath while struggling to escape. But they bit harder into his skin, taking him down and down into the depths below – the land of death and drowning. He wanted to shout out to Quetzal not to fall for their tricks; to run back into the daylight to the city and turn away from these sorcerers. But all his mouth gave out were bubbles of despair as the water took him to be hers.

Below him, at the bed of the lake, he began to make out shapes and buildings. It was a huge underwater city, and now he could see people waving to him, shouting encouragement, and beckoning him to join them. They were beautiful, like spirits who had never been touched by the greyness of life.

He realised he was breathing easily in the water and felt himself swooping down towards them like a bird returning to its flock. His bonds were falling away and he was naked, not as a man, but as a newborn baby, soft and pure.

They caught him in their arms and he felt their hands all over him, caressing him and stroking his skin, soothing him with the soft caress of their mouths. A hand brushed against his face and he turned and saw a handsome youth gazing at him with pure jade eyes. Their lips touched and he felt the boy's soft mouth open to receive his tongue. He wrapped his arms around the youth's muscular body and let his fingers run down the smoothness of his perfectly formed chest, exploring him and making him his own.

The boy's hands slid over his stomach and found their way into the hair around his cock. His fingers were cold like a spring breeze and they teased around the base of his shaft, making him hard and causing his cock to push out and up in the water.

The boy looked him in the eyes and smiled. Then he dived down and took Axatan's cock into his mouth, letting the water rush in and out of his lips as he sucked on the head and pulled gently on his balls with his fingers.

Axatan was in heaven, running his fingers through the boy's jet black hair and watching it wave like seaweed in the water as his mouth flowed up and down the length of his staff.

Another youth approached and took his face in his hands, swimming up so that he could let his half-erect penis brush across

Axatan's lips, leaving the salty taste of precome on the end of his tongue.

Axatan closed his eyes and let the soft flesh slide into his mouth. The skin was smooth on his tongue and the head gave off the true scent of man as he took the youth further into his mouth, sucking on the shaft and making the vein which ran along the bottom of his cock swell with pleasure.

A third youth approached, even more beautiful than those who had come before him, and guided his hands to his chest so that Axatan could feel the hard silkiness of his nipples rising up in the coldness of the water.

He let the cock slide from his mouth and took one of the youth's nipples into his mouth, rubbing his tongue over the tiny bump and pulling the skin gently between his teeth.

A tongue was now lapping at his arse. He felt the heat of the first boy's breath as he flicked his tongue over his hole, making it open with excitement to offer up the dark secret of his crack.

He stretched out as hands caught him from underneath, cradling him in a thousand arms, whispering in his ear and kissing his face and neck. He was in paradise.

'Stay with us.'

Their voices called in unison, and he found himself floating through a field of dreams.

'Stay and never fear again.'

He remembered then what his teacher had said.

'Be yourself. Always be true.'

He was not of this world. Not yet. He belonged on the earth, not in the Humming Bird fields of the dead.

'Stay.'

He began to panic, pushing them away. He was calling out.

'No, stop!'

But his voice was silent.

Hands reached out for him but he was already rising up through the water, the youths disappearing into the distance, their faces sad, their stares imploring him to stay. He started to taste the lake, brackish on his lips, and found his throat constricting as he broke the surface, gasping for air and coughing the water from his lungs.

The warriors had been waiting for him and they nodded in approval as he was hauled out of the pool, the ropes still around his wrists and ankles.

'You have resisted well, warrior. The first of your trials is done.'

He looked up. The Prince was standing above him, naked except for a black strap which wound around the base of his cock and made it swell and jut out like an angry snake. He gestured to the men around the side of the pool.

'My warriors are eager for you to succeed. Now you must move on to the trial of knowledge.'

All eyes were on him and he could see that some of them were already aroused by the sight of his naked, muscular form bound at the feet of their Prince.

A door opened in the wall and Axatan saw that behind was a cell encased in darkness.

'In the waters of temptation you did well to refuse. Now you must always accept.'

A door opened in one wall of the cavern. Inside was blackness.

'The trial of the Earth where time distorts and the Bundles of Years become one.'

They undid his bonds and pushed him into the dark. The door swung shut behind him and he fell to the floor, panting from his ordeal.

He reached out. He was in a small cell cut into the rock, no taller than a man and no wider than the span of his arms. The floor and walls were stone but they contained neither the dampness nor the cold of the caves he had been in. Instead, they held a comforting warmth that reminded him of being held by his mother when he was ill as a child.

He tried to keep his eyes open. In the darkness he could make out forms and faces coming towards him but never quite meeting his stare. He saw his family calling him from the small farm he had left behind. He saw Quetzal crying out for help – drowning in the lake, being burned in fire – but all he could do was laugh. A wild animal jumped up and bit into his throat, but he pushed it away with a shrug of his shoulders.

His teacher's voice echoed in his head.

'They will take you to a dark place and you will meet the spirits of your future. Respect them and honour them, for they are you.'

An acrid smell like burning rose out of the darkness and two dim, red eyes opened in front of him. He heard a growl like a wild beast and he felt his stomach contract with fear.

'Respect them and honour them, for they are you.'

In front of him stood a man taller than any human he had seen. His chest was covered with thick black hair and his legs were like pillars of stone. His arms were lifted up to the ceiling as if cursing the gods. Axatan looked up and saw his own face looking down at him.

He fell to the floor.

He saw the giant's feet, huge and solid in front of him, and impulsively began to lick them like a mother bear licks her cub. He ran his hands up the thick hair of his legs and looked up to see his cock growing in front of his face.

It was long and hard and Axatan hesitated for a moment, fearful that the giant would split him open. Would he be able to service such a god? He looked up. The man's eyes were burning with fire, but a smile played across his face.

Axatan opened his lips and took the thick shaft into his mouth.

The taste was bitter and musky, like the powerful scent of a beast who marks his progress through the world by leaving his trace wherever he goes. He felt it burn the inside of his mouth with its power, making him stretch up to keep it all inside him as the god started to buck his hips and ride his mouth.

He reached between his legs and took the giant's huge balls in his hand. The man growled in pleasure and Axatan worked them between his fingers, letting his tongue slide up underneath the giant's foreskin and round the heavy ridge of his cockhead.

The scent of the man's musk was swimming through Axatan's head and he felt his own cock leap up and send little spurts of precome running down its shaft.

He started to wank himself, lost in the force of the god's desire. He let the come rise up inside him, ready to make this place his own and mark his own point in time in the kingdom of the gods.

'The spirits of your future. They are you.'

The giant had taken Axatan's head between his hands and was slowly sliding his cock in and out of his mouth, filling him with his flesh and letting the scent of precome rush through the passages of his head.

He was growling, holding him tighter as he thrust his shaft in and out of Axatan's mouth. Axatan was pinned to the rock face by the force of the man-god's onslaught. A voice boomed through the cell.

'Axatan! Axatan! Achieve your destiny.'

He wanked himself harder, feeling himself grow so that he seemed to be as big as the giant who was his future. He thrust forward with his mouth and for a moment the two of them hung in perfect balance before the god pushed down and, letting out a roar which threatened to tear through the stone walls and hurl them both out of the side of the mountain, pumped his seed into Axatan's throat.

His head was filled with the sweet musk of the man's desire and his own come poured from his cock, splashing on to his chest and stomach and arms as he drank down the sweet juices of his future, taking inside him the seed of the giant he was to become.

He fell back and closed his eyes, tasting the white come within his mouth and drifting into a dream until at last the door was opened and the guards dragged him back out into the cavern.

He blinked in the light, looking up at the men clustered around him. He could see the approval in their faces; their desire that he succeed and their understanding that he had grown now and taken a step towards his destiny. He also felt their lust, and how they longed to take his body and make him one of their own.

They lifted him up. A line of dry come ran down his chest and stomach and one of the soldiers knelt in front of him and began to lick it off. Others dipped cloths into the water and cleaned him like a baby, stroking him gently and soothing him with soft words of encouragement.

The Prince held up his hand.

'Enough.' He looked at Axatan. 'You have done well, my warrior. The third trial will be your final test. You have refused temptation and accepted your future. Now you must control the one you love.'

Around him the warriors were playing with themselves, hard and magnificent, aroused by the adventure ahead. His body was taut and full of power. He had conquered the easy life and faced his destiny. Now he was ready to triumph in the ultimate trial.

They dressed him in a leather harness and thick leather boots, placing a beaded armband around his bicep, which gleamed in the flame of the torches.

The Prince clapped his hands and a thunderous explosion filled the cavern. The water parted and flames licked up from the deep pit which was revealed below.

A stone platform stood in the middle of the room. Steps led up to it on all sides and at its base braziers held burning fires which filled the room with their acrid heat.

Tied to a bench on the top of the platform was Quetzal. He had been stripped, and his arse was pushed up into the air, his hard cock sticking out below him. He was facing away from them towards the back wall, his strong legs bound to the wooden frame with thick ropes.

'Every Eagle Warrior is part of a pair.'

The Prince's voice echoed through the chamber. The other warriors were moving in on the stone altar, and Axatan found himself mesmerised by the beautiful sight of his friend tied up in front of him.

'Both men are masters of each other and both each other's servants. Some day you will find yourself subordinate to Quetzal's every need, but today you are his master and he is yours to control. His vow is the complement to yours: he will succumb to the one he loves.'

Axatan mounted the steps. In front of him, Quetzal's pale arse lay open for him, the thin line of golden hair promising the sweet beauty of his hole below. His back muscles were taut and his arms, tied tight, pulled against the ropes.

Axatan circled him once. He looked up and Axatan allowed him to kiss his hand as he stood in front of him. He stroked his hair, giving himself a moment to feel the soft golden locks which cascaded on to his neck and shoulders. He brushed his fingers across his face and let them rest for a moment on his lips, savouring their soft beauty and imagining the joy they would bring him later.

He smiled at Quetzal, who smiled back before looking down at the floor and Axatan's boots. They both knew their roles and they both relished the challenge ahead.

Axatan walked back to the front of the altar and stood in front of Quetzal's arse. The other warriors had formed a circle around them and were already playing with themselves, their cocks hard and thick in their hands.

He knelt and let his eye run up Quetzal's crack before leaning forward and running his tongue along the line of golden hair which nestled there.

Quetzal let out a sigh of pleasure, and Axatan ran his tongue up again from the base of his balls, along the crack and over Quetzal's soft, pink arsehole. The boy writhed within his bonds and Axatan let his tongue lick deeper, feeling the hairs moisten and lie flat against his golden flesh as he probed into the musky pleasures of Quetzal's arse.

He placed the tip of his tongue on his arsehole. The tight muscle was throbbing and he flicked the tip lightly over its surface. Quetzal cried out and Axatan pushed his tongue just inside, opening him slightly and letting his saliva drip into his arse.

He felt between Quetzal's legs. His cock was hard and his balls hung low and heavy below him. He looked down. His own cock was thick and solid, rising up out of the leather harness, making both of them hard with the pleasure he was giving to Quetzal's arsehole.

He pushed his tongue in some more and the boy squirmed on

his rack. His arsehole opened up and Axatan lapped his tongue in and out of it, licking the soft flesh within and making Quetzal's prick twitch with pleasure.

He stood up slowly, letting his tongue lick up the smooth line of his spine until he was nuzzling at his neck, his cock pushing up in Quetzal's crack.

'Fuck me, Axatan. Fill me.'

Quetzal's voice was barely a whisper but it echoed through their private world.

'I will, but not yet.'

He kissed him on the face and let his cock run up and down Quetzal's crack, teasing him with it and making the boy buck with pleasure.

He stood up, his cock sticking out like a truncheon, and walked round to position himself in front of Quetzal's face.

The warriors signalled their approval and he was thrilled to find himself performing for them and pleasing Quetzal at the same time. He let his cockhead rest just in front of Quetzal's mouth. Quetzal leant forward to lick it but he grabbed hold of his hair and pulled his head back so that he was just out of reach.

He looked deep into those soft eyes, which stared back at him, imploring Axatan to use him.

'You are mine now,' said Axatan. 'You are mine.'

The flames roared up around them as Axatan increased his grip on Quetzal's hair and ran his cock across his lips.

'Do you want me inside you?'

The question hung in the air. Quetzal's eyes were filling with desire.

'I want all of you inside me,' he said.

Axatan pushed his cock forward and past Quetzal's lips. At the same time he lifted his head up further so that his cockhead slid up across the roof of his mouth, probing the soft tissues of his throat.

Quetzal grunted with pleasure as Axatan made him open up wide and played his cock in and out of his mouth, brushing the ridge across his lips and hammering his gleaming cockhead down into the back of his throat.

Quetzal was bucking on the wooden frame now as his mouth was filled with the silken hardness of Axatan's shaft. Spittle was running down his chin as he serviced Axatan's cock, as his friend and warrior used his face for his own pleasure.

Axatan plunged deeper and felt the soft muscle of Quetzal's throat close around his cock, so that he was fucking him deep in his mouth, his cockhead encased in his friend's flesh.

He pulled out, his cock throbbing with pleasure. A thin strand of precome stretched between his shaft and Quetzal's mouth.

He let go of Quetzal's head and let it drop down in ecstatic exhaustion.

Axatan ran his hand over Quetzal's back. It was broad and firm and he enjoyed feeling the hard muscles under his smooth skin. He let his hand brush over Quetzal's buttocks, feeling the tiny golden hairs stand up under his touch. He stroked between his legs, probing the secret parts of his friend's firm body. He bent down and kissed his arse cheeks again and then raised his hand in the air and brought it down with a mighty slap.

The noise echoed through the cavern and a red mark spread across Quetzal's pale skin. He lifted his hand again and slapped the opposite buttock, drawing back his hand and letting fly a third, harder than the others, which caught the soft muscle of his arse and made his cheeks glow red.

He leant over and whispered in Quetzal's ear. 'I will take you to new heights of pleasure.'

Quetzal's voice was soft and full of desire. 'Take me where you will.'

He slapped down on to Quetzal's arse again as the others crowded round to watch, aroused and excited by the handsome boy being spanked in front of them. Quetzal raised his arse in the air to invite Axatan's hand, which he brought crashing down, sending another slap echoing through the chamber.

Someone handed him a leather strap and Axatan took two paces back and swung it round his head. His cock was rock hard with excitement. The blood was coursing through his body as he brought the strap down on to Quetzal's arse, making the boy cry out.

'No! No more!'

But he pushed his arse up further to invite the strap's fearful kiss.

'You will take six more,' Axatan said. 'And you will count them.'

Quetzal drew a deep breath and called out as the first slap came down on his buttocks.

'One!'

He flinched at the next, but pushed his arse immediately up into the air again to receive the third.

'Three!'

The stone floor below him was glistening with the product of his lust and arousal.

'Four!'

The strap came down on him again and Axatan felt like a god, delivering love and punishment in equal measure.

'Five!'

Quetzal's voice was quavering and a beautiful red welt was appearing across his buttocks. Axatan raised the strap above his head for the final time and swung it down onto Quetzal's arse with all his might.

'Six!'

He flung the strap aside and began to kiss Quetzal's buttocks, soothing them with his tongue, licking away the pain which had given so much pleasure and anointing him with his own spittle.

'You are beautiful, my friend. You give and you take and you make others beautiful too.'

He took Quetzal's head in his hands and kissed him deeply. He closed his eyes and for a moment they were alone again at the lake, caressing each other's bodies and bringing each other to beautiful climaxes which filled the water with soft, white clouds.

Axatan stood, and one of the warriors handed him a bowl of warm oil. He spoke out loud.

'Quetzal, Stable warrior, soon to be Eagle Warrior, you are my gift.'

He had rehearsed this moment over and again in his mind, where he would have to stand back and give away his friend to the lust of the other warriors.

'I therefore commend you to these men and enjoin you to serve them well.'

A horn sounded and he let a trickle of oil run down Quetzal's arse. He stroked his hair and whispered to him in his ear.

'Whatever happens between us I will always love you.'

Quetzal nodded, his face showing fear and desire in equal portions. He was about to become the Eagle Warriors' plaything.

Axatan gave the signal and the first warrior ascended the steps up to the stone platform they were on. The fires were burning strongly now and his body ran with sweat.

As was the custom, he bent low and kissed Axatan's hand and then positioned himself behind Quetzal. Axatan gave another signal and the warrior began to push his huge thickness into Quetzal's arse.

Quetzal bucked on the frame. The warrior pushed his cock in hard and Quetzal cried out, his voice changed by lust and desire.

'Yes, fuck, oh yes, fuck me.'

The warrior slammed his cock home and Quetzal rose to meet him as his hard length slid in, man and boy writhing in mutual pleasure.

The others formed a line behind him, wanking their cocks while they waited for their turn to fuck this beautiful arse.

With a roar, the warrior came and pulled out, leaving Quetzal open and ready for the next.

The second warrior mounted the steps, kissed Axatan's hand and at his signal thrust his shaft deep into the golden-haired boy.

Axatan looked on as his friend lost himself in pleasuring warrior after warrior. They were ploughing through his arse one by one, making him their slave. He looked at the array of men queuing up to use him. Some were broad and beefy, their cocks thick and long like parts of a tree. Others were more wiry, their muscles honed through running or the hunt, and others still maintained a soft strength, the cocks in their hands fat and eager for Quetzal's arse.

The air was full of the smell of come when the Prince appeared at the end of the queue, watching his Eagle Warriors in action.

He slowly pulled on the thick shaft which hung semi-hard between his legs, eyeing the passion which was taking place on the stone altar.

The man in front of him had just stepped up to take his portion of Quetzal's arse when the Prince called out.

'Guide him in. Fuck your friend with his cock, Axatan. Make him cry out in pain and pleasure.'

The man's cock was as thick as an arm and Axatan took hold of it and guided the head to Quetzal's arsehole. He nodded to the warrior, who began to squeeze it through the tight ring and up inside Quetzal.

Quetzal cried out. Its massive girth was stretching him further than he had ever been stretched before. Axatan felt the hard power of its length slide between his fingers and force its way up into Quetzal.

He glanced at his friend. His eyes were closed but on his face was an expression of perfect rapture.

The warrior began to slide his cock in and out of Quetzal's arse, making him rear up with the sheer size pushing in and out of him. Axatan took hold of his cock and began to bring himself to climax, but the Prince shouted out.

'No, Axatan, take the one who takes.'

He pointed at the warrior who was fucking Quetzal. He was young but broad and expansively muscled.

'Fuck him, Axatan. He is yours.'

The man grinned at him and Axatan took a moment to watch his arse pushing back and forth as he fucked his friend. Now he needed no prompting. He positioned himself behind the thick legs of the Eagle Warrior and opened his buttocks. His crack was hairless and the pink beauty of his arsehole shone back at him.

Axatan spat on his hand and rubbed the saliva across the

warrior's hole. The man groaned and reached round to take hold of Axatan's cock, massaging it with his fingers as his own thick shaft pushed in and out of Quetzal.

Axatan let his cockhead rest against the warrior's arse for a moment, not wanting to come too soon and this to end. He watched as the man pleasured Quetzal, the boy crying out in delight as the thick shaft pumped inside him. Then he put his arms around the warrior's thick chest and gently eased his cock inside.

The man let out a long, deep moan of pleasure as his prick penetrated the soft passages of his arse. For a moment he stopped fucking Quetzal to savour the feeling of Axatan's cock entering him. Axatan closed his eyes. Every part of his cock felt as if it were on fire, making him gasp as the waves of pleasure swept through his body.

The man tightened his arsehole around him and Axatan felt the vein along the base of his cock throb as the muscular warrior pumped him from within.

The man took up his fucking of Quetzal again, pushing deep inside the boy as his arse pulled away from Axatan's cock, and then thrusting back so that Axatan was deep inside him, filling him with his solid flesh.

The three of them were breathing in unison; fucking and being fucked, filling and being filled with cock.

The other warriors had formed a circle again and were wanking themselves to another climax. The flames from the braziers flared up around them and the room was filled with the heat and sweat of men pleasuring men.

Axatan felt the come stirring in his balls and he redoubled his efforts, fucking down into the muscular warrior's arse and grinding his hips into him until he cried out, begging for more. Quetzal was moaning and writhing in his ropes.

They were close now and the warrior in the middle clenched his arse and thrust down deep inside Quetzal in front of him. Axatan reached in front of him and found Quetzal's cock, hard and wet and throbbing with the come rising in its shaft.

He ran his fingers across the thick, hard head and then began to wank him roughly.

Quetzal cried out in encouragement and pushed his arse back on to the warrior cock inside him. Axatan could feel the come ready to spurt forth from his cock and he thrust deep into the warrior, shouting at the top of his voice as the thick white seed pumped out of him, making him gasp for air as his come filled the arse of the man in front of him.

The warrior slammed his cock deep into Quetzal and sent his come gushing into the boy's deep arse while at the same time Quetzal's cock splashed its hot seed out over Axatan's hand and on to the stony floor below them.

They lay there for what seemed like hours.

The flames died down in the braziers and the other warriors began to drift away.

Axatan pulled out and stood up, unsteady on his feet but sated and happy. The muscular young warrior in front of him smiled and kissed his hand. Quetzal was still fastened to the frame and the two of them set about untying his ropes.

Axatan kissed him. 'You did well, my friend.'

Quetzal smiled, stretching out his limbs and pushing the ropes away.

'We both did well.'

Axatan smiled.

On the bench behind them two Eagle Warrior headdresses lay ready for them to take.

The Prince had gone and they followed the others down the mountain path back to the city. The sun was setting and Tenochtitlan glowed in the rays of pink and orange from the west.

Axatan did not speak. Today he and Quetzal had reached another level in their friendship, but the day had also brought a far richer prize. Juan was free to be his.

Ten

Axatan rushed back to the Stable. It was getting dark and in the marketplace the traders were packing up for the day. The sun was setting behind the hills and a cool wind was blowing across the lake.

He pushed his way into the Stable courtyard. Some of the other warriors were preparing for the evening temple ritual. They looked at him in his Eagle Warrior regalia and called out words of congratulation. But he ignored them, hurrying instead to his own bedchamber and the prize that lay within.

He had fought the evil spirits of the underworld today to secure the man he loved and save him from death. He thought of Juan, by now delivered by the Prince's own escort to the Stable – his reward for his strength and courage.

Would he be well? Had they harmed him in the dungeons? Would he forgive him for not standing up for him in the courthouse? Was he now ready to spurn his advances and throw the love they had on to the fire because Axatan had failed him at his time in need?

He felt a cold fear rush across him. Would the Juan he was about to see today be a different man to the one he had left to his fate only a sunset before? He remembered his frightened eyes in the Royal Palace. But were they also eyes of hate, accusing him of betrayal in his time of need? He thought of the Prince's words. Why hadn't he interceded for him? Because he was afraid? Or because he had placed a *telpollo* above his friends, and they saw him as nothing but a traitor?

The courtyard had emptied and he realised he had been standing in front of the doorway to his room, as still as a ghost. Would Juan be happy to see him? Or would he be burning with the flames of revenge?

He pushed open the curtain and stepped inside.

His day clothes lay on the chest where he had left them. The water basin still held the water he had washed in that morning. The oil on the floor shone in the half light, reminding him of the fight with Tojo. On his bed was a dark red streak of blood.

His heart raced. Where was he?

His eyes darted around his room, as if Juan might appear suddenly, warm and smiling, welcoming him into his open arms. But the room was laughing at him, the shadows in the corner mocking him for his naivety. And above the jeering he heard the Prince's voice roaring with laughter, incredulous that a warrior could have been such a fool.

He tore across the courtyard, pushing people out of the way as he ran down the steps into the Great Courtyard and across to the Royal Palace. The last time he had made this journey he had been surreptitious and silent of foot. Now he was burning with fury, ready to bellow his anger out at any man who stood in his way.

The evening council had just ended and the Great Hallway was teeming with courtiers, each looking for ways to advance themselves and move up another rung on the ladder of petty officialdom.

They parted as he flew into the hall, his Eagle regalia making them scuttle out of his way as he swept across the blue-jade floor.

Before the guards could stop him, he pushed into the Prince's private chambers, letting the great golden door shut behind him and barring it with the heavy metal bolt.

Through the window he saw the Stable quarters, now pink in

the dying light of the day. Ahead of him was the doorway to the room he had been in only the previous night. The guards were hammering on the door. He swept aside the awning and stepped inside.

The throne was still against the wall. The cushions lay untidily over the floor and he felt a sickness rising in him when he recalled stripping for the Prince and the hypnotic pleasuring they had found between them. He had been seduced and tricked and he felt the heavy bile of shame rising in his throat.

The room was in the same dusky half light as his quarters and it gave up no secrets of Juan's whereabouts. He was about to leave when he made out another doorway in the corner, unnoticed before. He lifted the heavy curtain and peered inside.

The passageway beyond was dark and silent. He stopped for a moment. The only sound was the beating of his heart. He called on Huehueteotl to give him the fire in his eyes to let him see, and stepped into the dark.

The passage was old and the dust stuck in his nose, making him want to sneeze. He reached out and felt the stone walls on either side of him. The corridor was no wider than two men. He stepped forward. Huehueteotl had lit the flame in his eyes and he began to see further ahead of him ... the passage sloping away, a single door at its far end, a black grating the size of a man's face at eye level.

He walked towards it but it seemed to be alive in the dark, changing shape and moving around in the shadows, one moment only an arm's length away and the next tiny and out of reach in the distance. He thought he heard a footstep and froze, but it was only the beating of his heart. He was alone.

The door was made of thick wood and had no handle. He tugged on the iron grating but it remained still. He scratched at the doorpost, desperate to find a way in, but it remained unyielding.

Sweat was breaking out on his forehead and his eyes were full of tears of frustration. They had taken Juan and made him disappear. He had found this door, but there would be thousands of others and only one would give him Juan.

He beat his hands on his head and turned to head back to the Stable.

And then he saw it. On the floor, just in front of the doorpost, was a tiny glint of light. He bent down and felt the cold metal between his fingers. He didn't have to see it to know what it was. He was holding his Eagle Warrior ring.

He scrambled again at the door, clawing at the hard wood as if his nails could find a way to open the hard iron of the locks. He pushed his face to the grating, squinting his eyes to make out shapes in the gloom beyond, but all he could see were the ghosts of his imagination looking back at him, laughing and mocking in his face.

He turned back along the passage. Was there another door? Another way through to the Palace dungeons? The stone walls were cold to his touch and they dripped water as if they had never seen the blistering sun outside.

He felt in every crevice and every join between the unyielding stones until he stumbled out into the throne room again and saw that nothing had changed. The room's silence challenged him to find Juan. He felt the Eagle ring in his hand and remembered their pact to each other. He kissed it and saw Juan's eyes begging him to rescue him. At least now he knew where to look. He put the ring back on his finger and headed back to the Stable.

Quetzal was worried. The Stable was holding a banquet to celebrate their admission to the Eagle Warriors but Axatan had run off after the ceremony and not been seen since. Had something happened to him in that cavern? What had he seen in the chamber of his future? They had spoken, but briefly, after the ceremony and Axatan had even then seemed distracted. Now he was nowhere and the others were becoming impatient.

'Where is he?' Techuan whispered in his ear. 'It's time the feasting began.'

'I don't know,' said Quetzal. 'We began our march back to the city and then Axatan disappeared ahead of us. The last I saw of him was the top of his spear as he headed down into the valley. I don't know where he is.'

He looked Techuan in the eyes and for the first time Quetzal saw a softer side to his friend. Techuan was the rough one, the one who would always have one more drink to keep the party going. But now he was serious.

'You do know where he has gone, don't you?' Techuan said.

Quetzal felt his throat constrict. A thousand thoughts flooded into his mind.

He looked at the warrior. 'I have no idea.'

Axatan had to find a plan. Juan was somewhere in the Royal Palace and the wooden door would lead him to him. The Prince had tricked him, using the cover of the Eagle Warrior ceremony, to take him away and imprison him in the dungeons.

His mind was bleak as he climbed the rough steps which led up to the Stable courtyard. He felt sick and confused, and had no interest in the companionship of his friends. He knew they would be feasting now, celebrating his and Quetzal's accession to the Eagle Warriors, but he had no stomach for it. The thought of food and company nauseated him. All he wished for was Juan.

He entered the courtyard. From the hall, shouts and laughter told him that the banquet was in full swing. The rest of the Stable was in darkness and he crept slowly around the outside of the courtyard, heading for his bedchamber but uncertain what he would do there or why.

Quetzal was making a speech and he listened to him for a moment, weaving in and out of the beautiful Aztec rhetoric as if he was a lawyer, not a soldier. He was speaking about companionship and loyalty and Axatan felt himself blush when he realised how much of a man Quetzal had become and how much of a boy he himself still was.

He took another step and suddenly, out of the darkness, hands were round his neck and face, choking him and preventing him from crying out. He kicked out but his assailant squeezed his throat harder until he found himself losing all strength. He slumped to the ground, looked up and saw Techuan standing there in the shadows, his face as grim as stone.

Axatan put his hand to his throat. 'What do you think you are doing? You nearly killed me.'

Techuan was silent, his eyes boring into Axatan's skull, as if his thoughts would spill out for them both to see.

'Techuan. You are my friend.'

'And it is as your friend that I have come to see you. What are you playing at, Axatan, Aztec prince, so-called Eagle Warrior? Are you so noble that you choose to avoid the company of your comrades? Or are you so low that you have to sneak around the courtyard, hoping no one will notice you?'

He glared down at Axatan, shook his head and looked away.

'It is no secret, this love you have for the *telpollo*. The whole Stable is talking about it. Only Quetzal, your comrade in arms, your friend, your *lover*, denies that you have any feelings for him. When you were summoned to the court, he spoke for you in front of the whole Stable. Many were saying that you should have been killed yourself, that you took the life of an Aztec and should be made to pay for it in the Gladiator Ring. But he, loyal Quetzal, Quetzal your friend, stood up for you, argued that you must have acted nobly because you were noble of spirit. Noble indeed.' He spat on the ground. 'Sneaking around the shadows so that no one sees your shame. You are no more noble than the boys who fill the baths in the morning, who suck the courtiers off for a *tamale* and a new jewel to wear round their necks. If you love the *telpollo* then come clean. Otherwise, cast him from your mind and leave him to his fate.'

His eyes were burning red and Axatan saw there was no escape. A roar of laughter echoed across the courtyard and songs burst out from the hall. But here, in this dark corner, serious matters hung in the balance.

He stood up.

'Techuan, my friend.' Techuan turned away from him and Axatan saw the softness in those broad shoulders. 'I have acted badly. Sometimes I have felt as if the *telpollo* had put me under a spell, as if he brought with him the witchcraft of the underworld. But I know that the only spell is my own love for him. He is a stranger and a friend, my enemy and my brother. Yes, I have been sneaking around. And yes, I have done Quetzal wrong. I listened to him making his speech and I knew he was a man. But I have also been a loyal friend to you, to you all. Ready to protect those I love. Quick to destroy their enemies. I have killed a man in this very place. I have brought death inside the walls of the Stable. But I have also brought friendship and love and all I ask is that you acknowledge that in my time of need.'

Techuan looked at him, his brow creased with thought.

'Axatan, you are my friend. But you are acting like my enemy. You must go to Quetzal and ask *his* forgiveness, *his* acknowledgement. I cannot forgive you. It is he who you have hurt.'

He turned and walked back towards the Great Hall. Axatan paused for a moment and than ran to catch him up.

As they entered, a great wave of warmth swept over them. The Stable was together; drinking, celebrating, enjoying the solidarity of friends and comrades. Axatan saw Quetzal and Janza sitting together, laughing and talking across each other. He hovered in the doorway, unsure about proceeding. Were they really his friends any more? Or was he now as much a stranger as Juan?

He stood for a moment, watching the revelry, then Quetzal looked up and caught his eye. A beam of pleasure swept across his face and his eyes lit up with delight. Axatan felt embarrassed, but already Quetzal was rushing towards him, a broad grin on his face.

Others were looking round now and some of the warriors were toasting him and calling out his name. He looked around. Only Techuan remained grim faced.

'Axatan! I didn't know where you were. Where did you go? We were waiting for you.'

'I –' The words stuck in his mouth. Where did he go? Breaking into the Palace, feeling his way down a damp corridor, trying to scratch his way past thick wood and iron locks. What was he thinking of? 'I – I need to speak with you.'

Quetzal smiled. Was his face more knowing? Axatan wondered, or was it just the way the light played across his features?

'Come outside.'

They stepped into the courtyard. The night chill had descended and the gloom seemed to wrap them with its cold fingers, closing off the revelry they had left behind.

Quetzal slipped his arm through Axatan's and Axatan felt himself stiffen at the unwanted intimacy.

'You know what is happening, Quetzal.'

They walked in silence, the sentence hanging in the air like a finger challenging them to face the truth.

'I am in love, and it is not with you.'

He felt Quetzal tense beside him. He seemed a boy again, soft and fragile, needing Axatan's protection. Axatan remembered their first day together when Quetzal had arrived at the Stable. How they had grown since then, and how he had learnt no lessons in all that time.

'I don't know how to say it, but I love Juan and I need his love for me.'

The words seemed heavy and they dropped like stones from his lips. They walked on, their footsteps echoing through the empty courtyard.

Axatan's stomach was churning with fear and love. He knew he still loved this man and knew he was hurting him. But where else could he turn? Techuan was right. It was Quetzal he owed the most to. Quetzal who had stood by him from the start, loyal and caring, uncomplaining when he was moody, happy when they spent the days together swimming and laughing. And now he was grinding him under the sole of his foot.

It was Quetzal who broke the silence.

'I know of course about your love for the *telpollo*. He is a handsome man and he has captured your heart. I am not stupid. Everyone in the Stable is talking about it and although they try to hide it from me I hear comments and jokes about you and him.'

He turned away.

'But I want you to know I have been loyal to our friendship. I have stood by you even when you killed Tojo. Do you know how many people wanted you dead then? How many of your so-called friends were ready to condemn you to the Killing Stone? Too many, Axatan. Too many to bear contemplating.

'But that was when I realised that the bonds which bring us together as Stable warriors are so thin, so fragile. We live and laugh together, but we do not love together. When I saw your friends, *our* friends, happy to condemn you to death, I felt a cold wave of fear run through me. No one but you knows what happened in that room. But some of your friends have developed eyes which can see through walls. They know better than you do what happened between you and Tojo. And they are still ready to condemn.'

Axatan's heart was racing. He thought of the faces which had greeted him when he had entered the hall, the air filled with his name. What did it mean? Was it all a front? All to make him feel comfortable before an assassin's knife found its way between his shoulder blades and despatched him to the gloomy world of Mictlan for ever?

He shuddered.

Quetzal had untangled his arm from his own and they were walking side my side, man and man. He looked up at his friend's face. The smooth, soft features, the pale eyes and the golden hair had all taken on a hardness that he had not seen before. Or had he seen it but refused to acknowledge it? How long had Quetzal put up with the jokes about him and Juan? How long had he argued in his defence, knowing that his friend had withdrawn his love? How had he faced the truth?

First Techuan, now Quetzal. Neither needed to say anything. His accusers were within. His heart was a storm of black spirits, rushing to torment him with their spears of guilt. He stopped walking and turned to his friend.

'Quetzal. I still love you.'

Quetzal looked at him for a moment. In his eyes, Axatan could see waves of doubt and confusion. He held his breath, waiting for the golden-haired boy to forgive him, give him his blessing and free him from the bondage of their love.

Quetzal smiled and Axatan's heart sang for joy as he leant forward to kiss his friend on the lips.

It was only then that he saw Queztal's fist coming towards his face. A white light shot through his head and a ringing noise echoed between his ears. His left eye was closed and as he tried to open it, Quetzal hit him again, this time up under his chin, the impact making his teeth crash together and his neck snap back so that his whole body was thrown backward. He regained his balance and managed to stop another punch to his face, gripping Quetzal's wrists and holding him there, their faces just a hand's breadth apart. Quetzal's eyes were full of hate and their breathing was hard and tight between them.

'You are a traitor.' Quetzal's words came out like darts from his lips. 'I stood by you and you abandoned me.'

Axatan gritted his teeth, the pain from his eye spreading through his head. Was it true? He had no idea. Reality had become like smoke from the fire, formless and impossible. He felt himself in another place, away from the Stable, away from all his life, where his actions didn't matter. He squeezed harder on Quetzal's wrist and looked him in the eye. His heart beat with the love he felt for this man. It was as if all their time together had been mixed into one perfect moment which flowed like molten gold through his body. He saw now how strong Quetzal was and how he had changed from the boy who needed his protection. He saw courage in his eyes and he envied him. He fell to his knees.

'I have not abandoned you. If anything I have become unworthy of you.'

He bowed his head, tears running from his eyes on to the dusty floor below. Quetzal was motionless.

Axatan continued.

'But my love has changed and I must ask you for my freedom. I need Juan. You are strong now. I am still weak. Yes, he is a *telpollo*. But he is also a beautiful warrior in my eyes. I have made myself his slave, and like a slave who cannot find his master, I am destitute until I have him back. It pains me to ask you this, but I need your help to find him. You are the only one I can trust now. And I need to be able to trust someone.'

He looked up. Quetzal's face was serious, a mask through which Axatan could not penetrate.

'Juan is somewhere in the Royal Palace. I need to free him, but the task is dangerous and I cannot do it on my own. You are the only one I can trust. Who knows who is ready to turn me in? If you love me still, you will help me. But even if you hate me, do not stand in my way.'

'If I help you –' Quetzal's words cut through the air like the chill breeze which heralds the end of a summer's day '– and we free him, you will both have to flee the city. And then you will have gone for ever.'

Axatan remained silent, the sound of the feast mixing with the barking of dogs from the city below.

Quetzal was right. These would be his last days in Tenochtitlan. All would go – the Stable, the Prince, the lake, the Eagle Warriors. He would be stripped of everything. But he would have Juan.

At last he spoke.

'I need you to help me. That is all I can say.'

Eleven

From the window Juan could see the moon high in the sky and hear the sound of the nightwatchmen calling to each other through the deserted streets.

It was late and still no one had entered the room after they had dragged him from the Stable to the Royal Palace. The guards had been different from the warriors who had usually escorted him around the Aztec city, and they remained silent, refusing to answer his questions about where they were taking him.

Until today he had almost forgotten he was a prisoner. He was being fed, he had the friendship, and more, of an Aztec warrior, and he had even taken part in the games in the Stable. But as he entered the Palace, he began to have his doubts again and his heart beat faster against his ribs.

The room they had brought him to was large and low ceilinged. On the walls were tapestries like that in Axatan's bedchamber and the same wooden chest stood against one wall. It was dominated though by a tall metal cage that stood in the centre of the room.

The guards had pushed him inside and tied his hands to the bars that formed the roof of the cage above him. The ropes bit into his wrists and made him stand on tiptoes like a piece of meat in the market.

One of them had stripped off his loincloth and now took a long, lingering look at his cock and balls.

'Impressive,' he said. 'And does our *telpollo* friend perform for anyone or just the royals?' He leered at Juan and ran the edge of his fingernail along the vein on the underside of his shaft.

Juan fought against the sensation, but the feeling was irresistible and he soon found his cock swelling up to the man's careful touch.

The guard stroked along the vein again, making Juan's cock push out forward into his grasp. He was standing in the doorway to the cage but now he took a step back and let the metal grate shut tight, enclosing Juan on all sides. Only his hard cock pushed out from between the bars, inviting the guard's rough grasp.

The man scratched his fingernail along the base of his cockhead, exploring the sensitive skin there and making Juan twist in his bonds. A tiny drop of precome oozed from his slit and the guard used it to rub his finger around the thick head, flicking his hole with his fingers and squeezing lightly on the tight skin of his ridge.

Juan shut his eyes but the guard shouted at him angrily.

'Keep them open! I want you to watch.'

He let his tunic fall to the floor. He was tall and lean, with the strength of a hunter rather than a fighter. Little pockets of hair marked out his armpits and crotch but otherwise his body was totally smooth.

His skin was pale and his cock was enormous, rearing up now with lust and desire for Juan's body.

The man pulled on his foreskin. It was long and elastic and he slid it up and down his cockhead once or twice, the sweet juice of his precome making his cockhead glisten.

The other guard looked on.

'*Telpollo*. You are a prisoner of this city and I am one of its guards. Until now you have enjoyed the grace of the Prince, but now the Prince is away hunting, it is my pleasure to discover the hidden secrets of your body.'

He stepped forward so that their cockheads touched. Juan felt a wave of excitement shoot through him as the hot skin touched his pisshole. The man looked him in the eye and then took his foreskin in his hand, rolling it forward over his own cock and out on to Juan's cockhead so that it enveloped both their cocks in its tight skin.

Juan pushed forward, his shaft penetrating further the other man's foreskin. He felt its warmth around him, savouring the soft heat of the guard's cockhead against his own. He groaned, and the man squeezed gently on both their cocks, making their precome melt together as their hard flesh kissed in the man's strong grip.

The man pulled his hand back and Juan found his own foreskin rolling up over his cock ridge and stretching out on to the guard's glistening shaft. It felt as if he was being pulled beyond his endurance but as if by magic, his skin wrapped itself around the man's cockhead and his cock was filled with the man's hard flesh.

They stood like that for a moment and then the man rolled their skins back again, so that his foreskin was covering them both. Precome dripped on to the floor as the guard rubbed their foreskins back and forth, letting out tiny grunts of pleasure as their cockheads met inside one foreskin after the other.

They stood there for what seemed like an eternity, rubbing their cocks together, the skins sliding back and forth across them.

Juan looked up to see the other guard walking towards them.

He had stripped off. His body was solidly built, and while his cock was not as big as his comrade's it was thick, and the base bristled with sharp black hairs.

His eyes were filled with desire and he wanked himself as he watched Juan and his comrade fucking each other's foreskins.

He stepped over to the cage and pushed the older guard on to his knees. The man happily obliged, taking Juan's cock into his mouth and then his comrade's. The younger man turned and reached into the cage. He took one of Juan's nipples between his fingers and gently squeezed it.

Juan groaned and the guard took his cue to squeeze a little harder, causing a white heat to flash across Juan's chest. The guard took his other nipple between his fingers and pinched on them both, letting pain mix with pleasure.

Juan breathed in so that his chest expanded and his nipples were hard and prominent against his skin. The younger guard pulled his cock away from the older man and pushed it through the bars, rubbing it against Juan's thigh and leaving a little trail of precome on his skin.

The older guard was sucking Juan's cock and Juan felt his tongue push into his slit. He thrust forward and made the man open up his pisshole and lap up the precome which was oozing from it.

The younger guard pulled hard on Juan's nipples, making him fall forward and push his cock deep into the other man's mouth. He looked Juan in the eye, his face dark and handsome, and moved closer to his older comrade, letting his cock play across his face until the man let Juan's cock drop from his lips and again took his into his mouth.

The younger man positioned himself so that his arse was brushing against the bars of the cage, just out of Juan's reach. His cheeks were firm and muscular and he spread them so that Juan could see the soft ring of his arsehole.

Keeping his cock in the older man's mouth, he looked at Juan and beckoned him to fuck his arse.

Juan thrust his cock as far forward as he could but the bars were in the way and the man was standing just out of reach. The man reached behind him and opened his cheeks further. Juan pushed forward and the guard took a single step back, letting Juan's cock brush up against his hole.

Now Juan understood. The guard would ride his cock, taking as much or as little inside him as he wanted. By moving his arse he could control the amount of Juan's cock that went inside him and by moving the older man's head he could govern the feeling on his cock. He had taken two slaves and now he was going to extract his pleasure from them.

The guard pushed backward and Juan's cockhead slipped inside him, opening his hole just a little.

The guard gasped with pleasure and Juan felt his heart beating in his cockhead as the man's tight ring closed around it, squeezing him just below the ridge of his shaft.

At the same time, the guard gripped the older man's head and pulled it down on to his shaft so the whole of his cock was in his mouth. The older man grunted with pleasure.

Juan felt the younger guard's arse muscles spasming against his cockhead and then suddenly the guard had thrust back and Juan's cock was deep inside him, his ring massaging the base of his shaft and his balls banging against the man's hard flesh.

Juan cried out. The seed was churning in his balls and he felt he was going to come that instant. The guard thrust his arse forward again, letting Juan's cock slide out and ramming his own deep into the older man kneeling in front of him.

Juan was desperate to fuck him properly and he squeezed his cock forward so that it touched the man's hole. The guard cried out and pushed back on to his shaft, filling himself with it and making Juan buck backward with the force of his onslaught.

The older man was wanking his cock hard now, and from the precome running down his long shaft, Juan could tell that he was ready to come. The young guard positioned himself so that he could hold Juan's cockhead just inside his tight ring and he squeezed hard on it, making the seed seethe and boil in Juan's balls.

Juan begged him to push back but the guard stayed still, sending Juan into spasms of ecstasy as his come rose up his shaft. The older man was still sucking furiously on the younger guard's cock.

Juan felt the come rising in his cock when suddenly the younger guard pulled away and stepped to the side, leaving Juan to send an arc of come flying through the air and into the mouth of the older man kneeling in front of him.

The man gobbled up his seed and then came, sending spurts of white come up on to his face and chest and stomach. The younger guard looked on approvingly and wanked his cock for a few moments more before coming in great spurts of hot come over Juan's cock and balls and up on to his face.

He smiled and threw a cloth towards his comrade.

'Clean him up,' he said as he made for the door. 'The Prince will be back from the hunt soon.'

★ ★ ★

Axatan hugged himself against the cold wind which was blowing through the courtyard. Quetzal had wandered over to the ramparts and was staring out into the night sky. The moon caught the gold in his hair and even in the half light he looked like a spirit from another world.

Axatan walked over to him and placed his hand on his shoulder.

'My friend. We have been the closest companions since you first came to the Stable. We have shared so much together and now, if you help me, we will part. The truth of this shatters me. I feel a tempest rising in my head even as I say these things. But I know I must rescue Juan. I cannot leave him to die on the killing stone.'

Rain began to fall, a tropical storm, pelting the sides of the towers of the Great Temple, washing away the blood from that day's sacrifices.

Quetzal turned. His eyes were full of tears.

'I will help you, Axatan. But you must promise me one thing. Remain true to yourself and always follow your heart. I love you still, and if your place is here, then stay. But if you are destined to go, then do not delay in making your decision. Find your lover and flee the city. Hesitation will mean death.'

He looked at his friend.

'Now tell me the plan.'

Axatan led him towards the ramparts again and pointed across to the Palace.

'I have a friend within Palace walls. We have arranged to meet when the moon moves behind the great tower of Tlaloc. He will tell us where Juan is being kept and let us through the side gate into the Palace garden. From then on we are on our own.'

They looked down into the Palace compound. All the windows were dark and the clouds sent shadows racing up the stone walls like deathly fingers. They could see the gate and the path which led to the main building.

'We wear the clothes of the Priests of the Sun. The city is full of new priests come to take part in the Great Festival and many are quartered in the Palace. What's more, the priests' masks completely cover their faces so no one will recognise us from the Stable.'

'We enter the Palace and take the guards by surprise.'

He stopped. The rain had become heavier and was washing down on to the dark stone below, filling the Great Courtyard with little rivers which flowed down towards the marketplace.

'After that, I do not know.'

Quetzal was looking at him, serious and questioning, and Axatan felt cold under the glare of his scrutiny.

'I know. It is not a great plan. But it is the best I can do. More we cannot say until we know where Juan is being kept.'

Quetzal looked at him for a moment and then nodded. 'I am with you.'

He reached out and took Axatan's hand in his own.

Axatan embraced him.

'Then I will get the priests' robes. We will meet in an hour at the entrance to the Great Courtyard.'

They kissed, then Axatan ran down the steps which led into the city. Quetzal watched him go, his excited footsteps echoing through the night. He turned and headed back to his bedchamber, in search of parchment and ink.

The Prince pushed into the room, hot and drunk. The hunt had turned to revelry and the revelry had turned to lust.

Juan froze in his cage and the Prince's dark eyes burnt into him. He was still stripped from his encounter with the guards and the cold was making his nipples rise up and beg for attention, pushing through the black hairs that spread across his torso.

The Prince licked his lips and let his eyes rest longingly on the young captive who hung from his ropes, awaiting his desire. He closed the door behind him and opened the cage.

'*Telpollo*. Our time together has been too short. Tomorrow you face death on the killing stone. Your soul will go to a better place, but your body –' He ran his finger down Juan's stomach into the dark, wiry hair around his crotch '– will be cut into a thousand pieces and fed to the dogs. You are beautiful, but you are also my enemy. You are my enemy, but you are also my slave.'

He slapped Juan gently on the face, teasing him and fixing him with those dark eyes, which mesmerised him with their power.

Juan felt the same warmth, the same dark desire, rise within him. He met the Prince's gaze, defying him to hit him again, his eyes almost pleading with him to cover him again with blows of the whip and let him taste the power of his cruel strength.

The Prince leant closer and Juan could smell his hot breath; the scent of sweat and man. Their lips touched, the energy flowing between them of father and son, master and slave.

Juan felt the Prince's tongue slowly probe between his teeth, opening him up.

The Prince had wrapped his hand round Juan's balls and now he squeezed gently on them, hinting at things to come, and reminding him of the secret joy of true subordination.

Juan groaned and opened his mouth further, letting the Prince's tongue push into him and take control, filling him with his strength.

The Prince squeezed harder on his balls and Juan let out a tiny whimper of submission, giving himself up to the stronger man and abandoning himself to his dark power.

He closed his eyes and felt the Prince's finger on his nipple, scraping at it with his fingernail as his other hand continued to squeeze on his balls and his tongue probed deeper into his mouth.

Juan's cock was hard now, standing straight up against his belly, and the Prince let his fingers brush up against the vein on its underside, making it throb and swell.

Juan pushed his cock against his master's hand and began to rut him like a dog, letting his precome lubricate the movements between them. The Prince slid his fingers over Juan's cockhead, covering them with Juan's precome, before reaching up and pushing them deep into Juan's mouth so that the young conquistador found himself sucking on the sweet taste of his own spunk.

His cock twitched as the Prince squeezed more precome from

him and again pushed his fingers into Juan's mouth, filling him with the heavy scent of his seed.

The Prince stepped back and Juan watched as he stripped off, revealing his solid, muscular body, covered with black hairs, and his thick cock lifting up out of his pubes, ready to achieve its desire.

He reached into the wooden chest and took out a collar which hunters used for their dogs. He held it up in front of Juan's eyes. It was made of black leather and shone in the dim light of the oil lamp.

Juan smiled, hoping to indicate his acceptance, but the Prince remained serious and put it round his neck without a word. A metal ring hung from the collar and the Prince threaded a thick rope through it, tying the other end to a bar of the cage.

Then he reached up and untied the ropes around Juan's wrists, setting him free from his bonds.

'Get down on all fours.'

Juan obeyed.

The stone floor was cold to the touch. He looked ahead of him. The Prince's powerful legs rose up in front of him.

'Lick me, dog. Lick my feet.'

Juan leant forward and ran his tongue across the top of the Prince's right foot. He licked gently, as if he were caressing a precious object, leaving a trail of saliva glistening in the half light.

The Prince ran his fingers through his hair.

'Good dog. My hunting dog.'

Juan moved his tongue to his other foot, stroking between the toes, cleaning him and tasting his master's sweat.

He kissed the Prince's ankle, rubbing his cheek against the sharp hairs that covered his legs.

'Lick me,' commanded the Prince again.

Juan ran his tongue up the Prince's calf, feeling the outline of his muscle and the strength of those legs made to hunt and command.

He knelt up and reached the Prince's inner thigh, kissing it and licking it to please his master. The rope was tight but he strained at the leash to reach higher up the Prince's body and push his tongue into the dark beauty of his crotch.

The Prince gave him some more slack on the rope and he knelt up so that he was facing the Prince's cock and balls.

His cock was long and heavy, ringed with dark hairs, and his balls were round like oranges, awaiting his tongue.

He bowed his head.

'You may kiss them.'

Juan pushed his face forward into the thick bush of hair, breathing in the dark scent of manhood while he let his lips brush against the taut skin around the Prince's heavy balls.

The Prince breathed in sharply and Juan ran his tongue along the crack that lay between his balls and his leg, tasting the sweat and making the Prince's ball sac contract with pleasure.

The Prince's fingers were pushing into Juan's scalp, directing his tongue as his cock reared in front of his face.

'Suck me.'

The soft firmness of the Prince's cockhead pushed between his lips. The foreskin had rolled halfway back and Juan could feel the ridge of the man's cock nestling under its outer sheath.

He licked across the smooth surface of the Prince's cockhead. Precome was oozing from his slit and Juan licked it up greedily, swallowing the salty nectar.

The Prince's cock was stretching his lips into a big round 'O' and Juan let him push his shaft gently in and out of his mouth, massaging the softness of his lips and tongue.

The Prince pushed his foot between Juan's legs and pressed up into the crack of his arse. Juan opened his legs to let the Prince in and sighed as the firmness of the Prince's foot pushed against his hole.

Juan pushed his head down on to the Prince's cock and let the thick majesty slide inside him. The Prince slid a toe up inside Juan's arse, making him writhe with pleasure as it pushed open his soft hole and burrowed inside.

Juan reached between his legs and pushed a finger inside him next to the Prince's toe, stretching open his hole so that he was fingering himself as he took the Prince's cock deep into his throat.

'Yes, dog, pleasure yourself.' The Prince's voice was firm and decisive. 'Pleasure yourself for your master.'

He stepped back, pulling his cock from Juan's mouth. Juan was left kneeling, the saliva drooling from his lips.

'Play with yourself, boy. Show off for me.'

Juan pushed another finger inside his arse, opening his hole as he rode up and down on his hand.

The Prince was wanking his cock while he took in the hard beauty of his young body.

Juan wanted nothing more than to satisfy this lion among men.

Saliva was dripping down his chest and the Prince stepped forward and scooped some on to his fingers.

'Put your arse in the air.'

Juan leant forward and got on all fours again. He felt like a dog, a handsome hunting dog, and he wanted to be fucked like one.

The Prince moved round behind him and touched his fingers to Juan's arse.

Juan cried out with desire.

'Yes, master, please!'

The Prince pushed one finger inside him and then another and another. Juan arched his back as the Prince opened his arse, preparing him for the onslaught that was sure to come.

Juan's cock was throbbing between his legs. The Prince had pushed a fourth finger inside him and was opening his hand so that his ring was stretched. Juan felt the cool air of the night rush up inside him.

'Master, take me.'

He was drooling with desire, his cock twitching against his stomach, and he shouted out at the top of his voice when at last the Prince's cock pushed into him, filling him with its molten strength and pounding into the very depths of his soul.

★ ★ ★

The courtier was late. The moon had long passed the tower of Tlaloc when the short, overweight figure scuttled through the shadows, waving to them frantically across the Great Courtyard.

'I'm sorry I am late!' he said, panting after his exertions. 'But I have news which will help your plan.'

He handed them the masks and robes of the Priests of the Sun.

'You have chosen your disguise well. From the full moon until the end of the month no priest may show his face. The gods have given you the perfect disguise.'

They wrapped the dark robes around them and put on the black and gold masks. The heavy leather covered their faces entirely and Quetzal found himself looking at the man through deep eye sockets as if staring down at him from a high roof.

'The Prince is returned from hunting and has gone straight to his bedchamber. The young *telpollo* is there already, caged and waiting for him. The Prince is lusty and will be using the *telpollo* for his desires even now.'

Quetzal turned towards Axatan, but all he saw was a sun mask gazing back at him with a neutral inscrutability.

The man continued.

'The Prince has given orders, and this is your cue, for two slave boys to be brought to his rooms, so that he can continue his pleasures . . .' Quetzal saw that the man was uncomfortable. Even in the moonlight, a flush of red was growing in his face. '. . . his pleasures with four of them. To that end he has ordered that the side door to his chambers be left unlocked. I have made the arrangements.' His voice became cold and serious. 'You are those slave boys.'

He unlocked the small gate into the Palace garden and ushered them through.

'One more thing.'

He glanced up and down the moonlit lawn.

'You will need clothing for the boy. In the bedchamber is a chest. There you will find the robes and mask of a novice priest. The three of you will attract no suspicion.'

He nodded to Quetzal.

'The best of luck. The hunter is returned. Now you are hunting the hunter.'

He knelt and kissed Axatan's hand respectfully, like a son might kiss his father. Quetzal watched through the deep holes of the mask as the two of them whispered together. Axatan bowed low and the courtier turned to scuttle back across the Great Courtyard.

They crossed the garden, trying to keep in the shadows as much as possible, and entered the Palace through the back gate. The Palace was sleeping and they met no one as they crossed from room to room, crept down stairs and felt their way along dark passages. Not a soul stirred. It was as if the whole building was under a witch's spell.

Suddenly Axatan stopped and held up his hand. They were in a small corridor, just wide enough for the two of them to stand side by side. An oil lamp burned on the wall and beside it a small wooden door stood slightly ajar.

The light from the room within spilled out a bright wedge on the floor and from inside they heard the unmistakable sound of muffled pleasure.

What lay behind the door? Quetzal wondered again if they could trust the courtier. Was he one to lead them into a trap? Did he want a reward for foiling their plan? Axatan had seemed certain of him, but what had they said to each other before the man departed?

His reverie was broken by Axatan, who turned to him and gave the signal to proceed. Quetzal nodded. Axatan pushed the door open and they stepped inside.

The room was long and low ceilinged. Its stone walls were hung with tapestries and a dark wooden chest stood against one wall. In the centre of the room, in front of a low couch, stood a metal cage. Its door was open and next to it the Prince was fucking Juan, with his back to the door, the *telpollo* on all fours facing away from them.

The two men were in a state of abandon, lost in their desire. Both were naked, and the Prince's broad, strong back was like a wall of muscle, rising and falling as he fucked the boy in front of him. The rhythmic slap of flesh on flesh and the grunts of the fucker and the fucked were punctuated with moans of pleasure and encouragement. The Prince was running his hands up and down Juan's smooth back and muttering words of love.

Axatan gave the sign and Quetzal moved swiftly behind the Prince and pulled a blindfold around his eyes. The Prince did not falter, but simply smiled because he was expecting the slave boys. He carried on fucking Juan.

'Ah, reinforcements!' he said. 'Boys for your pleasure and mine, my beautiful one.'

Quetzal ran his hand across the Prince's buttocks and then brought it down with a great slap across his flesh.

'Oh, yes!' cried the Prince. 'Make the master the slave and let the slave have domination.'

He pushed his buttocks out further, for a moment almost withdrawing from Juan, before Quetzal brought down another mighty slap on to his arse cheeks and the Prince plunged his cock deep into Juan's arse again.

Quetzal stripped off his robe, his golden skin shining in the light of the oil lamp. He was half hard, and he stepped forward and brushed the end of his cock against the Prince's crack.

'Yes!' cried out the Prince, reaching behind him to open his cheeks further. 'Fuck the master!'

Quetzal spat on his hand and began to wank himself, pulling his skin up and down his cockhead to make the blood flow into his thick shaft.

Meanwhile, Axatan had moved round in front of Juan. Quetzal saw him lift his mask for a moment so that the boy could see who he was, and in that instant he felt the river of love and joy which flowed between them. He knew he would never see Axatan again.

Axatan opened his robes and Juan reached up and caressed his already hard cock. The Prince was lost in the pleasure of fucking Juan and having his own arse teased by Quetzal's cock, and Quetzal easily pulled his hands behind his back and tied them with a rope so that he couldn't remove his blindfold.

Now Juan leant forward and took Axatan's cock in his mouth. Quetzal heard his friend sigh with delight as the boy's tongue caressed the cockhead and found its way to the sensitive skin underneath.

Quetzal was hard now and he pushed his cockhead slowly into the Prince's arse. His heart was pounding in his ribs. This man, who he had always thought of as a god, was begging him to thrust hard inside him, to fuck him deep and strong. He looked at the Prince's hands tied behind his back and checked his blindfold before thrusting his cock straight inside him, letting his shaft find its target as the Prince cried out and pounded his own cock deep inside Juan.

The four of them took up the rhythm: Quetzal pounding his pale flesh deep into the Prince's dark, hairy arse; the Prince echoing Quetzal's timing by pulling out of Juan's arse just in time to plunge back deep down inside him; Juan drawing his mouth up and down Axatan's cock, moaning with pleasure as the two thick shafts filled him from both ends.

Quetzal looked over to Axatan. They had found their quarry and the hunt was going well. He smiled behind his mask, but his heart was filled with sadness.

He looked down again at the Prince, who was almost bent double over Juan's back as Quetzal's cock ploughed in and out of him.

Juan was gobbling greedily at Axatan's cock and Quetzal watched his friend's muscular torso rise and fall as he slid his shaft in and out of Juan's soft lips. The Prince was fucking Juan harder now, rising in energy as he felt himself begin to come. Quetzal, taking his cue, slammed his cock harder into the Prince's arse so that the slap of flesh against flesh echoed round the stone walls.

The Prince was making a strange sound – half a warble, half a moan of delight – as he pounded his cock in and out of Juan's arse, faster and faster, and then suddenly Quetzal felt his arse tighten as he came, filling the room with a great roar and setting the oil lamps shaking on their metal stands.

Quetzal twisted his cock one more time inside the Prince and let forth a torrent of come into his arse, his heart pounding away as if it were pumping in the hot seed itself.

Axatan was stroking Juan's hair and Juan was wanking at his cock furiously as he sucked on his lover's shaft, drawing out the come until the two of them came together, Axatan's spunk falling from the boy's mouth and mixing with Juan's white seed which ran across the floor like a gleaming river.

They fell on to the couch, a mixture of tired limbs and sweaty, muscular torsos.

Quetzal checked the Prince's bonds again. They were still tight and he gave the signal to Axatan to wait. They lay there in the silence until the unmistakable sound of the Prince snoring told them it was time to escape.

Quetzal stood up quietly and put on his black robe. All was quiet, only the Prince's snores piercing the night air. Axatan was stroking Juan's hair and whispering words of comfort.

Quetzal opened the wooden chest and took out the novice's uniform. A gleam of metal caught his eye. A knife, sharp and deadly, lay among the clothes. He picked it up and slipped it into the pocket of his robe.

Quetzal led the way back out into the Palace garden. Dawn was upon them and the sky was glowing with the first soft rays of the sun. In the trees, birds were beginning their morning calls and Quetzal knew that men were stirring in the Palace. Which eyes were watching them now as they made their way towards the door that led to the Great Courtyard? Which eyes saw not two priests and their novice but a pair of traitors who were spiriting away the Prince's prize captive?

The door was still unlocked and they slipped through into the Great Courtyard, bathed with the milky light of the first moments of the day. In one corner, the women were making *tamales* as they always did, but they did not call out. They knew well enough to leave the priests to their lives of sacrifice and mortification, looking death in the face to preserve the life of mankind.

They hurried down into the marketplace. Dotted across the

broad square, a few stallholders were already laying out their goods, their tiny oil lamps burning like stars in the night sky. But the square was virtually empty, most of the traders not expected until the sun was high in the sky.

The twin towers of the Great Temple loomed down on them, black against the lightening sky, and Quetzal made the sign of protection, begging the gods not to betray them and praying especially to Our Mother Earth to give the fugitives sustenance on their way.

And then they were at the city gates. A single guard was checking people coming in and out of the small wicket door which opened on to the lake beyond. They pushed past and he took no notice – just three more priests going about their business as the Great Festival approached.

They stepped on to the wooden causeway. A cool, damp wind blew across them from the east. To their right, across the lake, the sun's rays were beginning to push up over the mountains in the east. To their left, the ancient city of Tlacopan was still sleeping through the last moments of the night.

Ahead of them, cutting through the choppy waters, the long wooden line of the north causeway stretched out into the lake and to the lands on the far shore. For Axatan and Juan, this was the road to freedom. For Quetzal, it marked the loss of the one man he held dear.

He slipped the knife up his sleeve and walked over to where Axatan and Juan were gazing out across the lake.

'My friends,' he said. 'It is time to bid farewell.'

Through the dark eyeholes he could see that Axatan was crying, and tears began to well up in his own eyes.

Axatan put his hand on his shoulder.

'Do not grieve my friend,' he said. 'I leave you now in person, but my spirit stays where it belongs – in your heart. We will be wandering, fugitives from the anger of the Prince, always hoping for the news that his wrath has cooled, that we are welcome back into the city. Until then I will be thinking of you every day, longing for the time we can be together again. Wait for me, my friend. Do not forget me.'

Quetzal's heart was swamped with a drunken mixture of anger and love. Axatan threw his arms around him and as they embraced for the last time, Quetzal let the knife slip quietly into his hand and from there into the pocket of Juan's robe. It would be their protection along the way.

Quetzal and Axatan stood looking at each other through their heavy masks, the tears streaming down their faces. And then Axatan turned, took Juan by the arm and set off down the causeway into the swirling mist.

Twelve

As soon as they set foot on the causeway they began to run. The wooden boards rose and fell beneath their feet like a great river taking them to safety.

The wind had picked up and the mist blew into their faces as they ran towards the far shore. Ahead of them, the causeway stretched out into the mist, the far end just visible in the pale light of dawn.

Juan pulled his robes tighter around him. It was cold even when they ran and he felt as if the savage gods were rising off the lake to bite into him with their razor teeth. He had heard much about the witchcraft of these people and was sure now that the Prince would set their devils on him to bring him back.

Axatan was ahead of him. He had hitched his robes up around his knees to run better and Juan did the same, feeling the wooden planks fly beneath his feet as they raced to the far shore and freedom.

As they approached the shore, Axatan slowed down and held up his hand.

'Put on your mask again,' he said. 'There are guards at the end of the causeway and we must be careful. No one has passed us so they will not know yet of our escape, but we must look like Priests of the Sun, otherwise they will stop us.'

Juan put on his heavy leather mask. From inside it the world shrunk away, leaving him to the sound of his own breathing and the distant aspect of everything around him viewed through deep, black eye sockets.

He looked at Axatan, who had also replaced his mask. His face had become the sun and only his eyes, through the dark holes, betrayed any sign of life.

They were ready.

They walked on, shoulder to shoulder. The guards stood idly at the point where the causeway became a ramp leading down to the shore's edge. They looked like father and son: one short and a little fat round the middle, his spear dwarfing him and his headdress too large, and the other tall and stronger looking, with an air of suspicion which comes naturally to those new to guard duty. They were looking in their direction.

'Halt.'

It was the older one. He ambled towards them, leaning heavily on his spear.

'Where are you going?'

Juan looked at him through the eyes of his mask. He was terrified to speak in case the guard recognised his accent. He was looking right at him, waiting for an answer. But then Axatan spoke.

'I am taking my novice to Tulpetlac, to the temple there, to take part in the rites of Our Mother Earth.'

The guard looked them up and down. 'Remove your masks.'

'You know that is impossible,' said Axatan, a touch of irritation in his voice.

The guard looked agitated. 'Remove your masks,' he repeated.

Axatan continued, spelling out the words as if speaking to a child. 'We cannot remove our masks until the morn of the Great Festival. The gods forbid it.'

The guard's face twisted with fury. 'I said, "Remove your masks"!' His voice had risen to a shout.

Juan's mouth had gone dry. The other guard was close to them now. He looked them up and down and turned to his comrade. 'They can't remove –'

'Silence!' The older guard was furious. 'Remove your masks, I say, or I will remove them for you!'

What happened next took them both by surprise.

Juan put his hand in his pocket and found a knife. When had that been put there? Had someone known that they would face this problem? He clutched it. It felt cold and menacing in his hand.

With his left hand, he reached up as if he was going to comply and remove his mask for the guard. But in an instant he shot his right hand forward and plunged the cold metal into the soft flesh of the older man's stomach.

The blade hesitated a moment, pushing against his skin before sliding forward, cutting through the man's flesh and burying itself in his innards. Juan barely felt the warm blood flowing out on to his hand. He just stared ahead until the man started to scream and then, as if guided by an unseen force, he twisted the blade in the man's guts until the guard fell back, narrowly missing his comrade who was running towards them swinging his blade-encrusted club.

Juan pulled the knife out and without hesitation plunged it into the younger guard's eye, ducking sideways to avoid the downward swing of his club.

The man let out a roar of pain and Juan found himself fascinated by the spurt of blood which flew up into the air and down on to his black robes.

For a moment, the man looked surprised, as if he had been slapped in the face. Then he lifted his club high above his head and brought it down on to Juan's shoulder. Juan dodged sideways and the club grazed his arm, throwing the guard off balance and sending him teetering towards the edge of the causeway.

The knife was still sticking out of his eye and for a moment Juan wondered whether he should get it back. Then the guard let out a final roar and toppled into the lake, taking Juan's knife with him and leaving only a pool of red floating on the water's surface.

They stood for a moment, dumbfounded by what had happened. Axatan grabbed Juan's sleeve and dragged him down the ramp and on to the soft mud of the shore. Juan felt confused, but Axatan was screaming.

'Run! We have to get away!'

Juan's heart pumped strength into his legs as they ran away from the causeway and the fat guard who was still writhing on the ground. They pulled at each other to run faster through fields already planted with the autumn crop, into woodland, and finally – who knew how long it had taken them? – deep into the jungle with its green canopy and strange sounds and safety.

They fell on to the ground, rolling deep in the undergrowth as if the leaves themselves would make them invisible and protect them from the vengeance which was sure to come.

Axatan was grim.

'You acted bravely,' he said, 'but you did not need to kill them.'

Juan looked at him. He felt ashamed. He knew Axatan was trying to play down his mistake, trying to be generous. But Juan had acted in too much haste. Even if they had removed their masks, the alarm had still not been raised. The guard would not have recognised them. Now he had attacked two enemy soldiers but left them both alive. Captain Joaquín would have had him court-martialled.

He bent his head.

'Axatan, I meant well, but I acted rashly. You should not be gentle on me. We are both warriors; men of war. We know the rules of survival.'

Axatan smiled.

'All is not lost. We have made it to the jungle. The Prince will have awoken and an army will be assembling to hunt us down. But finding anything in the jungle takes luck and courage – and we have both.'

He held Juan in his arms.

'I have not brought you out of captivity to let you perish in the jungle. We will find safety.'

His face had taken a softer aspect.

'We are heading for the Tarascan kingdom in the east. For years now the Tarascans have refused to pay tribute to the Aztec Princes and in return they have been subjected to cruel and bloody campaigns. I was an Aztec Prince, but I have Tarascan blood in me. And now we are fugitives, it will be the Tarascans who will help us find a new life away from Tenochtitlan, away from the Stable.'

He looked away.

'Of course it will be a hard life. In the Stable I asked you if you wished to make your escape. You can still return to your people. If we separate you can make it back to your camp. It is my death the Prince wants most. They will concentrate their hunt on me. So I ask you again: will you come with me to the east or will you head towards the setting sun and find your own people again, the pale-skinned *telpolli* who have brought such destruction to our country?'

Juan looked at him. The brave man who had rescued him from the Prince's quarters seemed so lost in the hugeness of the world. He thought of his friends in the camp, his family expecting him home and his promises of gold and fame when he returned.

And then he thought of Axatan. The one man he had ever truly loved. The man who formed the other side of his soul.

He reached out and stroked Axatan's hair.

'There is no question. Your destiny is mine. We will make our lives in the east and we will make them well.'

Axatan stared deep into his eyes.

'I am glad,' he said, embracing Juan with a soldier's grip. 'I am glad.'

They continued up into the jungle.

The sun was rising now, but its rays hardly penetrated the thick greenery above them. Around them, strange beasts gave out their morning cries. Birds in the branches above them called out in plaintive songs. Everywhere was damp and warm and buzzed with the sound of a million insects.

They trekked deeper into the green. Small streams showed them the way uphill, away from the lake, away – for the moment, at least – from danger. They hardly exchanged a word, brought together by the silence with which they faced their fate.

Axatan reached out and touched Juan's hair, but Juan pulled away, his mask hanging from his neck, his robes torn and dirty, his face angry and defiant. He didn't want to be touched.

'I needed to kill him,' he said. 'Not just injure him. I needed to see him suffer from his wounds; see the lifeblood seep away from him.'

There was disappointment and anger in his voice.

Axatan smiled.

'What you did was enough,' he said. 'We are on the run and killing one won't stop the others. They will be hunting us like dogs hunt their quarry in the fields. We are vermin for them now. Our only hope is that Quetzal sets them on the wrong scent.'

The name caused Juan's blood to well up inside him.

'Quetzal!' he said, spitting on the floor. 'Quetzal cares nothing for me. If he could, he would have handed me over to be torn to pieces by the dogs in the marketplace. All he wants is for you to come back, to be part of his life again, to be part of the Stable. I saw it in his eyes. I saw it in his embrace. Did he embrace me at the gates of the city? Did he wish me the protection of your gods? No. He does not see me. Or rather, he sees me and wishes I was dead.'

His words shocked them both. Axatan said nothing and they turned and pushed on through the jungle.

The going was hard. Juan found himself short of breath, lagging behind Axatan, who seemed to cover the distance like a mountain goat.

He cursed under his breath. His feet were catching in the creepers and great insects buzzed across his face, making him thrash out in horror. The noises of animals, birds and strange ghosts rose up in the distance, only to vanish into the carpet of green that stretched out as far as the eye could see.

There was so much green. The trees were green; the floor was green. Even the sun, high above them now, seemed to be sucked into the green as if they were beneath the surface of the sea.

Juan remembered the Prince's threat. 'Leave me and you will wish you were never born.' Were they walking into their own living hell?

Axatan had seemed confident of the lead they had on the warriors, but he had warned him not to dawdle. He knew this time there would be no mercy; just the terrible hooks of the hunting lassos biting into their flesh and dragging them back to the city.

Ahead, Axatan had found a stream and was drinking from its clear blue waters.

Juan ran up to him and bent down to taste the sweet refreshment.

'Can we stop for a moment?' he asked.

Axatan looked around as if he could see through the trees to where the Aztec warriors were starting their hunt for the fugitives.

'For a moment,' he said, his face sad with worry. 'For a moment.'

They sat by the edge of the stream. The water caught the tiny rays of sun that pushed through the thick roof above them and sent them tumbling over the rocks in the stream like pieces of silver.

Juan thought back to his days in the fields in Spain. Would he ever see Spain again? Would he ever see his sister or his parents? Were they wondering where he was and when he would return? Or were they like old Dona Jinaldo? The old widow had taken her son's possessions and burnt them in the village square when he had gone off to the wars, saying, 'I have no son now. There is no son in our family.' And then she had shut herself up in her house with her daughters and none of them had ever gone out again. Most people thought she was mad, but Juan knew that her son would probably never return to their tiny village.

He leant up against Axatan and put his head on his shoulder.

★ ★ ★

The sun was low on the horizon by the time they emerged from the jungle into the scrubland which led down into the valley. Juan looked around him and realised that they had been climbing all day. Behind them stretched the jungle and in the distance, catching the last golden rays from the west, lay the lake and the city they had fled.

All seemed so peaceful. There were no armies on the move, no calls of hunter to hunter. Only the sound of the birds circling overhead and the soft hush of the wind played in their ears.

Ahead lay the east, dark already, and stars were appearing on the horizon.

'That is where we are headed,' said Axatan, placing one arm around Juan's shoulder and pointing into the distance with the other. 'The lands of the Tarascan and the sea.'

Juan could see nothing but rolling hills and small pockets of forest and jungle spreading out ahead of them.

Every so often, smoke rising in the wind showed the position of a settlement or a farmhouse. The land around them was barren, with only spiky cactus plants dotted here and there to interrupt the flow of the dry, red earth.

It was like the land around his village and again Juan felt the pull of nostalgia and yearned for his family, his friends and his home.

They trekked on towards the darkening horizon, their shadows now long in front of them.

Axatan was muttering under his breath. These were the Dead Lands, he said, the lands where ghosts of warriors who had been murdered and forgotten, never mourned or avenged, were at large. They roamed these lands, weeping for their fate, and attacked travellers who lacked the protection of the gods. That was why, he said, it was important to pray to Quetzalcoatl, that great warrior himself, to grant them his protection. And why Juan should pray too if he wanted to be saved.

Juan said nothing.

They walked on, looking for shelter for the night.

And then they saw him.

In the shadows, a man was watching them. He was about their height and covered from head to foot in strange white markings. In his hand he held a spear, and where his head should have been was nothing but a grinning white skull.

They froze and Juan felt a spasm of terror grip his heart. Axatan stopped his mumbling and gripped Juan's hand.

'We must walk quietly. He may not have seen us. Sometimes the spirits walk in their sleep.'

They stepped sideways, fixing their eyes on the ghostly skull. It was looking in their direction but the eye sockets were empty as if he wandered the country never seeing what was in front of him. Juan felt almost sick with horror. Had he seen them, or would they be able to escape down into the valley without the terrible ghost running after them in pursuit?

They continued to their left and then the skull man took a step forward, lifting his spear into the air.

Juan felt Axatan brace, alert now like a wild animal, smelling the air for danger.

Another step forward and now Juan could see a face. The skull had been painted on, like the rest of the markings, and behind the sockets were two green eyes darting back and forth.

The creature moved forward again, sizing them up, and then he lifted his spear once more and threw it on to the ground.

Axatan burst into laughter and fell to his knees, bending his body so that his forehead touched the ground.

They exchanged words in a language Juan had never heard and then they both sat up, laughing and embracing like old friends.

Axatan turned to Juan.

'We have found our shelter,' he said.

The three of them set off down into the valley. The skull man was called Totec, Axatan said, and he was a Tarascan hunter. He was painted like that because the spirits of the hunt would come to him, thinking he was a spirit like them.

Juan could see him properly now underneath the white paint. He was young – about their age – and well built. His hair was short like the warriors in the city and he was wearing a leather bag and a small loincloth round his waist. His feet were bare.

'Totec's people have lived here since the Second Age,' said Axatan, 'and they are sworn enemies of the Aztecs. He says he will help us.' He paused to mull on his words for a moment. 'He will help us evade the hunters.'

Night was closing in on them and Juan was glad of any shelter. A light rain was blowing across the hillside and he knew surviving in the open would be hard. Ahead of them, a thin plume of smoke rose into the sky and he could just make out two or three small white huts clustered around a fire.

'What are you thinking,' asked Axatan. 'Are you afraid?'

Juan was afraid, but whether he was afraid of the Aztecs or of Axatan he could not tell. Only this morning he had been a prisoner in the Aztec palace. Now they were approaching a strange encampment with a man whose face was painted like a skull. It was as if this adventure was running away with them; as if their destiny had slipped from their control.

'I am not afraid,' he said, turning to face Axatan. 'I am a soldier.'

He knew that neither of them believed him.

Totec was telling them of the Aztec movements and Axatan was relaying the information to Juan.

'He says they have come out of the city and are marching north towards Tenyuca. He has seen them and the Tarascans have been alerted. The army is big and it is heavily armed. He says he is surprised they are looking for us as they seem prepared for a long campaign.'

Totec spoke again and Axatan translated.

'Totec says if we are fleeing them we must have committed a terrible crime. I told him our crime was to love each other when others loved us.'

Totec looked on and then spoke again.

'What is he saying?' said Juan.

'He says the ways of love are more dangerous than the ways of the soldier. He has seen men die nobly in the midst of battle, but love can bring with it a long, agonising death which leads straight to the cruel shadows of Mictlan.'

Totec nodded sadly and touched the end of his spear in the way many of the jungle dwellers did when they talked of bad things.

Axatan watched him for a moment and then barked a question. The man shook his head and gave him his reply.

'I asked him,' said Axatan, 'if that was a good enough reason not to love.'

'And what did he say?'

Axatan smiled.

'That there is never a good reason not to love.'

The wind picked up. Totec stiffened and began to speak hurriedly.

'There is a storm on the way,' said Axatan. 'Tonight the army will camp at Tenyuca and we will shelter in his village. Tomorrow, though, we must continue on our way. Totec is worried about the Aztecs finding us. If we are caught in his village, the Aztecs will kill them all.'

Juan felt his stomach turn. He had forgotten the dark force they had unleashed.

The hut was tiny.

Totec had washed off his skull markings and was smiling broadly, pointing to the rush mat in the corner of the hut, the small jug of water next to the door and clean straw he had brought in for bedding.

The other villagers were crowding in the doorway, smiling and laughing at their new guests. Juan had already lain down on the straw and Axatan was trying to bid them goodnight so that they could eat a little and then sleep.

'Thank you,' he said, as more villagers brought food and drink and a short, balding man began to sing a song of welcome. 'Thank you, but –'

He turned to Totec, who was looking on and beaming with pride, his deep green eyes full of friendship and life.

'My friend, we are always in your debt for the shelter you have given us, but now –' He waved towards the fat man whose singing was filling his head '– we need to sleep if we are to be strong in the morning.'

Totec looked at him for a moment, his face puzzled and uncomprehending, and then suddenly he broke into a smile and, nodding his head, began to shoo the other villagers away from the hut, until only the three of them stood in the small wooden shelter.

He turned to Axatan.

'You are a brave man to risk your life for love,' he said. 'I am proud to help a brave man. Sleep well. I will bring provisions in the morning.'

He stepped out into the dark and let the heavy drape fall across the doorway. Axatan let out a long, deep breath of relief. 'At last,' he said, turning to Juan, 'we are alone.'

He lay down beside him and they embraced, feeling the warmth of each other's bodies under the tattered priests' robes.

Their lips met and for an instant all the worries of the day disappeared. Axatan looked at Juan.

The day had changed him. For the first time, Axatan could see that he was no longer a boy; that they were now equals, man and man, venturing forth to build a life together.

They kissed again.

A wave of warmth and joy spread between them, forging a bond which, Axatan knew, no man or god could break. Their tongues met, welcoming each other into the depths of their love.

Axatan ran his fingers down Juan's face, stroking the rough stubble that had grown there. He pulled away for a moment and looked into Juan's deep brown eyes and was awestruck by their beauty and the trust they placed in him. He gave him unconditional love and felt the same in return. He was no longer the *telpolli* captive – he was his lover and his friend. They were both strangers now, ready to forge ahead and build a new life wherever they could.

He ran his hand across Juan's nose, small and smooth, and down across his lips, letting him lick his fingers and kiss the palm of his hand.

They sank down on to the straw and kissed again, this time more urgently, their breathing becoming shorter and more hurried.

Axatan ran his hand down Juan's back, pulling at the torn robes and lifting them up around his waist. He ran his hand up over his legs and across his strong buttocks.

Juan moaned with happiness as Axatan brushed lightly at the tiny hairs that spread across his skin. Their cocks were hard and pressed against each other through the black robes which hung from their bodies, challenging each man to give himself up to the other.

Axatan tore at Juan's robes and the fabric came away from his body, revealing the thick mat of hair and dark skin of his torso.

He leant forward and took one of Juan's nipples in his mouth. Juan pushed his head down on his chest so that he could bite harder on to his nipple and tease it with his tongue.

Axatan ran his hand down into the small of Juan's back, holding it there for a moment and then plunging down across the soft skin of his buttocks. He breathed in deeply to savour Juan's special scent and taste the sweat on his chest, drinking in the essence of his lover.

Juan was moaning out loud and calling his name, ready to give himself up to him.

Axatan pulled at his own robe and tore it off so that they were both naked, their cocks touching and their chests and stomachs rubbing against each other as if they could become one in their ecstasy.

Juan reached up and kissed Axatan on the lips, pushing his tongue inside him and abandoning himself to the wild energy of their love.

Axatan was on top of him now and he let his cock slide between Juan's legs. Juan moaned through their kissing and lifted his knees slightly so that Axatan's cock could find its way down into the darkness of his arse.

They paused for a moment, looking into each other's eyes, their smiles betraying their lust.

Axatan locked his eyes on his lover's and pushed his cock slowly forward, burrowing in between Juan's arse cheeks.

Juan raised his knees some more, never letting his eyes leave Axatan's. Axatan's cock pushed in a little further and they both gasped as the head touched Juan's smooth ring.

They held that position, Axatan's hot cockhead pushing at Juan's soft arse.

The words rose in Axatan's mouth of their own accord.

'I love you.'

Juan stared back at him. He closed his eyes and let Axatan's cock slide gently into his welcoming arse.

He was breathing like a child; moaning as if he were dreaming.

Axatan felt the heat of Juan's arse close around his cock. He let himself relax as the sensations of love and power flowed through him, enjoying the feeling of his lover's body and the way Juan gave himself to him so that their love could be sealed in this beautiful act of oneness.

His cock was almost all the way in and Juan's breathing became more pressing. Axatan looked down. He loved Juan's chest, covered with thick black hair, making his nipples shine pink and tempting against his brown skin. He loved his face, so soft yet so noble. He loved the strength of his torso and legs, a body made for fighting and, Axatan knew now, for loving.

He pushed deeper inside him and watched as Juan tossed from side to side, clearly relishing the beauty of Axatan's cock within him.

Axatan felt the last part of his cock sink into Juan's arse, and as it touched that magic spot inside, Juan cried out with pleasure, scratching at Axatan's chest and pulling on his nipples, making Axatan push in further and harder as they rose into the rhythm of their fucking.

Axatan put his hand under Juan's body and lifted him up off the ground. Juan's legs were balanced on Axatan's shoulders and

Axatan could look down and watch his cock sliding, dark and thick, in and out of the pink smoothness of Juan's arse.

Axatan leant forward and kissed him. Juan's lips parted and Axatan let his tongue slide softly into the sweet beauty of his mouth, tasting the nectar of his lips and caressing him with his tongue.

Juan opened his eyes and they looked at each other, both delighted and lost in what was happening between them.

Axatan locked his eyes on Juan and teased his arse with his cock by pulling out all the way and then plunging his shaft down inside him so that his lover called out with pleasure and his cries filled the old wooden hut which was their shelter for the night.

Juan sat up slightly and reached between his legs, brushing his hand across Axatan's balls before pushing a finger into his arse, next to Axatan's cock.

Axatan gasped with pleasure, twisting his cock in and out of Juan's arse, loving the touch of his finger against his hard shaft. Juan rubbed up and down his cock, sending waves of lust running through him.

Juan pushed in another finger and Axatan thought he would explode as his lover caressed his cock while it slid in and out of his arse.

He was close to coming and felt that low, dull stirring in his balls.

He kissed Juan again and looked on as he took his own cock in his other hand and began to wank himself, his fingers still in his arse caressing Axatan's shaft.

Precome was oozing from Juan's slit and Axatan bent down and licked across the top of his cockhead, tasting his seed and taking the scent of his arousal within him.

Axatan felt as though Juan's arse was swallowing up his cock. Juan's fingers had found the vein which ran up the underside of his shaft and he was squeezing it, making the come rise. At the same time he was wanking his own cock, gasping for air as he thrashed back and forth in the straw.

At last Axatan could hold back no longer. Juan's fingers pushed deep into his arse, squeezing Axatan's cock and letting the hot come fly up inside him, filling him with the salty beauty of his sperm. Feeling this, Juan wanked harder and the air was suddenly full of his come, flying high before their eyes and raining down on the dark hairs of his chest like a thousand pearls.

They collapsed on top of each other, Axatan's cock still inside his lover, kissing and stroking and laughing with joy because they had found each other and they had found freedom.

At Tenyuca, the camp would be seething with soldiers ready to hunt them down, but for now, Axatan knew, nothing could disturb the paradise they had made for themselves here in the valley.

Juan awoke early and looked around him.

The night had been cold and they had huddled close together to stay warm and give each other reassurance against the strange sounds which came echoing out of the darkness.

Axatan was still asleep and Juan let his eyes linger on his lover's face. He traced the profile of his nose, so straight and majestic, and took in the deep red lips which he had kissed so often, every time losing himself in their soft sweetness. He saw the stubble pushing up through his smooth skin, throwing a shadow against his mahogany chin. He let his eyes wander down across his strong arms and chest to his stomach, where his belly button lay like a perfect jewel, and down, following the line of fine, black hair, to his cock, lying gently against his thigh, soft and still as he slept.

He touched his face and Axatan opened his eyes, gazing up at him with the bemused adoration Juan had now got used to seeing in him. He smiled and Axatan smiled back, stretching out his arms so that Juan could nuzzle in and lay his head against his lover's chest, listening to his heart and smelling the morning beauty of his body.

They lay there listening to the birds until they heard Totec calling to them from outside the door.

Axatan sat up and bade him enter.

'I have some food for you,' Totec's voice called in from beyond the doorway.

He lifted the drape and Juan squinted as the morning sun streamed into the wooden hut.

For a moment, the great hunter stood silhouetted in the entrance, his broad shoulders almost filling the doorway, his bulk blocking out the sun. Juan sat up, feeling groggy but happy to be away from the city and the Aztecs.

Totec stepped into the hut, followed by a small boy carrying a tray. The great hunter waved him in and the boy unloaded bowls of cheeses and *tamales*, honey, milk and fruit on to a small table which he placed next to Juan and Axatan. When the tray was empty he looked unabashedly at the visitors, bowed low and scurried out into the daylight. Totec let the drape fall closed.

Then Juan realised how hungry he was. They hadn't eaten the night before, having been too tired even to stay up with the villagers, but now he attacked the food like an animal who has been starved for too long.

Axatan laughed and he and Totec exchanged some words in their strange language.

'He says you eat like a warrior,' said Axatan. 'That you will always be ready for battle.'

Totec was grinning at him and Juan saw how white his teeth were and admired the strong line of his face. He had green eyes and straw-coloured hair and his face shone like that of an angel.

He sat down next to them, letting the curtain fall closed again in the doorway.

And now Juan was aware of his presence; his easy-going strength and the sparkle in his eyes. He felt himself captivated by this young hunter and his love for life. Strength seemed to run through his veins, and his eyes shone with an excitement which was infectious.

Juan put down his food and stopped to listen to Totec's voice, his strange words framed with a sweet accent which made him sound soft and vulnerable.

Totec was wearing a high-necked tunic which showed off the

strong line of his chest and the breadth of his shoulders. His forearms were thick and sinewy as befitted a man who hunted for most of the day, but his skin had the same softness as his voice, which gave him the air of an innocent child.

He was sitting cross legged and Juan let his eyes run down his strong calves, which were covered with light, sandy-coloured hair.

Totec and Axatan were talking animatedly, sometimes serious, sometimes breaking into laughter as if they had shared a joke or suddenly understood something which was eluding them.

Juan could not take his eyes off Totec. He imagined them naked together, swimming in the sea, embracing and kissing as the water crashed around their taut bodies. He wanted to look into those deep, green eyes for ever.

He felt himself getting hard.

He looked up. The conversation had stopped and both Axatan and Totec were looking at him, smiles playing on their lips.

He looked from one face to another – faces which had seen the world and made him feel a boy again.

In the distance, he could hear the villagers calling to each other, but here, in the hut, all was silent.

Axatan leant forward and kissed him on the lips. Totec let his hand brush across the hairs of his thigh. This was what they had been talking about. This was what the laughter had been for.

Juan leant back, stretching out on the soft straw. Thin beams of sunlight were pushing through the cracks in the roof and they caressed him with their warmth.

Totec was eating him with his eyes. He saw him look up and down his hairy torso and relish his long, thick cock which now lay hard against his stomach.

Axatan bent down and began to lick his right nipple, biting on it gently so that Juan felt great waves of pleasure rush through him. Totec's fingers were making him shudder as his hands moved up towards his crotch and the soft skin below his balls.

Then the two men bent forward and, as one, began to lick on his balls.

He closed his eyes. The ends of their tongues flicked up and down his hairy ball bag. He felt his cock lift up off his belly as his balls throbbed with the thrill of their moist breath. He longed for them to take his cock in their mouths, to suck him dry, and he arched his back to push his flesh towards them.

They had both stripped off and he looked at their strong bodies, powerful in their nakedness. Axatan, smooth and dark, always the gypsy boy, his short black hair crowning a noble face, was lost in the pleasure of sucking his balls. His cock was rock hard, its purple head pushing out of his foreskin.

Totec was paler, almost golden, showing hard muscles under soft skin. His hair was so light it seemed to shine in the half light of the hut. His thighs were huge and between them lay his cock, half hard.

He lay back again, as one of them – could he tell which one? – started to lick up the shaft of his cock. He felt his flesh engulfed in hot, moist breath and the urgent strokes of a tongue making the vein on his shaft swell and throb.

The other man had taken both his balls in his mouth and was playing with them with his tongue. He relished the feeling for a while and then, at last, felt the warm embrace of a mouth on his cock. He pushed upward, letting his cockhead slide between the eager lips and feeling the man's tongue slide across his hard flesh, brushing over his cockhole.

He pushed in further and the soft mouth opened up to him, letting him control it and allowing him to push his cock in as far as he could until he knew he was fucking the man's throat, his cockhead touching the soft muscles at the back of his mouth.

He sighed with perfect ecstasy. And still he kept his eyes shut, imagining a blend of Axatan and Totec, a perfect union of dark passion and soft, open love of life.

Hands were holding him now. He felt them take him, gentle but firm, and turn him so that he was lying face down on the straw.

The same fingers caressed his buttocks, softly brushing across the hairs on his arse. He kept his eyes closed and lifted his arse up a little, so that one hand could slip between his legs and take hold of his balls.

He felt a tongue lick over his crack and he pushed his arse further up to open his cheeks. The hot tongue delved deeper, making the hairs of his crack moist and pushing down to the soft sweetness of his hole.

Hands were pulling on his balls and cock and he felt a second tongue push into his crack and the stubble on a man's chin scrape across his buttocks.

Totec and Axatan were breathing more heavily and the hut was filling with the scent of their desire. He heard their deep grunts as they licked up inside his crack. He knew they would both be hard now, men aroused by the beauty of his arse and each other's lust and passion.

And then two strong arms wrapped around him and he felt himself being lifted up off the floor. He opened his eyes. Totec was lying below him, his cock, solid and magnificent in his hand, his eyes filled with desire. Juan knew what he had to do.

He straddled Totec's broad torso and let the end of the hunter's cock brush against his arsehole. Axatan was behind them and he felt his fingers tease at his soft, pink ring, making it ready to take the strong hunter inside.

Totec was looking up at him, a smile playing on his lips. Juan ran his hands across the broad expanse of the hunter's chest and took his nipples between his fingers.

Totec closed his eyes and threw his head back as Juan squeezed and twisted them, feeling Totec's cock rear up against his arse.

And then he eased his arse back, letting Totec's cock press at his hole. He opened up easily and allowed himself a moment of total pleasure as the thick head pushed inside him, the ridge stretching open his ring and the thick shaft sliding up into his arse.

Totec bucked and writhed beneath him and Juan twisted his body back and forth on the hunter's massive cock. They had become one, taking and giving pleasure in perfect balance.

Juan would lift his arse up so that Totec's cock would all but slide out and then Totec would pound his cock deep inside the Spanish lad, making him gasp for breath.

They fucked like this for a while, and then Juan felt another cock probing at his arse. Axatan was rubbing up against his crack. Juan sat up and reached behind him. He knew now that he wanted them both inside him. He wanted to be filled with the hard flesh of two lustful men.

Axatan pushed his cock against Juan's hole, where Totec's shaft was already stretching him wide open. His ring was tight but slowly Juan felt Axatan's thick cockhead ease inside him, opening him further than he had ever been opened before and stretching him as if a fist was pushing up inside his arse.

He took hold of his own cock and began to wank it as Axatan pushed deeper inside him. Totec was groaning at the feeling of another cock pushing up beside his own and Juan pushed down, desperate to be filled by these two beautiful men.

Axatan's cock slid all the way in and the three of them held still, relishing the perfect union of the moment. Then Juan began to ride up and down on the two cocks inside him, wanking his own cock as he used the two men as a massive dildo.

Slowly they took up his rhythm, fucking him in unison so that their cocks slid in and out of him with perfect timing, opening his hole as far as it would stretch and then pounding their flesh deep inside him.

Juan was in another world. He had never felt such strong feelings before. The two men were grunting with lust as they ploughed up into his arse.

Totec reached up and took Juan's balls in his hand, squeezing them and pulling down on his sac so that Juan wanked harder, letting the big hunter stir up the come in his balls and bring him closer to climax.

The two men were fucking him as hard as they could now and Juan wanted to cry out in the wild ecstasy of the moment. Axatan grabbed him from behind, squeezing him hard, his breathing becoming faster and faster. Totec was thrashing around the floor and Juan longed to let his come stream out over his beautiful broad chest.

They fucked for what seemed like hours; three men in perfect harmony. But it was Axatan who came first. With a great cry he plunged his cock deep inside Juan and pumped his hot, white come into his arse and up over Totec's hard shaft.

Feeling this, Totec reared up and came too, slamming his cock into Juan's arse and filling him with the hot sweetness of his seed.

Juan felt the two men's cocks throbbing in his arse and he wanked his cock harder, making the come rise in his shaft. Totec gave his balls one final squeeze and great streams of come flew up out of Juan's cock and down across Totec's neck and chest and hard, flat stomach, leaving a sweet pool of spunk which ran across the hunter's golden skin.

They fell into a soft, calm sleep, limbs tangled together, hands caressing faces, their breathing settling into a quiet rhythm. Juan looked first into Axatan's eyes and then into Totec's. Their faces told of an unspoken bond that had grown between them. And for a moment he felt he could see into their souls.

At last they stirred. Totec sat up and reached for his tunic. His face was sad.

'You must go now. The Aztecs are advancing through the jungle and they will soon be here. Our people will do what they can to hold them off but they are closing in and they must not find you here. It is time to say farewell.'

He looked at them both, tears rising in his eyes.

'Our time has been brief. But I want you to know that you will for ever be in my heart.'

The three of them sat in silence for a moment. It was Axatan who spoke.

'You have treated us above our expectations. We are in your debt and we will go at once. We do not wish to place the village in danger.' Totec had brought them new clothes and he picked up a white tunic and placed it over his head. 'But let me make you a promise that, when all of this is over, we will return with greater forces to help you with your fight against the Aztecs.'

Juan looked at him. He knew how painful it was for a soldier to give up his allegiance. And yet he understood. He himself knew he would never see Spain again or be a Spaniard in anything but name. He knew he would have to find new loyalties and a new sense of belonging. He said a prayer for his family and the friends he had lost for ever.

The three men embraced. They were all fighters, living with both fear and pride. He knew they would never see Totec again but he was certain that they would never forget the help he had given them.

Totec kissed them both on the cheek.

'I wish you luck,' he said, and disappeared through the doorway.

The sun was high in the sky when they stepped out of the hut. A fire was burning in the middle of the little square which marked the centre of the village, but no one had come out to see them off.

'We are probably too dangerous now,' said Axatan. 'If we were caught here this whole village would be burnt to the ground and its inhabitants dragged back to be slaughtered on the killing stone. It is better that we are leaving.'

Juan thought back to the terrible stone monsters which lined the steps up to the top of the temple, steps which shone with the blood of countless victims.

Many a time in the city he had lain awake at night thinking about his own death at the hand of the Aztec priests. Someone had told him that he would be drugged first and would feel nothing as the flint knife bit into his flesh. But he shuddered still in those early hours imagining himself stretched across the bloodstained altar, the knife raised above his chest, the priest's eyes burning behind his mask of death.

And now they were far from the city, yet his life was still in danger. Axatan was hiding nothing from him. If they were caught, he said, they would be bound and tied like the quarry of the hunt.

Their old friends would spit upon their bodies as they were dragged back to the city and their skin would be scraped away by stones and thorns. And then the priests would cover them with salt and burning lime and leave them in a pit for days. Axatan had seen fugitives punished like this before and he had seen one man remain alive and in agony for seven days until his kinsmen had come one night and beaten his emaciated body to death with clubs. It would be better, he had said, to die here in the jungle than as common criminals back in the city. At least here death would be swift.

They set off along the path that led east out of the village. The land here was barren and dusty, but ahead of them a line of green marked the beginning of the jungle again.

They barely talked as they walked, the sun burning down on them, and only the sad cry of vultures punctuated the silence of the day.

Every so often they stopped and Axatan took out a small pitcher of water which Totec had given them. It was already nearly empty and they took only a few drops each to soothe their parched mouths.

The jungle shimmered and blurred in the heat. At times it seemed to be almost upon them; at times it was as far away as it was when they had set out from the village.

Juan felt a hunger rising inside him. Totec had given them fruit and bread, but neither of them knew when they would find food again, so they had agreed to walk until sunset and only then to eat into their provisions.

The road was hard and their feet were bleeding. In his mind's eye, Juan dreamt of running water and cool brooks which would soothe his thirst. He desperately wanted to lie down and rest, away from the fear of being caught.

Axatan walked on resolutely, his expression fixed on the jungle ahead, and Juan wondered what thoughts were going through his mind and if he had any clearer idea about their future than he did, or what would happen to them once they reached safety. His heart was beginning to fill with doubt and confusion when Axatan held out his hand and said softly, 'They are close.'

They stood still, holding their breath. The tiny moan of a conch shell came towards them, carried on the wind.

'It is them.'

On all sides all they could see was the dark red earth stretching out away from them. And then it came again – the low moan of an Aztec hunting horn, this time from their right. They both scoured the horizon but saw nothing.

Juan turned to Axatan and saw for the first time real worry on his lover's face.

'Come, we must move quickly,' said Axatan. 'The jungle will give us cover, but we must head further south to keep the distance between them and us.'

They turned towards the sun and began to trek across the bed of the valley. The jungle began on the next ridge and they could see a craggy path winding its way up the hillside towards the dark, green world which would give them the protection they needed.

Axatan was muttering to the gods, sending up strange prayers and touching his chest. Juan felt he should pray too but his mouth was empty and all he could do was look at the heavens so that the Virgin Mary could look into his heart and see his distress.

And then they saw them. Arrayed along the high ridge to their right, a line of Aztec warriors which stretched as far as they could see. Their many-bladed clubs glinted in the sunlight and the conch-shell horns sung out their terrible cry, so close now and threatening, as if the army had covered a day's journey in an instant.

They turned away from the warriors and began to run towards the cliff ahead of them. The hillside was not high but the path wound back and forth up it and the stones cut into their feet as they scrambled up towards the protection of the jungle.

Juan glanced behind. He was filled with terror. The Aztecs were flooding down into the valley and he could almost feel the flint blades of their clubs eating into his flesh.

Some of the advance guard were almost at the foot of the hill.

He could hear their shouts and saw them pointing up at them, urging on their comrades.

Axatan had reached the top and Juan pulled himself up on to the ridge. The Aztecs had begun climbing the hillside and he and Axatan turned and ran headlong towards the green mass which was the jungle and their friend.

They had almost reached the edge of the trees when Axatan stopped, his face drained of blood. Juan opened his mouth to ask him what the matter was when Axatan let out a cry of horror and began to push him back away from the jungle and sideways along the ridge.

Juan was stunned. This was the wrong way! They had to take cover in the trees! The Aztecs were behind them. The jungle was their only hope. He looked to where Axatan was pointing and saw only trees and branches, the perfect cover for them to escape. Axatan was blubbering, trying to say something but unable to make words come out of his mouth. He was pointing into the trees and Juan squinted to see what he was trying to show him.

And then his stomach turned to water. Hanging from a high branch, his body swinging lifeless in the wind, was Totec's servant, the boy who had brought them wine and bread. His flesh had been hacked to pieces. And below him, his eyes black with fury, stood the Prince.

They turned in unison, imploring their feet to fly across the stony ground. The world became a blur and ahead of them the sun turned everything pure white.

The conch-shell horn sounded loud in their ears and they could feel the force of the Prince bearing down upon them. The soldiers were rushing up the embankment towards them and their only hope was to lose them in the thick of the jungle.

Juan pushed himself harder. The blood was coursing through his veins and he felt every muscle in his body reach out to take him forward and away from the Prince. It was as if the trees on their right were flying by, the ground rushing below them like a fast-moving river of earth. Their feet hit the ground together, propelling them along and pushing them harder until all Juan could hear was the lightning quick thud of their feet as they flew across stony ground.

And then they stopped.

The path had run out.

Far below them, stretching as far as the eye could see, was the deep, blue expanse of the ocean. On all three sides, steep cliffs led down to where the white foam crashed against the sharp rocks. Behind them, the Prince was advancing down the rocky outcrop, his club raised above his head.

They knew now what they had both secretly known ever since they had fled the city. He was a god and no human could escape his omnipotent grasp.

They looked into each other's eyes. Juan's heart was pumping with love and fear. Their bid for freedom had failed and their time with each other was coming to an end.

He held out his hand. Axatan, tears streaming down his face, took his hand in his and squeezed his fingers.

Their love streamed out towards each other and their eyes never left each other's faces until they stepped off the edge of the cliff and fell fast and silently into the deep water below.

The Prince was standing at the edge of the cliff when Quetzal caught up with him. He watched in silence as the waves closed over the heads of the two fugitives.

His face showed a grim satisfaction.

'It is done,' he said, and turned back to where the other warriors were waiting.

Epilogue

Down, down he fell, the light changing from sapphire to jade as the ocean filtered out the sun and drew him down into its depths. The water was warmer than he had imagined, caressing him like a mother, stroking his body and holding him as it returned him to her realm.

He thought first of Quetzal, and then of Juan. How the two men had shaped and turned his life, how he had grown from stubborn independence to the ability to love and be loved, whatever the risks.

He remembered nights sleeping in Quetzal's arms. The boy's soft skin, golden against his own. How Quetzal used to sigh under his breath as he slept. How his utter devotion had strengthened him and let him flourish even in the Stable. And how he had stood by him to the last, even when Axatan had betrayed him so completely.

He continued to fall. The waters were brushing at his eyes, giving him sleep, filling him with a blissful calm and taking the strains away from his limbs.

He saw Juan, falling too, betrayed at the last by a lover who knew not what he was doing. His body, once strong, now scrambling in the water, useless against the ocean's insistent hands.

He saw the Prince, angry but loving, his black eyes burning red as his protégé's final moments were taken from him. Axatan heard him speak but his words were swallowed up by the waters and all that was left was blue and cold and clear.

He had no need for air. The waters would hold him; the waters would love him like he had tried to love. He had tried. But each time he had had to run away. In his heart he cried.

He could hear Juan's voice in the distance, pleading, calling. And with it the voices of all the captives he had taken in battle, all the men he had betrayed in love, all the responsibilities of his life.

He felt light now. It didn't matter if he kept his eyes open or not. All was cold and dark.

There was music in his ears: singing, like the singing of the priests in the Festival of the Sun. A woman appeared and put a tamale in his mouth. It was his mother and he saw that he was just a child. He smiled at her and she smiled back, her face filled with light, cutting through the dark waters. Quetzal was there too, golden in his beauty, giving light and strength, and Juan like a bright torch, making his eyes strain, showing him the way, until the greens turned to blue and the blues to sapphire, and suddenly he was surrounded by white and gold and air and the wind was blowing in his face and he lay bobbing on the surface of the water gasping for air.

His head sang, yet he couldn't believe it. He breathed in great lungfuls of air and a smile spread across his face as he realised his good fortune. He was alive. The gods had sent him back to this world. The ocean had spat him out. His time had not yet come.

And then his heart was gripped with panic. Where was Juan? Had Juan been saved too? He looked around him, frantically scouring the choppy waves for a sign of his beloved. He called out his name and dived back down under the surface to see if he could see him. But only the gulls returned his cry. On every side the water was clear, the plaintive cry of the birds mocking him in the void.

Tears welled up in his eyes, splashing down into the ocean to mix their saltiness with hers. He started to hit the water, shouting at the top of his voice, calling Juan's name. But as far as the eye could see, only small choppy waves broke the flat surface of the sea. The water had taken its prize.

Slowly, he swam back to the shore.

The sandy beach was almost in reach when a hand grabbed his foot.

He bucked against it, feeling it pulling him back and down below the surface. But another hand had clasped around his leg and he felt himself being dragged back into the blue night of the ocean.

He kicked out again, but the hands held him tightly, and then he felt arms wrapping themselves around his body, squeezing him hard, stopping him finding the surface.

And then lips on his lips and a mouth breathed air inside him. He opened his eyes and saw the deep brown eyes of his lover smiling at him, welcoming him back. Juan was alive.

His heart sang and, as they broke the surface, he found himself laughing uncontrollably. Juan was running his hands through his hair and across his face, his face a watery smile. And their cocks touched under the water, hard with passion and relief.

They were both crying, kissing each other as the jewel they each thought they had lost was returned to their hands. They kissed again and swam together to the tiny beach which lay at the bottom of the cliffs.

Axatan opened his mouth to speak, but Juan bade him be silent.

They pulled each other up on to the sand and Juan straddled Axatan, looking down into his face.

His cock was hard and tiny drops of seawater were caught in his black pubes. Axatan took hold of it, feeling its heat even through the cold of the ocean. Juan smiled and positioned himself so that Axatan's cock slid smoothly up inside him.

Axatan felt his heart explode and he was filled with an intense love and desire. He pushed his cock deep into Juan's arse and leant up and kissed the Spanish boy softly on the lips. They looked into each other's eyes, bursting with love, secure that their future had begun.

High above them, Quetzal watched them climb up on to the beach, safe from the ocean's grasp. He smiled and turned back along the path to the Aztec troops. His friends were safe.

At the point where the jungle met the cliffs stood Nuatl, a young warrior who had joined the Stable only the night before. His eyes were fixed on Quetzal and he was slowly rubbing himself through his breeches.

Quetzal smiled. One adventure ends, he thought, and another is only just beginning.

IDOL NEW BOOKS

Also published:

THE KING'S MEN
Christian Fall

Ned Medcombe, spoilt son of an Oxfordshire landowner, has always remembered his first love: the beautiful, golden-haired Lewis. But seventeenth-century England forbids such a love and Ned is content to indulge his domineering passions with the willing members of the local community, including the submissive parish cleric. Until the Civil War changes his world, and he is forced to pursue his desires as a soldier in Cromwell's army – while his long-lost lover fights as one of the King's men.

ISBN 0 352 33207 7

THE VELVET WEB
Christopher Summerisle

The year is 1889. Daniel McGaw arrives at Calverdale, a centre of academic excellence buried deep in the English countryside. But this is like no other college. As Daniel explores, he discovers secret passages in the grounds and forbidden texts in the library. The young male students, isolated from the outside world, share a darkly bizarre brotherhood based on the most extreme forms of erotic expression. It isn't long before Daniel is initiated into the rites that bind together the youths of Calverdale in a web of desire.

ISBN 0 352 33208 5

CHAINS OF DECEIT
Paul C. Alexander

Journalist Nathan Dexter's life is turned around when he meets a young student called Scott – someone who offers him the relationship for which he's been searching. Then Nathan's best friend goes missing, and Nathan uncovers evidence that he has become the victim of a slavery ring which is rumoured to be operating out of London's leather scene. To rescue their friend and expose the perverted slave trade, Nathan and Scott must go undercover, risking detection and betrayal at every turn.

ISBN 0 352 33206 9

HALL OF MIRRORS
Robert Black

Tom Jarrett operates the Big Wheel at Gamlin's Fair. When young runaway Jason Bradley tries to rob him, events are set in motion which draw the two together in a tangled web of mutual mistrust and growing fascination. Each carries a burden of old guilt and tragic unspoken history; each is running from something. But the fair is a place of magic and mystery where normal rules don't apply, and Jason is soon on a journey of self-discovery, unbridled sexuality and growing love.

ISBN 0 352 33209 3

THE SLAVE TRADE
James Masters

Barely eighteen and innocent of the desires of men, Marc is the sole survivor of a noble British family. When his home village falls to the invading Romans, he is forced to flee for his life. He first finds sanctuary with Karl, a barbarian from far-off Germanica, whose words seem kind but whose eyes conceal a dark and brooding menace. And then they are captured by Gaius, a general in Caesar's all-conquering army, in whose camp they learn the true meaning – and pleasures – of slavery.

ISBN 0 352 33228 X

WE NEED YOUR HELP . . .

to plan the future of Idol books –

Yours are the only opinions that matter. Idol is a new and exciting venture: the first British series of books devoted to homoerotic fiction for men.

We're going to do our best to provide the sexiest, best-written books you can buy. And we'd like you to help in these early stages. Tell us what you want to read. There's a freepost address for your filled-in questionnaires, so you won't even need to buy a stamp.

THE IDOL QUESTIONNAIRE

SECTION ONE: ABOUT YOU

1.1 Sex (*we presume you are male, but just in case*)
Are you?
Male ☐
Female ☐

1.2 Age
under 21 ☐   21–30 ☐
31–40 ☐   41–50 ☐
51–60 ☐   over 60 ☐

1.3 At what age did you leave full-time education?
still in education ☐   16 or younger ☐
17–19 ☐   20 or older ☐

1.4 Occupation _____

1.5 Annual household income _____

1.6 We are perfectly happy for you to remain anonymous; but if you would like us to send you a free booklist of Idol books, please insert your name and address

_____
_____
_____
_____

SECTION TWO: ABOUT BUYING IDOL BOOKS

2.1 Where did you get this copy of *Conquistador*?
    Bought at chain book shop ☐
    Bought at independent book shop ☐
    Bought at supermarket ☐
    Bought at book exchange or used book shop ☐
    I borrowed it/found it ☐
    My partner bought it ☐

2.2 How did you find out about Idol books?
    I saw them in a shop ☐
    I saw them advertised in a magazine ☐
    I read about them in _____
    Other _____

2.3 Please tick the following statements you agree with:
    I would be less embarrassed about buying Idol books if the cover pictures were less explicit ☐
    I think that in general the pictures on Idol books are about right ☐
    I think Idol cover pictures should be as explicit as possible ☐

2.4 Would you read an Idol book in a public place – on a train for instance?
    Yes ☐   No ☐

SECTION THREE: ABOUT THIS IDOL BOOK

3.1 Do you think the sex content in this book is:
    Too much ☐   About right ☐
    Not enough ☐

3.2 Do you think the writing style in this book is:
      Too unreal/escapist   ☐   About right   ☐
      Too down to earth   ☐

3.3 Do you think the story in this book is:
      Too complicated   ☐   About right   ☐
      Too boring/simple   ☐

3.4 Do you think the cover of this book is:
      Too explicit   ☐   About right   ☐
      Not explicit enough   ☐

Here's a space for any other comments:

SECTION FOUR: ABOUT OTHER IDOL BOOKS

4.1 How many Idol books have you read?

4.2 If more than one, which one did you prefer?

4.3 Why?

SECTION FIVE: ABOUT YOUR IDEAL EROTIC NOVEL

We want to publish the books you want to read – so this is your chance to tell us exactly what your ideal erotic novel would be like.

5.1 Using a scale of 1 to 5 (1 = no interest at all, 5 = your ideal), please rate the following possible settings for an erotic novel:

   Roman / Ancient World   ☐
   Medieval / barbarian / sword 'n' sorcery   ☐
   Renaissance / Elizabethan / Restoration   ☐
   Victorian / Edwardian   ☐
   1920s & 1930s   ☐
   Present day   ☐
   Future / Science Fiction   ☐

5.2 Using the same scale of 1 to 5, please rate the following themes you may find in an erotic novel:

- Bondage / fetishism ☐
- Romantic love ☐
- SM / corporal punishment ☐
- Bisexuality ☐
- Group sex ☐
- Watersports ☐
- Rent / sex for money ☐

5.3 Using the same scale of 1 to 5, please rate the following styles in which an erotic novel could be written:

- Gritty realism, down to earth ☐
- Set in real life but ignoring its more unpleasant aspects ☐
- Escapist fantasy, but just about believable ☐
- Complete escapism, totally unrealistic ☐

5.4 In a book that features power differentials or sexual initiation, would you prefer the writing to be from the viewpoint of the dominant / experienced or submissive / inexperienced characters:

- Dominant / Experienced ☐
- Submissive / Inexperienced ☐
- Both ☐

5.5 We'd like to include characters close to your ideal lover. What characteristics would your ideal lover have? Tick as many as you want:

Dominant	☐	Caring	☐
Slim	☐	Rugged	☐
Extroverted	☐	Romantic	☐
Bisexual	☐	Old	☐
Working Class	☐	Intellectual	☐
Introverted	☐	Professional	☐
Submissive	☐	Pervy	☐
Cruel	☐	Ordinary	☐
Young	☐	Muscular	☐
Naïve	☐		

Anything else? _____

5.6 Is there one particular setting or subject matter that your ideal erotic novel would contain:

_____

5.7 As you'll have seen, we include safe-sex guidelines in every book. However, while our policy is always to show safe sex in stories with contemporary settings, we don't insist on safe-sex practices in stories with historical settings because it would be anachronistic. What, if anything, would you change about this policy?

_____

_____

SECTION SIX: LAST WORDS

6.1 What do you like best about Idol books?

_____

6.2 What do you most dislike about Idol books?

_____

6.3 In what way, if any, would you like to change Idol covers?

_____

6.4 Here's a space for any other comments:

_____

_____

_____

_____

Thanks for completing this questionnaire. Now either tear it out, or photocopy it, then put it in an envelope and send it to:

Idol
FREEPOST
London
W10 5BR

You don't need a stamp if you're in the UK, but you'll need one if you're posting from overseas.